THE JERICHO DANCE

The Jericho Dance

by Jim Marcus

March 2026

This book is set in Lato Regular 9/13
Titles in Lato Heavy 16/20

Cover:
Harem
by Jim Marcus 2024

Edited by Hilary Shroyer

ISBN 979-8-9936679-1-1

www.pulseblack.com

For more information on Usher Syndrome and how to raise awareness, visit the **Usher Syndrome Coalition** at https://www.usher-syndrome.org/

PULSEBLACK

Lyrics throughout from the song

L'Oiseau et l'Enfant

by Joe Gracy

1. Prologue - The Bird and the Child	9
2. The Boat and the Waves	27
3. The Blood of the Poet	47
4. When mornings pluck petals off dreams	65
5. The Bird, It's You	83
6.The Girl of the Shadows	101
7. My Sun so Dark	119
8. Dark are the misery, the men, and the war	137
9. The Land of Love has no Borders	155
10. A child with their eyes filled with light	175
11. The blue bird soaring above the Earth	193
12. The City with Heavy Eyes	211
13. Night changes to day	229

1. Prologue - The Bird and the Child

Comme un enfant aux yeux de lumière
Qui voit passer au loin les oiseaux
Comme l'oiseau bleu survolant la terre
Vois comme le monde, le monde est beau

Just like a child with eyes full of light
That sees the birds passing in the distance
Like the blue bird flying over the earth
See how the world is... the world is beautiful

It's midnight and I'm sitting propped up outside her door. I can smell her somehow, but that's not surprising. I fell in love with the way Turk smells a long time ago. Maybe on that first day. I never did figure out if you love someone, in part, because of how they smell or love them and then fall in love with that exact smell.

It's hard to tell.

I know where she's leaning on the other side of that door, back to the smooth black wood, bare legs curled up with her arms wrapped around them. She's barely breathing, which scares me, but she's still crying.

Which is my fault.

To understand it all, I need to go back about a year.

My name is René Mäkelä. My last name means, pretty much, "Hey, check out that farm on that hill." From here on, I will forgive you if you lose all the doodles riding on top of all the letters. If you couldn't tell by the messy blonde hair, perky girlish cheekbones, and green eyes, I'm Finnish, not French.

And we don't care.

Although my father, king of all francophiles, would slap the pen out of your hand. He goes by his middle name "Milan" just so people will suspect he is French. Nobody cares, really. But it matters to him. On my 25th birthday, I understood why.

Anyway, a year ago today, May 7th, 1977, I was sitting there, holding Milan's hand while we listened to his French idol, Marie Myriam, at Wembley Conference right next to the Arena, sing at the Eurovision song contest with her winning version of "L'Oiseau et l'Enfant," – "The Bird and the Child."

Since then, every single line of that song has come to mean something to me. It's strange how that works. She had recorded that song in five different languages, one of which being her own, Portuguese. It was also the fifth time France had won, which was a record, if you are a fan of coincidences.

Which I am.

We were two of the 2000 people in attendance, watching that performance. We were in the fifth row, rounding out that run of convenient synchronicities, if you were keeping track. Get a pad of paper if you need to.

Milan was 59 years old that year, with his 60th just around the corner. He would want me to tell you he was a handsome man, with skin about two shades darker than mine, a tightly groomed salt and pepper beard and a thick rush of greying hair making him look wiser than he suspected he was. He was slim and tall and could always be found in a colorful shirt, open at the neck, with a silver necklace or two on top of his furry chest, generally frolicking in the sun, near water.

To me, he was everything. He was my bear, my dragon, my saint. Milan was fun. He was the first and best person I ever played hide and go seek with. If he didn't want to be found, that man would not be found. But he was my heart, too. When I was six and my mom disappeared, he instantly picked up the slack, making me feel like I was missing nothing. He took me everywhere, without concern for what anyone would say.

I remember one night, I was a six-year-old girl in thick plaid pajamas, unable to sleep at 2 AM, when Milan took me bowling with his friends. Staying up until the morning, laughing, eating bar food, and cheating wildly – so much so that I actually won. I slept the whole next day, my fingers feeling the tingle of the inside of the ball while the crack of pins falling rushed through my head like a fucking sonnet.

I felt like a part of the world.

And he was there when the world was taken away from me, too. Three years before that concert, in an antiseptic white doctor's office – a stranger's office. He held my hand then, too.

Happy birthday.

But you should get to know me a little better before I tell that part. For now, I need to give you some information that will help you figure out what kind of story this is.

So, take a look in front of us, in the first row.

Right there. Not the woman. Although, not terrible.

The older man. In his 70's. He's Greek, by ethnicity, but you can probably tell. He's a statue, a bony throwback to Hephaestus, blacksmith hammer notwithstanding. He's big and robust. His face is olive and his hair is bright white, painted across his head, face, and torso, in haunting contrast to that Grecian skin. He looks solid. In fact, you can only really tell his age when you see him next to his son, standing one seat over, applauding, ready to sit back down without reaching behind himself. Ready to jump on stage or through a window, or anywhere seemingly.

He's a jumper. That's Nikola Karras. I've never met him but I've seen him out in seedy neighborhood windows and across dark pool halls. And his father next to him is Anton Karras. If he handed you his card, it would say that, in silver print, massive Roman letters. And beneath it, with a flourish, the words, "Art Dealer."

But, in reality, he's the same as us. And that's my way of letting you know what kind of story this is.

We're thieves.

I saw Milan watch the older man's hands carefully as he applauded. Until, finally, Karras lifted his right arm over his head. He made two quick symbols with his hand, the first looking like the universal symbol for the hitchhiker, his thumb pointed outward. The next a symbol resembling the Devil Horns that had become so popular lately with music fans.

Milan whispered to me, "did you see?"

I nodded. It was in LSF – Langue des Signes Française – French sign language for "A" and "H."

"AH is the farthest box, right?"

He smiled. "Yes, it is."

I looked around, "Who else do you think is here?" I hadn't seen another larron since we had come in. I promised myself I wasn't going to toss around French words here and force you to follow. Larron is what we called ourselves. We're thieves of the mind. We like to think that we hurt no one. We win through cleverness. So we get a slightly clever word. And, since it was brought up, the fancy boxes to the side of the stage were all numbered with two letters, the farthest one being AH.

Out of the way.

"I've seen no one." Milan was doing that thing where he looked all over without making it appear that he was noticing anything. He patted his pockets for a matchbook absentmindedly, appearing to have lost it. I still had a lot to learn from him.

That's when Turkana showed up. She was 28, a year older than me, with dark skin and a pouf of natural hair in a near perfect globe framing her face. If 1977 had a face and a shape it would have been hers. She walked with casual confidence, jaunty and bouncy, velvet bellbottoms snaking down her beautiful legs and expanding at the bottom like the majestic trunks of oak trees. But unlike those trees, there was nothing hard or unyielding about Turk. When she slid her hand into mine, it fit perfectly. When she kissed my neck, her lips slid across the surface like a warm cloth, forcing my nerves to slink toward the softness, to sink into her.

She was this whisper everyone turned toward. Especially me.

"What did I miss?"

Milan made a point of looking faux annoyed. "You missed the song and you missed the kiss on the cheek." He leaned in for her to graze his cheek with those near purple lips.

"I'm sorry, pops. I saw Aggie back there."

He nodded as we sat down. "Agnes is here?"

"I see more." Turk looked around obviously. She wasn't one for hiding anything. Aggie was Agnes Bernard, a fellow larron and gymnast who had wanted to work with Turk in the past. She might have had a bit of a crush on her. I put that away.

We watched Karras and his son stand back up as Marie Myriam left the stage after thunderous applause. They stepped out the side doors leading to the stairs while the next artist stepped onto the stage. I looked at Milan and he nodded.

The three of us excused ourselves and slid down the aisle toward the doors.

The Wembley convention hall was a smaller building built right next to the Arena. But it wasn't tiny. It had gravity of its own. Still, it was small enough you could hear the music all over. As we walked to the stairwell, we listened to the German Eurovision offering, a band called Silver Convention. They were performing a catchy disco song called "Telegram."

Milan froze for a moment, his hand on the door. "Do you hear that?"

Turk cocked her head at him. "What is it?"

"Listen. The sounds." He could hear the morse code in the song, interrupting the rhythm. The song was about a telegram. And the morse code spelled something out. The dots and dashes were out of sync. They sounded wrong.

She tried to listen. "Do you think it means something?"

"I think everything means something," he laughed. "But is it something useful?"

Up the stairs, we stepped down the hallway to the box. It was open and airy and the carpet felt deep under my feet, like there might have been a layer of rubber beneath it. It masked a bit of the sound, but I could still feel the beat below.

I still worked.

At the door to AH, I knocked, locking eyes with Milan. A moment later, a tiny Judas window opened and a man's face appeared. He was a dark, Latin man with a face full of stubble, close to my age. His hair, however, was perfectly styled. It wasn't the first time I saw the illusion that men often created where they made themselves look partially unkempt, rough, in order to lure you in. He smiled.

"'Since you've gone I'm all alone.'"

Milan laughed quietly. He called out, "stop. 'Just can't make it on my own.' Stop"

The Morse code for the song. Stop. Turk squeezed my hand, moving it slightly toward her. I turned to see another woman walking toward us. She was thin and airy and dressed in black. She stood behind us and waited.

The face disappeared and the door opened a moment later. We stepped through the doorway and the woman followed.

Karras had taken over the box. It wasn't large, but he had made it his own, removing the seats and pulling the curtain closed. You might have been able to see through it a little, to the stage, but we were keenly aware that no one could see here, into the darkened box.

So, here is where my deficits are going to make this a little hard for you, the reader. I'm currently 27 years old. Three years ago, on my 24th birthday, I was diagnosed with Type III Usher syndrome. If you know what that is, a lot of things here are going to make more sense.

People from Finland have a sexy little accent. They are more likely to be blonde and have blue or green eyes, like mine. But, as well, due to some evolutionary logjams, they are more likely to carry various genetic diseases. My disease, Usher syndrome, is a classic Finnish one.

I was born with average sight and hearing. At 24, I went to see the doctor, noticing that my balance was off. If I got up quickly, I might find myself falling over. I had good days finding my balance and, well, I had bad ones. On the very bad ones, I sat down a lot. On the extremely bad ones, I sat down in a wheelchair. But that wasn't the primary problem. Usher syndrome is the leading cause of congenital deafblindness. I learned on that day that by the time I reached 30, I'd likely be totally deaf and completely blind. It was progressive and there was no cure.

As my sight diminished, I found myself unable to make out shapes at night. And, again, I had good days and I had bad ones. My hearing was possibly more intrusive. Not only was my balance affected, but my ability to process sound was degrading. I had good days, like today, when I could make the most of a beautiful French song while holding my father's hand. I was even able to lift a wallet or two from the people in the audience, although no one was really paying attention. I could have stolen their pants, as well.

But on bad days, I felt cut off. Unable to do much of anything. A world you can't hear is a world you aren't really in, it seems.

So, I'm going to try to explain to you what I heard as I sat in that darkened room.

Anton Karras was at 12 o'clock, right in front of me, gruffly introducing the people in the box. He was there, of course. To his immediate right was his son, Nikola-Nik. On his other side, the left, was the man who had let us in. His name was Rialtos. His voice was smooth and velvety, with that slight swish suggesting that he might have been gay. I smiled, in spite of myself. It made it much more likely to me that his precisely calculated three days of beard stubble was a misdirection, a subtle affectation. It said, "I am rough, don't expect precision out of me," so that he could better be precise in his own evaluations and actions without fear of being sussed out.

He was a con man, too.

The other woman, who came in behind us, was an American who went by the name of Noemie. I wasn't sure what her job was on this adventure, but she didn't look like a crook.

She looked like a gothic fairy, ready to dissolve in the half light, to slip into the nothingness that defined the edges of the room for me.

Turk wrote the letter A in my hand as Rialtos opened the door again. It was Aggie. Crush on my girlfriend notwithstanding, Agnes Bernard wasn't a bad choice for a job. She had never lost her gymnast's build or her ability to snake into and out of anywhere. She was dark and sleek with tiny braids, a smallish woman whose smile was still overwhelming. As I had expected, she leaned against the wall near Turk.

Anton continued the introductions, painting the picture of my family. How my father, the master criminal, had brought up his only daughter to be a pickpocket and consummate thief herself. And how that girl, at 16, had come across another girl, living on the streets and stealing, and taken her in, making her one of the best safecrackers in the world. He missed the part where Turk and I fell in love, but I think that was mostly our story to tell anyway.

And he missed someone else.

Karras continued. "If you agree, the six of you will accompany my son on this job."

Milan shook his head. "Seven."

Nik raised his hands. "No. No way. He's not even here."

"He's in the van outside. And he goes with us or we stay home."

I don't know if any of us could make out what Nik and his father were whispering about. But it gives me a chance to explain what the problem was.

My father's best friend and partner had been a cat burglar by the name of Christo Lafitte. When he was killed in a fall from a job they were on, his ten-year-old son, Devique, came to live with us. He was 30 now, and in those darkened pool halls where I'd remembered seeing Nik? He was usually losing to Devique–something Nikola tolerated once or twice before erupting in a drunken rage.

The two of them weren't close.

But Anton Karras still nodded. He put his hand over his son's and the gesture was clear.

This wasn't the time.

Devique was waiting for us outside in the van. He was a large man, quiet and kind. He was the closest thing I had to a big brother and I loved him. His family had come from Nigeria, like Turk's, and he wore that on his face–the smooth, dark and mysterious face of some ancient nobleman or king. People were always surprised at his quirky sense of humor, his almost imperceptible sarcasm. He had a regal air about him. But he had the attitude, very often, of a jester.

Right now, he was probably cleaning the van. Devique had taken the lessons of both Milan and his father to heart. Don't let chance get in the way.

Control what you can control.

It feels strange telling you what I'm going to tell you next. This was a room filled with secrets. This was a place where any loose application of that secrecy could get us all thrown in jail.

Separate jails.

But if you want to understand it all, I think you have to hear it all. I'm not sure it makes any sense any other way.

So we stood in that room, the seven of us, and an old Greek art dealer told us how we were going to get rich.

"Now that everyone is here and you all know who the people around you are, I want to tell you a story. If, after you hear this story, you want to walk away, well, we might have a problem. So, does anyone want to leave before I start?"

Turk spoke up. "How do we know this is worth it? Before we hear your story?"

Karras continued, "because I have bags here, for each of you, that contain a half a million francs. This money is yours, even if we all fail. Even if the job falls through. It's money that will allow you, I hope, to sit and listen for the time it takes me to explain."

Rialtos began passing messenger-bag-sized brown satchels around to everyone except Nik. I opened mine. It contained what felt like a paperback book the size of a bill.

Five hundred 1,000-franc notes in a paper wrapper. They were new.

Untouched.

You could feel the tension release in the room. He had our total attention. He'de just spent three million francs to buy it, regardless of how well we did on the job.

So what was the job?

He went on. "I want to paint you a picture. It's 9000 BCE. The giant ground sloth is going extinct. There is no modern language, modern law, or modern clothing. But there is something. Something that predates all that.

There is a bank. A place where people put things that are too valuable to keep at home. And this bank, lost to the machinery of time, is the very first one. It sits in the site of the oldest continuous human habitation. At first, it's a simple hole in the ground. Then, once agriculture is invented, once thatching is invented, a modest building. Soon, stonemasonry is developed. Thousands of years ago, it is a building. It grows upwards. But twice as quickly it grows downwards."

Aggie's voice rang out, "where is this?"

"This is in what is likely the oldest city on Earth. Jericho, in Palestine. At first, nothing but a pit to hide wealth. Even as our understanding of what has value changes. Then a deeper and deeper hole, even as the building on top rose up. Today it is part of the Tell es-Sultan, the oldest artifact of a city on the planet."

Milan's interest was clearly piqued. "And what is in there?"

Karras laughed. "Anything. Everything. Precious metals on one level. Bearer bonds on the other. Priceless art on the next. My son will be bringing me what I want – a priceless piece of art. But he can't make it down there to the vault beneath the city alone. That's where you all come in. For your help, I will pay each of you two million francs. On top of that, you can keep anything that you are able to scavenge."

I tried to work it out in my head. "If it's a significant challenge, I don't see us being able to carry much. Even the gold would be less than these satchels here.

Karras smiled, “René, is it? Yes. You aren't thinking big enough. Let's say that bearer bonds aren't interesting to you. A woman your size should be able to carry about 25 kilos in a backpack. Twenty-five kilos of rhodium would be about...”

He turned to Rialtos. “Ray, it would be?”

The younger man smiled. “Almost two million francs, Anton.”

“Rhodium, platinum, gold. And there is more down there. Billions of dollars of the most valuable assets that anyone has ever seen. You can keep anything you can carry. And if it's art, I will move it for you, for less than my customary fee. A simple clay bowl could net you tens of millions. What you do down there is up to you. What you take is up to you. You are people of imagination.”

Aggie looked excited. It did sound like something worthwhile. “What kind of security are we talking about?”

Karras pointed to Rialtos. “Ray, would you like to explain?”

Rialtos stood up. “The top few floors have some of the most sophisticated alarms known to man. Or not. We don't know. We have solutions for them, but we're skipping those. We're more interested in what we can dig down to. Below the third sub basement, the alarms and security devices are more... interesting.”

Turk laughed. “I don't like the sound of that.”

“I meant that in a bit of a laughable way. I don't know much about your upbringing, but let's say that the rest of these devices aren't really technology based.”

Karras pointed to Noemi. “Noemi here, Miss Noel Mason, is one of the leading lights in the American Wiccan movement. She is... well, she is a witch.”

I felt Milan brush by me as he stepped toward the door. “Nope.”

Karras called out, “are you afraid, Auguste?”

He seemed to wince a bit. "Fuck, no. No offense, I'm sure she is quite a capable witch. But do I believe that there are mystical protections on this vault? No. More to the point, do I want to be in business with people who do? I don't think so."

He turned to Noemie. "Again, no offense, Ma'am."

She nodded. "None taken, Mr. Mäkelä."

He started toward the door. What happened next was small, but it hit me pretty hard. The woman, Noel Mason, lifted her hand and a tiny ball of light appeared in front of her. It was no larger than a golf ball, but it glowed brighter until it lit the room. It raised up to the ceiling of the enclosed box and sunk into it, spreading across the entire top of the structure in a way that I could barely follow. For me, a girl whose vision was dependent on light, it opened up the room completely.

I could see.

I could see everyone in the room. Everyone but Karras and his son were looking up in amazement. I heard Turk next to me.

"Fuck me."

Karras went on."I had asked Ms. Mason to prepare a spell or two to hopefully convince you all. She is familiar with all of your skills but I recognize you are less familiar with what she brings to the table."

Noemie spoke. There was something about her that felt otherworldly. And her voice had an air of elusiveness. It was male in parts, female in others. It was quiet and purposeful. "I promise you all I won't let you down. I've studied this vault area for over a year, with Anton's help. I don't think there is anything down there we can't handle."

Milan looked down, surveying her face. I could tell he saw what I did. "You don't think."

Karras's son spoke up. There was a real respect in his voice that may have meant more than his words. "I'll be honest with you, Milan. That's all any of us have. We rely on our abilities. I trust yours, for sure."

Karras stepped over, putting his hand on my dad's shoulder in the newly-lit room. "We have six months. We'll be back in Marseille, then here. We can work together on addressing any contingencies. We can iron it all out."

I felt like raising my hand. The atmosphere in the room had gotten more hopeful, as though the new lighting had liberated everyone as much as it had me. But, unlike everyone else in the room, I had a clock inside me, ticking. Six months was a long time. "Why six months?"

Karras turned and smiled. His teeth were white and chalky looking, unreal, artificial. It's interesting what you notice about someone and when. "Ah, Ms. Mäkelä. I was about to get to that. Twenty-seven kilometers southwest of the City of Jericho sits another very important site."

Milan nodded. "Jerusalem."

"That's right. And on November 17th, the president of Egypt, Mr. Anwar Sadat, will arrive at Ben Gurion Airport to spend 36 hours in country, with one hour spent talking with the Israeli government."

Turk looked at Karras. "I haven't heard anything about that."

Karras circled the room like a panther. "No one in the press will. Not for months. But this visit will be one of the most complex security issues in the area. The Palestinian government needs it to be peaceful. The Israeli government needs it to be peaceful. Hell, the Egyptian government needs it to be peaceful."

Aggie added, "it's a logistical nightmare."

Karras laughed. "That's right. And that's why every eye, every security force, every human being past the age of majority in the country will be focused on Jerusalem on November 17th."

Nik shrugged. "So that's our window."

Turk thought out loud. "Every person with a camera is going to be in Jerusalem."

Karras nodded approvingly at her, "That's right, Ms. Moreau. If we play our cards right, it will be weeks before anyone notices what we've done."

All eyes were on Milan. His reputation was why he was in this room. He nodded.

"Okay."

Karras threw up his hands. "Fantastic."

Rialtos stood up straight. "We have a few things to do once we get back to France. Things to streamline and prepare over the next few months."

The aging art dealer next to him dismissed that with his hands. "Yes, yes, of course, we will be in touch, we will work it all out. But the important thing is that we are all here. All of you, I hope, will enjoy your time here in London. I suspect that all of us won't be in the same room together until we meet for final planning."

Milan nodded, "That makes sense."

"So, have fun."

We talked amongst ourselves for a few minutes and then filed out. The last act was on stage but none of us were really interested anymore. We had gotten what we came for. I leaned against the silver railing and looked out over the sea of faces rising over the red velvet chairs. This was what we were depending on for this job. The power of attention. Every eye was tied to the stage as if by some unseen cord, making it impossible for anyone to look away.

This was why this would work.

We stepped outside into the London evening. Although it was 10 PM and foggy, the street lights built a web of light that filled the streets for miles in every direction. I looked up, wondering and thinking about what I'd seen in that box. A simple trick, likely. Something a stage magician could do. But in that room, it felt so real. Milan spoke into a tiny metal ball at the end of his necklace, tucking it back into his shirt, and, moments later, a dark green van rounded the corner.

The side door slid open and Milan stepped in. As I suspected, the interior was spotless. Devique never seemed to concern himself with things being in the right place. He just made sure they were. He smiled widely at me as I pushed Turk in and piled in over her.

Devique looked at Dad. "Looks like she's winning. Over 150 points."

Milan patted him on the shoulder enthusiastically. "Ha. That's right, son. It's the world working out."

My father never missed a chance to make sure that both Devique and Turk knew they were as much his children as I was. He sought out those opportunities. He put everything into that word, "son." Whenever he could. Whatever else he was, master thief, hedonist, con man, he was a father first and last. Even as the hedonist in him slid off his shoes, always the sign that it was time to relax now.

"Ok, thoughts?"

Turk jumped in first, leaning against the side of the van and putting her feet in my lap. "Well, I think I'll be a magician when I grow up."

Milan laughed. "First of all, young lady, nobody gave you permission to grow up. Second, anyone seen that trick before?"

Devique had only been listening. He hadn't been in that room with us. "What happened?"

I tried to make sense of it. "Some kind of magic light ball. It lit the room up. It had to be a trick."

Milan nodded. "A good trick at the right time."

So, that was it. Her trick hadn't convinced him that she was magical. It had, however, convinced him she knew how to con a room full of people. And that was enough.

I thought for a second. "I call bullshit, though. Banking eleven thousand years ago? It just doesn't track. It's not what we learned historically. Maybe 2000 BCE. In Mesopotamia. It doesn't add up. "

Devique nodded. "That's fair. It's a pretty big hole."

"Okay, all right. What if banking is one of those things – discovered, lost, discovered again." Turk shrugged.

I looked at Dad. I worked pretty hard to call him by his name and not "Dad." But he was right. On jobs, it didn't ever help to let people know what your emotional relationships were. "What do you think?"

"I think it's one of many plot holes. We've got six months to figure it out."

"Oh, and..." Milan pulled out a brown bag and handed it to Devique. I was unsure if it was the one Milan was given or if he had just taken another one. I like to feel that he had possibly lifted it from Aggie. Did that make me a bad person?

"Spend it all in the same place." Milan winked at him.

"I'm not quite sure how to do that."

Milan looked him in the eye. "Hey. Do not buy anything for a job. Buy fun things. This is for you, payment for sitting in the van."

"You know it's a pretty comfortable van... wait." He turned up the radio.

"...and with 168 points, and for the fifth time, France wins with Maria Myriam's execution of "L'Oiseau et L'Enfant." The radio rang out.

We all yelled out. Milan cheered, drumming on the side of the van. "Sonofabitch."

"It was a good fucking song."

2. The Boat and the Waves

Beau le bateau dansant sur les vagues
Ivre de vie, d'amour et de vent
Belle la chanson, naissante des vagues
Abandonnée au sable blanc

Beautiful's the boat, dancing on the waves
Wild of life, love and wind
Beautiful's the song, coming from the waves
Abandoned to the sand so white

By July, we were back in Marseilles at the depot in Le Cours Julien. The Depot was our name for the large apartment space originally designed as storage for the many shops below. Milan had bought it outright years ago and built out rooms and spaces within it for all of us. The water pressure sucked and it was noisy as hell. But from the street, it still read as storage.

I was sitting backwards on a chair, topless, on the balcony overseeing the weekend shopping below while Devique tattooed my back. If I could have felt anything at all through the pain, I would have said that the wind felt like a procession of floating heated feathers drifting lightly over my skin and the sunlight was nearly wet and dripping warm like wax across my face.

So, remember that for when I'm not being tattooed. I can be poetic when not in pain. I leaned into the walkie-talkie next to me.

"So what are you wearing?"

Turk's voice came through as a whisper. "What are you, a cop?"

Devique snorted, "busted."

Turk went on, "you know you have to tell me if you are."

I shook my head. "Nope. I do not."

"Don't move." Then into the walkie, Devique validated me. "She doesn't."

More loudly now, Turk's voice still had a secretive tone. "Whaaaat?"

Devique spoke into the walkie, "that's a wives' tale, cops are allowed to lie as much as they want."

"Gotta say, I don't like that much." She replied. I could hear Turk at work on the safe.

I didn't either. "I hear you."

"Almost got the last tumbler number." She was across town taking the weekend to test her skills against the safe of a local banker. He was out of the country and had committed the cardinal sin of bragging about his new high-tech safe. That is never a good idea.

"The answer is always three," I whispered.

Devique shook his head. "It's not."

I laughed. "Men are downers."

"Meh. They get stuff off high shelves. And...I'm in."

"Anything good?" I prodded.

"Do you need a new necklace?"

Devique leaned in again. "After this heals."

"I can't wait to see it."

We had designed a tattoo for my back of the alphabet. When my senses wane, people would be able to use the chart on my back to talk to me. It was designed to maximize communication, with a series of rows showcasing the 26 letters of the alphabet, a row of numbers, a period, an interrogative, a space and one other character.

"That looks good." Milan walked onto the balcony in a pair of pajama pants, wiping his hands on a towel.

Devique steadied me. "It doesn't matter what it looks like."

Turk's voice was louder now over the walkie. "Excuse me, that's my girlfriend's back."

I scrunched up my face. "It kind of matters."

"Well, it looks good. This will be good. This is important." Milan reached in and I recoiled.

"Ouch. Still sensitive."

"Right. The center, right above her tailbone. That one, son."

"I got it, pops."

"Damn, your father was such an artist. Nothing he couldn't make or build, draw, design. Nothing. This place is mostly him, you know."

Devique nodded. He knew.

"And now, look at you." Milan patted him on the back lovingly.

"I'm almost done with the white."

Turk's voice sounded like she might have been back in the car. It was easy, brighter. No semblance of a whisper. "I don't get why the white ink?

Milan leaned into the walkie. "It's actually no ink. He's going over it over and over again for the main stems of the characters. We need to build it up. We don't chase scars. We want ridges that people can feel when they use it."

"I'm going to be ridged."

"You will, little girl. People will be able to feel the letters. At first, they can trace them. Eventually, you will know the letter from placement." Milan tossed the rag back inside.

Devique finished. "hypertrophic ridges. They'll hurt a lot at first, but won't reduce sensation in the long run."

"Wow. You guys want anything on the way back. Besides this fancy necklace. And what looks to be about 1700 francs and some condoms?"

Milan smiled. "Dibs on the condoms."

"Am I getting tipped?" Devique asked.

I shook my head. "Sorry, no. You're just hurting me. That's your prize."

"I should have enjoyed it more."

Milan looked more closely. "Here. Like the 'Q'. make sure that tail is long enough. It has to feel intentional."

"Got it, pops."

"You know what you're doing."

Turk jumped in. "Yeah, I think I need some more stuff done, Dev."

He laughed. "You have almost no room left." He wasn't wrong. Turk's arms and legs were covered in tattoos, brilliant brightly colored tribal pieces with thick black lines tracing her muscles. Devique had done most of the work on her and just about all the tattoo work on himself.

Milan knelt in front of me. "The lower back ones are just a bit bigger. This is to compensate for reduced sensitivity."

I nodded. I joked about this because a part of me felt like crying. So much of my life right now was preparing. So much was me reclaiming my body before parts were lost.

"And the vowels have a little dot on top. This helps the typist center. The letters curve slightly with the shoulder blades. They should feel straight to you."

"You really thought this out." I ran my hand over his beard.

He grabbed my hand and kissed it. "Nothing crosses the central axis of the spine. We can use the spine as code – the vertebra as symbolic sort of morse code. And the 40th character, right above your tailbone is the heart. It means –"

"I love you." I knew what it meant. Milan made sure I knew over and over.

"This is the most important character. You understand?"

My eyes filled up. "I do."

"We can still use your hands to write in. We will practice that, too. We have LSF tactile, We have Lorn alphabet. We have print on palm. This is for us."

"I know."

He stood up and ran his hands through my hair. It was longer now, down past my shoulders. But it was still wild. My hair could never be controlled. How often I envied Turk's precise globe–the fuzzy black beautiful planetary shape that made everything look like a satellite to her.

"Good." He started back into the depot. "I'm going to get cleaned up. When you are done, meet me downstairs."

***

Devique wrapped my back up and I wiped myself down a bit, throwing on a black t-shirt. Turk always joked that all my shirts had holes in them in places all over but none were the exact right places. One day I finally told her that I did that on purpose. I was taught to take advantage of every gift I had. And I knew that if I stood in front of someone, fiddling with my shirt, a shirt with holes that were constantly threatening to expose my braless chest, that there would be much about the conversation that person might miss. In fact, I could expect them to not really remember my face at all.

Use what you have.

I sat crosslegged on the stone in front of the Depot, watching the people go by. It was bright and alive. Today was a good day. My vision responded well to the bright French sunlight and I felt like I could hear forever. On days like this I almost felt that the doctors were wrong.

And maybe they were.

Milan drove up in a metallic blue Alpine A110 Berlinette, rear-engine coupe. It was a beautiful thing and I'd never seen it before.

"Come on.... get in."

I hopped up and ran over to the passenger side, sliding in.

It felt amazing. "Whose car is this?"

"For right now, it's ours. You like?"

I did like it. It was small and lithe, with only two doors. It rode low to the ground like some kind of a spaceship and the blue metallic sheen reflected light in every direction.

Everyone on the street stared. It wasn't hard to feel pretty in a car like this.

"Where are we going?"

He smiled. "You'll see. I wanted to have a chance to talk. Just you and me."

"Ok." I tilted the seat back. It moved remarkably smoothly. "This is sweet."

"It really is." He aimed toward the Route de la Gineste.

I looked up. "Are we going to the D559? Cassis?"

He laughed. "Very good. You make an excellent passenger."

"Well, you could let me drive..."

"Maybe on the way back." He wound his way through the roads to hit the Avenue du Prado. He opened it up a bit.

"Ok. I'll call you on that." We were going about 90 kph now. That was likely over the speed limit for this Avenue. Milan was an excellent driver. I said that to myself in my head a few times, I remember.

"I wanted to talk about your mom a little." His voice dropped an octave. We rarely talked about this. The fact that he wanted to do it now, while we were heading off to parts unknown was a bit jarring.

"I'm game. Dad." We turned the corner around the 9th arrondissement, probably a few kph too fast. But the car cornered perfectly. It was beautiful. I leaned over to see the speedometer. It was on 110 kph. Had there been other cars around, I might have been a bit more worried.

"How does your back feel, baby?"

"It's good. It doesn't hurt that much." I clicked my seat belt shut.

On any other day, I might not have bothered. But it seemed prudent.

"This is a beautiful day."

We hit the curve at marker 223, again, faster than we needed to. Milan didn't slow down.

"Dad. What are you doing?"

"I'm making a point. Do you trust me?"

"Of course I trust you."

"Do you trust us?"

I was confused. "In this scenario, who is us?"

He laughed. "You, me, together, in this car. The entire thing."

"Oh." I hadn't had the chance to think of it that way. Did I trust this car– this system?" I didn't know.

"It's you. You trust you. It's me. You trust me. And the car, who wouldn't trust this fucking car?"

"It's beautiful." I thought out loud. It was beautiful. And it cornered like something out of a sci-fi movie. "I do. I trust us."

"Okay. Then you are on board."

"I'm on board."

"Good." Milan opened it up. He hit the Gineste with everything the car had. I saw the speedometer dial move to 130.

"Shit." I laughed, leaning back. I tried to adjust the seat to the upright position. It felt weird leaning back when we were moving so fast.

"Your mother. You know how much I loved her." He raised his voice. We could hear the wind racing past the windows.

"I do, Dad. I do."

"I hope she knew. I wanted her to know. She was afraid. I think she trusted me. I believe she did. I don't know if she trusted us..."

"Why do you say that?" I raised my voice a bit, too. I could see the speedometer rise again. It was slowly making its way upward to 140.

"I told her that we could handle it. The disease. That even if she felt like she could not, we were something different. A system. A closed system, like this car. Like a boat. People can't float, but a boat does."

"I do. I float a little."

"My baby, you are an excellent swimmer. And so was your mom. But, you know..."

"I know, Dad." I didn't mean to say it like that. I reached over and put my hand on his leg as his foot dipped deeper onto the accelerator. To our right were mountainous walls, rising up, and to our left was the drop.

The fall from the clifftop.

I tried not to think about it as we sped forward. The speedometer hit 150 kph. We'd gone faster than this, but never on the Gineste. The road narrowed and curved. The speedometer kept rising.

160

"She took herself away. She didn't want to be a burden."

"I know, Dad."

"Because she didn't trust our system. What we had made. The people, the car, the boat, whatever. The system that would make it work."

"She didn't want to burden you."

He hit the wheel with the palm of his hand. "Now, here I am burdened by the hole she left. Do you see that? Nothing was going to be worse than the hole."

"I don't think she saw it that way."

"I don't give a shit what she saw." He leaned back, pressing down hard. The speedometer hit 170. His eyes were pinned to the road as he took every curve, almost supernaturally, without hesitation. Without stopping to think. It felt like the car was anchored to the middle line, like we would stay attached no matter what– a toy car connected to a ridge riding in the center of the street.

180.

"She took herself out of the world. And the system collapses."

"I won't do that, Dad."

"How can I get you to trust us? Trust the system?"

The speedometer passed 190 and prepared to dig itself into the far end of the gauge. It would stop at 200, but the accelerator would go on.

It would keep getting faster.

I felt myself pinned to the back of the seat. Out of nowhere, my back began to throb. I yelled out. "Woooooooooo." I remembered the tattoo. This was my signal to him that I was going to stay in the world. And this is why he was so invested, designing it, plotting it.

He yelled out, too.

There were no cars anywhere. Had we lucked out, at this time of day, nearly all the way to Cassis, to not have encountered a single car?

We cornered way too fast around Les Cigales. I realized I wasn't afraid anymore. And I loved this car.

Whomever it belonged to.

We passed the Hotel les Jardins de Cassis at over 200 kph and slowed, pulling into the parking lot and scattering a family on bicycles. Milan was laughing as we parked at the far end of the lot.

I sat in the car for a minute.

"I'm not going to leave. Or hurt myself. Or take myself out of the world. I promise you I love this world."

He looked ahead. "Good."

I turned his head toward me, tugging at his beard. "Do you believe me, Dad? We're going to finish this tattoo. We're going to learn what we have to learn. We're going to go hang out with a witch and make a shitload of money and then we'll be together without worrying about it.

"We will." He kissed my hand again.

"I'm not Mom." I needed him to understand that. "I trust the system. I trust the car, the boat, I trust you."

"I love you."

I leaned in and we stayed there for a few minutes. I realized that my hand had been clutching the door for the last 15 minutes.

I let go.

***

Devique and Turk were in the hotel cafe laughing when we walked in. Somehow, they had beaten us here. That felt unlikely to me.

"Hello, white people." Turk pulled me into the chair next to her.

Milan sat down next to Dev and picked up a menu. "I could eat that car."

"It's a beautiful car." Devique passed him a glass of orange juice. "Did you wipe off your fingerprints?"

"I barely even have fingerprints anymore. But, yes."

"Did you guys drive top speed here in that van?" I was honestly curious.

Turk looked over at Dev and tipped her head. "Were we going fast?"

"Well, Turkana, I certainly don't think so."

Milan put the menu down. "I'm going to just have a giant piece of meat. I'm not here to play around."

Suddenly, my back was suggesting to me I should have breakfast. I didn't want to let it down. "I'll do some pancakes."

Milan waved to a surly looking dark haired waitress who sullenly began to approach.

I looked around the table. "Does anyone know why we are in a hotel in Cassis?"

"Ooh, I do." Turk took a big drink of her tea.

"Are you allowed to tell me?"

"He bought a boat." She pointed to Dev.

"I bought a boat. He gave me a frivolous and irresponsible amount of money and I bought a boat." He pointed to Milan who was handing the menu to the waitress. She looked at it with disdain before taking it from his hands.

"She will have blueberry pancakes and I will have just a big steak."

She sighed."What cut?"

"The biggest one. I do not care what part of what cow it comes from. The cow must be dead. I'm firm on that."

"How do you want that cooked?"

"Medium rare, please, Miss."

She sighed once again and stepped away from the table.

"She knows she works here, right?" Turk pointed.

"Where are we going in this boat?" I took a drink of water.

Devique went on. "This is what I like about this plan. We aren't going anywhere. We're going to go to the Plage de la Grande Mer, where I will pick up said boat and then, if possible, float around the Balearic Sea until that is boring.

Turk broke in, "maybe go to Barcelona for their very first gay pride parade since I killed Franco."

I smiled. "That was last month. But should you be saying that out loud in a cafe?"

"Oh, no one cares. He was an asshole. Too soon?"

"You guys missed the horrors of this full conversation," Devique went on.

Milan unconsciously followed the waitress with his eyes. She was just miserable. "I bet."

"But..." Turk moved forward, "Now that Getty is gone, we should have asked Karras where the ear was."

Milan winced. "Ouch."

"I'm serious. Don't you want to know?"

She was referring to millionaire J. Paul Getty who had recently died. His grandson had been kidnapped years ago and his ear had been cut off. The child was returned not long after but the ear was still missing. And rumors were that Karras had instigated the whole thing.

And maybe had the ear.

"All I want is to eat my giant piece of meat."

"I know, but aren't you curious, pops?"

"Call me Milan in public, strange disco girl." Milan took the cup of coffee handed to him by a different waiter, possibly the one who had murdered the sullen waitress in the kitchen, hiding her body in the bisque. I scrunched up my face and made a note to avoid the bisque. "And, yes, I'm curious, but..."

He seemed like he didn't want to really talk about Karras. Honestly, he was one of the things he didn't like about this job. Karras was an opportunist. Besides his son, he would sell out any one of us. Milan had gotten used to working with family.

Something felt off to me. I looked at Dev. "Why did you really buy a boat?"

He smiled. "Okay. Hear me out."

Milan looked at him. "It was for the job, wasn't it?"

Devique nodded. This was what had felt so odd. Dev was not a frivolous irresponsible person. This wasn't about floating around the Balearic Sea. This was for a purpose.

"You want to hear it?"

Milan nodded.

"Ok. I'm looking at maps. I don't like any of the ways we get out of Tell es-Sultan. The way I see it, we're landlocked and trapped. Nikola wants us to go east. We get airlifted out of Jordan. We don't have any control of that at all."

"Right." I interjected. "But we go west, we go through Jerusalem, through the airport, We're in the middle of the shit. And still, where do we get airlifted?"

"We don't. We plant our own truck at Ein Al Sultan. Get to the Aqabat Jabr, 457 to 60 to Birzeit."

I shook my head. "I am so lost."

Milan nodded. "We go in a wide circle around Jerusalem and the airport."

"We don't cross the path between the two at all. We head right to Rishon LeTsiyon Beach."

Milan looked up, thinking.thought "What is that? Eighty minutes?"

"About." Devique continued. "And the boat is waiting."

Turk nodded. "That's not bad."

"We have it stocked." I said.

"Yes. Then, it's past Cyprus, to Heraklion."

Milan leaned back. "Karras's island."

Devique looked satisfied."What do you think?"

I leaned in. "It's better. It's a lot better."

Milan thought. "We own it. The escape route, the vehicles."

"No strange planes and pilots." Turk added.

"Pretty fucking good." Milan looked up, grabbing his steak from the waitress' hands. She had apparently survived the kitchen coup. "To Devique. Woot."

We all cheered a bit. I took the blueberries on the side and piled them up into the center of the stack of pancakes. This was how we do things around here, I thought.

It was beginning to get a bit darker as we left the cafe. Turk saw me walk and did that thing she does where she pretends to lean on me playfully but is really supporting me. There is a moment of panic that happens, sometimes when you lose your balance. It's hard to explain to people who don't experience it. A year before that, I had been swimming in a pool and had lost my balance underwater. This was the panic. I suddenly couldn't tell which way it was to the surface. And it was too dark to see it. I could have let myself drift to the surface.

But I panicked.

We walked to the port at Plage de la Grande Mer. The sky was deepening into reds and violets. And right at the first dock sat Dev's boat.

"So, this is it. No name yet."

"That's bad luck, right?" Turk teased.

"We have a little grace period. It's new."

Milan nodded, impressed. "How much was this?"

Devique looked at him. "Three hundred thousand francs. Give or take. Still a lot left over to stock it."

Turk shook her head. "Damn. I just bought a skirt."

"It's a 1977 Hatteras 53 motor yacht. Extended. Sleeps eight easily, but about twice that can comfortably hang out. Lots of storage. Solid wood work."

Milan laughed. "American boat. No one will ever think..."

"Exactly."

He reached over and pulled Dev closer, kissing him on the head. "You amaze me. Still."

"So, wait. It's not stocked yet?" I asked.

Devique laughed. "Well. Not entirely. But..."

We made our way into the boat, stopping in the rear cabin for a moment.

It turned out that the only thing he had yet stocked it with was alcohol. And there was a lot of it. Each of the storage containers were filled with bottles of wine and liquor. And that seemed consistent across the entire boat. We toured the cockpit, the upper area, the skybridge, the front and lower cabins and the bedrooms. It was huge. Not nearly as big as the Depot, obviously, but for a ship, it would definitely work.

Even if it took us a week to reach Heraklion, we'd be comfortable.

"So we have a family boat?" Turk said with a wink.

"We have a family boat, Turkana. And it's full of booze." Devique laughed and opened one more storage area. This one held a number of bottles of brandy. Turk grabbed one and held it up.

"How do we know these are even real?"

The lower cabin was red and plush and comfortable. Turk, Milan, and I each had a bottle of our own as we sat around the room, each in a different plush chair. Devique had decided he would be the designated driver, although none of us had planned to see the boat actually move tonight.

"We can drive it around tomorrow," Milan said, taking a swig of brandy.

"I mean, I'm sure it works fine." Turk tried to match him, taking a swig from her bottle of vodka. My bottle was a chilled Riesling and I was keenly aware that I would need to up my game if I wanted to keep up.

Bringing wine to a liquor fight.

"It does, indeed, work. I drove it around before I bought it."

"It's so white. And red." Turk noted. It was extremely white. It was fiberglass and smooth, white and sleek. And every place that wasn't white was padded with a soft red type of velvet or designed with a beautiful wooden inlay, like the doors. It was homey. It made you want to lie down, to fall asleep in it.

Milan lifted his bottle again. "To the captain, Devique."

We cheered and drank as he laughed. "I didn't buy this so I could be captain."

I lifted my wine. "To our reluctant captain, Devique."

We all cheered again and drank.

Turk looked up. "Wait, am I XO? Because I have no training."

Milan lifted his bottle again. "To our naturally skillful yet dubiously untrained XO, Turkana."

We cheered. At this rate, yes, I would be drunk very shortly.

Turk stood up. "I want to make a little speech."

She arranged herself. "If I had to go digging under some magic ancient city for hobbit gold or some shit, I could not think of a better group of idiots to do it with."

I raised my bottle along with everyone else. "Here, here."

Milan took another drink and pretended to cry, "That was a beautiful speech."

The sun was dropping and it was near dark out the windows. The only thing I could see was in this room, in this space. And that was enough.

We sat up all night drinking and making toasts. I managed to finish off a pretty good bottle of Pinot as well, although some of that might have spilled all over me. We all could have gotten to the bedrooms, but falling asleep together, in that one room, seemed to make more sense. At least when drunk off our asses.

By the time I woke up, we were moving. Turk was cuddling my legs, on the floor, leaning against the chair. I slid down and kissed her. "Hey, sunshine. We're moving."

"Are we being kidnapped?" she responded, half asleep.

"I think so. Very slowly."

"Good. We'll have time to respond." She fell back, curling up on the rug. Milan was asleep, shoeless, across the room in another chair, looking comfortable.

I got up. I looked around for blankets. The side storage space had a couple of red plush blankets that perfectly matched the furniture and rugs. I slid one each over Turk and Milan and climbed out of the cabin into the topside cockpit. It was called the sky bridge on these boats and I admitted that was a cool name. Devique was at the wheel, driving the boat out.

The air smelled like morning on the sea. I'm not sure anything else smells like that. It was alive and accessible and it made you want to see it. It made you want to be a part of it.

"Oh Captain, my captain."

"I'm never escaping that, am I?"

"Oh, suck it up. What's a little Whitman between friends?"

"Is everyone still asleep?" He let go of the wheel for a second to stretch. He was still shoeless.

"For a bit, I bet. I was drinking a bit lighter than the room."

"I saw that. But French and classy."

"Always."

"Hey, did you know Dad was going to drive at 200 kph down a windy mountain overpass to convince me that he had my back?"

"I did not. And that's really him, isn't it? How is your back?"

"It's good. You really got in there."

Dev laughed. "I did. Good thing I know you aren't fragile."

"He didn't tell you anything?"

"He is cagey. But, hey, I secretly bought a boat. So, I win."

"You do." I moved out toward the opening in front of the cockpit. "What do you think the trip to the Greek islands will be like? Genius idea, by the way."

"Thank you." He turned the wheel and we headed out. "I think kind of like the Odyssey but without godly wrath."

"That sounds comforting."

"No, it's going to be good. It may be cold for some of it on the way back. That time of year. I'm going to make sure to stock sweaters and stuff."

"Yes, red ones."

"Of course, all thematic and matching." He took a deep breath. "But I think it'll be good. The rest of it, I'm in the dark."

"I'm worried about a few things, too. Tonight, I say we get around a table and put it all down. Let's figure out what scares us?"

He nodded. "Right. Let's do it. There are some things that don't add up yet."

Milan stepped out and kissed me on the forehead. He leaned in and kissed Devique on the shoulder. "You two got this beast under control?"

Dev smiled. "Yep. I got stuff for breakfast here. Or we can go back in."

Milan breathed in the seaside air. "I'm good either way."

Turk stepped up behind me, still wearing her blanket. "Hey, guys."

Milan gave her a hug. "Why are you awake?"

"I think I'm the early witch warning system?"

I looked at her. "What?"

She handed me a set of binoculars. On the dock, where the boat was tied, sat a woman dressed in black.

It was Noemie.

"I guess we should see what she wants." Devique pulled the wheel and we aimed toward the dock.

It took us a few to make it back to the dock, and she had stood up and was waiting for us. Turk was the first one down the ramp, followed by Milan, then me. By the time Devique had tied the boat up, she had spoken to us already.

He stepped off the boat. "So what's up?"

Turk waved at her presentationally. "Well, let's gather 'round."

Noemis looked up at Devique and told him what she had been telling us for the past five minutes.

"I think this job is a bad idea. We're all going to die."

3. The Blood of the Poet

Blanc l'innocent, le sang du poète
Qui en chantant invente l'amour

White, ever innocent, the blood of the poet
Who invents love just by singing

Milan had pulled out an elaborate tea set from somewhere and brought out tea for us as we sat around the dining table at the Depot. I hadn't managed to get much out of Noemie in the back of the van on the way home, but it looked like his tactic was working. She seemed more relaxed now with a row of arcane teas and infusers sitting in front of her. Since I was a child I had been impressed with his ability to read a room.

Turk filled a glass with hot water, tea and honey, stirring it slowly. "So, Karras doesn't know you're here?"

Noemie shook her head. She was dressed head to toe in black – a dress that would have been sweltering if it hadn't been nearly transparent, billowy, wraithlike. Small gusts of breeze from the open balcony doorway forced it to swim around her like smoke around an ancient witch aflame.

"I'm sort of tied to Karras in a way."

For a moment, she looked around the table, into our faces. I could tell how guarded she was and how difficult all of this must be.

"I'm a transgender person. In New York... in America, getting hormones is hard. To be...me."

I reached out for her hand. "Is it easier here?"

She slid her hand into mine. "In a way. It's easier if you have money. Karras has money."

Milan nodded. "So, you stick close to him, you get to be you?"

She took a breath. "More or less. I'm saving money. I've saved money."

Devique interjected, "but you aren't quite ready to leave?"

She nodded.

Turk licked the spoon and took a drink. "And let me get this clear. I, myself, die? Do I die? Because I've got plans to change."

Noemi looked down, smiling despite herself. That was the effect Turk had on people. "It's what I see. I don't see you specifically." She looked at Milan. "I see that you die."

Milan leaned back into his chair, crossing his arms. "Well, it wouldn't be the first time someone saw that."

Noemie moved forward for a moment, delicately pointing to Devique. "And you..."

Dev winked at me. "But I'm the captain."

I squeezed her hand. "How about you?"

"For me. It's dark after a certain point. I don't step off the boat."

Turk shook her head. "Uff. That is dark."

Milan looked up. "Interesting."

I could see what he was thinking. As far as I could remember, no one had told her we were using the boat for the job.

So how did she know?

I looked over at Dev and widened my eyes. He nodded. "So you see that in particular? You are on the boat, my boat, after the job?"

"And I don't see myself stepping off."

"And at that point, the blonde one and I are still alive?" Turk licked her spoon.

"Yes."

I tried to catch Noemi's eyes. It seemed like she wanted to climb inside herself and disappear. "You have been close to Karras?"

"In a way."

Milan stood up and made his way to the refrigerator. "And this Rialtos? Him, too?" I remembered how much Karras had leaned on him to explain back in the box.

"His name is Ray Turrico. He is helping to plan, yes. They are together a lot."

Devique leaned in. "Okay, how about this, then. Do you know what Nikola is bringing back from the site?" He looked at Dad, who nodded. This was an answer that might decide the whole thing.

"I don't."

I whispered, "do you see anything?"

She closed her eyes and tried to remember. She seemed frightened but it wasn't by us.

"It's a box. Slightly reddish. With symbols all over. Maybe a foot and a half by three feet long."

A box. Half a meter by a meter long. Red with inscriptions. I closed my eyes.

Nothing.

Milan spoke up. "That doesn't sound like any well known piece of art I can think of off the top of my head."

Devique finished the thought. "And it's worth the entire trip. The whole ride, for him. Millions of francs, months of time?"

She shook her head. She didn't know. But now we knew more.

"Okay, now the fun stuff. Do you see anything else? I'm talking big stuff." Turk grabbed her other hand and squeezed.

The woman in black looked up for a second and whispered to her.

"Elvis Presley dies next month."

That one was pretty believable. "He's not looking great."

Turk looked around the table. "I think we all know now what we have to do now. Save Elvis."

Milan pulled a cheesecake out of the icebox and stepped back to the table, placing plates in the center. A number of forks clattered on the plates as they hit the tabletop. He cut a piece and placed it in front of Noemie.

"Noemie, it's going to come as no surprise to you that I don't believe in any of this. Do you understand?"

She picked up a fork and ate a bite of cheesecake, without blinking, staring at him as he continued.

"But. I believe you. And I don't stay alive by ignoring information. And whether that information is coming from a walkie-talkie, magic, female intuition or just a good hunch, If it talks about my death or the deaths of the people I love, I will always listen. Do you get that?"

"I do."

"Good. We are on the same page. Now, where are you staying?"

"Karras has me in a hotel in La Roucas-Blanc."

Turk laughed. "So, like a fixer upper?"

Milan shook his head. "Would you like to stay here until you decide what you want to do? It's not La Roucas-Blanc, but..."

Noemi nodded. A gust of wind picked up her hair and wrapped it around her like a cigarette gone out. She was pretty, but in a way that seemed fragile, ephemeral. I found myself afraid she would fade away.

My dad tapped Dev on the shoulder. "Dev, would you mind setting our friend up in a room, find out what she needs?"

I let go of her hand as she stood up. "Thank you so much."

Devique offered her his arm and the two walked off down the hallway. I widened my eyes at Milan.

He shrugged. "She related to you. But she eyefucked him."

He wasn't wrong. I still felt like I would have been the best one to get more information. Turk grabbed some sugar and dumped it in her cup.

"To be clear, does the XO go down with the ship, too?"

Milan paced, passing by Turk to kiss her hair. "I don't think that's a rule, sweetheart."

I looked up at him. "You believe her?"

"She's scared. I just don't know what of right now."

"It's not us. I can't even make a cup of tea." Turk took her job of putting people at ease very seriously. But, yes, the tea thing was driving me crazy.

I grabbed her cup and began making her a proper cup of tea. "Is she afraid of Karras? Afraid of the job?"

Milan nodded. "It can be both." He looked over at Turk. "What did your guys find?"

"Literally nothing. She has no record. Noel Mason is actually her birth name. She just changed the pronunciation. Which is thrifty, I think. Noemie is her work name. She also goes as Madame Noël to read Tarot and haunt the rubes. She's telling the truth about coming from New York. She's been here since the meet in London. She's not dating anyone. The boobs are natural. Kind of."

I nodded and handed her back her cup. "So, she's essentially being straight with us?"

"Thank you." She made a kissing motion at me. "Yes. You can see right through that top."

Milan made a shuffling hand motion. "But about the rest?"

"As far as the local police and the other guys know. I'm still waiting on a couple of calls back."

He looked off thoughtfully. I could tell there were a million things going on in his head. The cheesecake had a little ribbon of raspberry on top in a very appetizing swirl. I noticed that some pieces had more raspberry than others. This wasn't a store bought cheesecake. I shook it off as Devique stepped back in the room.

Turk turned to him, pointing at Dad. "He honeypotted you."

"I got that. She's settled in. I showed her how to lock the door, which seemed to make a big difference."

"Good man. You feel free to come and go if you control the lock on your own door." Milan started to wrap up the cake. "This isn't breakfast."

"I think she's honestly afraid of Karras, but terrified of the rest. Like terrified."

I nodded. I had gotten that sense, too. "I don't really buy the magic part, but the intuition part I get."

"Agreed. I'll make some breakfast and then we put it all out on the table." He slid the cheesecake back in the refrigerator and turned back to us.

What happened next was my fault. My chair was facing the balcony so it was my responsibility to see it first. But when I saw the shadow, my brain processed it as one of my shadows– what I saw when my vision was impaired.

I didn't call it out. I didn't stop it.

When that man stepped into the kitchen from the open balcony door with a gun pointed at the back of my father's head, I didn't stop it.

And that's on me.

His voice was part growl, with a bass note that I didn't expect. He had a slight lisp that was even more unexpected. All in all it sounded like it hurt for him to talk, a wound deep down in his throat. But he spoke anyway.

"Or you all just stay in your chairs and you don't move."

Milan stared ahead. He hadn't turned yet to see the man. "And who the fuck are you?"

The man was dressed in a black pair of pants and a black turtleneck. He was probably 45 or 50 years old, Latin-looking, with skin that looked like it had been too long in the sun. There was some sort of burn on his neck and I could see he walked with a limp in his left leg. He held a new Sig Sauer P230 with a heel magazine release, and decocker.

These had just been released so the shiny new gun look was likely not just for show.

It was in his left hand.

He stepped around the table, keeping his distance, aiming the gun now at Devique. This was a common criminal behavior. If you have one gun and a few people to keep still, aim the gun at the person that most of your targets least want to see shot. He chose Dev, meaning he knew about our family situation. He also knew that it removed any lingering perceptions we might have had that he wouldn't shoot a young woman.

This is exactly what I would have done. And I hated it. Now, his job was to behave reasonably enough that we all thought we could give him what he wanted.

"My name is Ruach. And you work for me now."

I could see Turk trying to get his attention. She raised her hand, "What kind of benefits are we talking about?"

Milan stood up. "It's okay. Point that at me. I'm in charge here. Let's figure it out. What do you need?"

"I need you to sit down. Where is the witch?"

Turk continued. "You really have to bring your own fantasy characters to a party."

He finally pointed the gun at Turk. "Shut up. I saw her come in with you."

Milan waved his hands. Right here. Look at me. She's in her room. She's locked in her room."

"Get her out here. I want to talk to her, too."

Devique responded, calmly, "I'm pretty sure she's sleeping right now. Why don't you make your pitch to us and she'll follow along later."

Ruach stopped for a moment. A shadow washed across his face. I could see something in his skin, under his skin, like a wave, right below the surface. It ran from his chin to his forehead, so imperceptibly that it might have been a trick of the light. And just as quickly, and possibly unreal, as it passed the upper part of his face I saw something else.

Something impossible.

His eyes, for just a second, glowed yellow. It wasn't a jaundiced yellow or a glint that hit the light as yellow gold. It was some kind of inhuman color, something horrific and unreal. And it happened too fast to prepare for.

But his eyes glowed yellow.

He lifted the gun so that his arm was straight and sent a single bullet into my brother's chest.

Turk yelled out and rammed her head into his chest, past his gun. He fell backward a meter or so before gaining his footing and lifting the weapon again, pointing it at her head. Milan dove to the floor and huddled over Dev as I tried to stand.

At that moment, my balance went out. My foot had slid into the deepening pool of blood gathering around Devique and for a moment, up and down seemed to switch places. I hit the floor with a wet thud, watching the table obscure my line of sight to Ruach and Turk. I looked over to see Milan holding his hand to the hole in Dev's chest and desperately trying to staunch the flow of blood to the floor.

So much blood.

I pushed the table aside to see Turk. She had managed to grab a knife and was holding it out at Ruach. They were close enough that she might have been able to stab him even as he shot her.

He growled, "Okay. Okay. Now we can ease back a bit. You don't have any love for Karras."

Milan yelled out angrily, "he gave us a few million francs. You shot my son. Guess which way we're leaning?"

"Okay. He's the carrot. I'm the whip. Keep his money. Keep what you find down there. But when you get the red box, use this."

He reached into his pocket with his right hand and pulled out a small black pager, tossing it on the floor right near us.

My hands and legs were covered in blood. I called out, "what happens to us, then?"

"If you give me what I want, nothing. You live your lives. If you don't, you all die."

Dad was pumping Dev's chest, trying to get him to breathe. Turk was close to pouncing. He would shoot her, too. I crawled to where the pager sat, right outside the pool of blood.

"Go. Go now. I've got it. Go now."

He looked at me for a moment and bolted for the balcony. Turk turned and slid behind the door, trying to see where he went. She looked at me and shook her head.

He was gone.

I crawled to Devique, trying to help dad. He was breathing hard, tears in his eyes. He wasn't ready to watch him die. As I looked down, my peripheral vision seemed to peel away, leaving a reddish black lined tunnel in front of me, pulling my eyes toward the wound in his chest.

I put my hands on his chest, applying pressure so that Milan could work on his breathing. His heart was pumping blood like a firehose. I felt his thick broad chest under me and it was impossible to believe he was dying.

I could hear my dad's sobbing, a long, drawn out plaintive cry, with no beginning or end. It sounded like an animal, wounded, on the side of the road.

Dying.

Into the circle of my vision I saw a pale hand, longer and thinner than mine, stonelike. It was cold to the touch. It pushed my hands away and then, somehow, impossibly, began to push open the tunnel. The hand was joined by another one and I heard a connection, a kind of electrical snap that preceded a white glow. It grew from the hands in front of me, widening and dispelling the blood walls of my visual tunnel, illuminating the entire space in front of me.

I looked up to see Milan sitting back on his knees, Noemie in front of him, a brilliant light emanating from her hands pouring into Devique and across the plane of the room.

The light built a new level in the room, just 20 centimeters above the floor, rooted in the surface of his chest, a thermocline across the kitchen and beyond that cut through everything there. It felt electric across me, tingly, alive, as though my whole body was touching both poles of a nine volt battery.

Devique began to choke, spitting up blood that fell down the wells of his cheeks onto his neck. His hands shifted and moved and his chest rose into the air as if connected by an invisible rope to the ceiling. There was an electrical hum that rose, piercing the air around us and, finally, a different snap, a bigger one, as though an electrical transformer were being sharply turned off. The room went back to normal but for me, the change endured.

I could see.

I could see Dev reaching out to hold Milan, who was patting his head and crying. I fell back into the blood and looked up at Turk. it was rare that I ever saw her confused or without some kind of comment but she stood there, staring downward, her own tears still wet.

I reached over to Noemie and fell into her. I held her, crying. Clinging to her black gossamer dress.

And I listened to my brother try to calm my father down.

***

Noemie stood to my right as we watched Milan and Devique investigate the balcony. I had no idea what they were looking for but I recognized they had to do it.

"Is your dad ok?"

"Well. Thanks to you. I think he wants to brick up every window, though." I stared toward the kitchen. It had taken almost two hours for all of us to clean. And then to clean ourselves. Nobody wanted his blood on them. Nobody wanted to see it.

"Not a bad idea. I think."

"How do you think he got up and down from the balcony? I mean. You know things, right? How would you do it?

She breathed out. I could tell she was exhausted and I felt bad for even asking. "Well. I would prepare a spell to levitate or something."

I turned. "You can do that?"

"Yes. It's a hard spell and it's not fast. It doesn't seem like that's what he did."

"So, Ruach, any idea at all?"

She shook her head. Either she was being honest or was a fantastic liar. I was starting to think she had been honest about everything. "He knew I was here? How?"

"He admitted he'd been watching us. He knew about the job, about us, about you. Let's assume he knew everything. Do you think he knew that you could save Dev?"

"I don't know how. That spell is one I keep prepared. I can keep five of them. But I've honestly never had to use it, except for a bird once."

I imagined this wispy gothic fairy on the floor of some grand mansion, breathing life into a little bird with an elaborate lightshow and smiled to myself. "Well. Thank you again."

I heard the door slam as Turk made her way into the room and wrapped her arms around me from behind. "Did you know you looked like that?"

I laughed, "Like what?"

She licked at my neck. "Like yummy."

"Hm. I did not know."

"None of the peasants around here saw anything." She grabbed my hand.

"So he levitated on and off the balcony and nobody saw?"

"Who knew our neighbors knew how to mind their own fucking business."

She reached out and grabbed Noemie's hand. "Okay, Samantha Stephens, let's you and me go scavenge up an actual French breakfast and bring it back."

Noemie smiled and they rushed toward the door, holding hands. I watched as Milan and Devique gave up and returned through the balcony door.

"Nothing. We'll keep the door shut, though." Milan seemed to have an invisible cord attached between him and Dev. It wasn't much longer than five centimeters.

I breathed in. "Okay. Scenario A. That whole thing was a con, to get us to trust her."

Devique jumped in. "I'll play. I don't see it. Too risky. That was a real bullet. And it fucking hurt. And she really has something."

Milan nodded. "Agreed. There would be easier ways. It's too much. And I don't think she's that."

I considered. "Okay. me, too. I think she's been straight up. Scenario 2: Karras used this Ruach guy to test us. But why?"

Dev was scratching at his chest. "Yeah, how paranoid is he? Don't answer that."

"Could be a lot. Does that itch? Let me see." Milan reached to help him take his shirt off. He slid off his dark green shirt to expose a tiny bullet wound, looking nearly completely healed.

He shook his head. "This is insane. It only itches a little."

"Scenario Delta, all this is really happening and Ruach expects us to get him the box."

"That's my vote." Devique sat down on the couch, his shirt over his lap, with Dad not far behind. "It felt pretty real to me."

Dad had washed the blood from his hands, but he was still looking for errant spots. "It comes down to the same thing for me as before."

Dev nodded. "What is in this box?"

“Exactly. It’s the whole thing. We’re going to help someone get this box. I need to know what they think is in the fucking thing. Nothing’s changed.”

I sat in the conversation pit, across from them. We’d all had the chance to shower, but I was still in a pair of shorts and a robe. I couldn’t wash my back in the shower yet so I wasn’t feeling 100%. I pulled my feet up. “If I tell you guys something, I hope you won’t think I’m nuts.”

“I already do.”

“No, go ahead, sweetheart. Did you see something?”

“Yes. I did. As he shot Dev – right before – his eyes. They went yellow.”

Dad sat up. “Like a reflection?”

I shook my head. “No. Like something unreal. Like something not natural.”

Dev laughed. “Well. Unnatural seems to be the theme of the day.”

“He’s not wrong. None of this is normal.”

I heard the door open again. Turk and Noemie were laughing as they came into the living room with bags. Noemie seemed lighter now, more girlish, even. She let herself down inelegantly on the couch right next to Dev. I saw him put his hand on her knee to pull her up into the cushions, as though he’d known her forever.

Turk slid into the space in front of me, sitting on the floor, laying the bags out in a circle. “Bread, Chocolate, Fruit, Coffee. The four food groups.”

Milan reached for one of the bags, tearing it open. “Coffee.”

I pulled Turk over and wrapped my legs around her. “We don’t have a fucking library anymore, do we?”

Dev shook his head as he pulled fruit from a bowl he shared with Noemie. “Nope, the Alcazar is closed. There are smaller ones. But nothing we can use for this.”

Milan cocked his head, “Noemie, could you draw what this box looks like? I mean, do you actually see the box in your mind?”

She seemed to think for a minute. I was starting to get accustomed to her American accent and wasn't so shocked anymore hearing the voice of a cowgirl coming out of this ephemeral gothic waif. "I think I could."

"I love art time." Turk shot up to grab art supplies.

Noemie looked at me. "She's a hoot."

***

We spent the afternoon eating and prodding Noemie to draw what was in her head. Turk drew next to her at the living room table while the rest of us drank coffee and called the few antiquities experts we trusted.

Turk held up a piece of paper covered in a scene that revolved around a large rabbit. It wasn't bad. "This is a giant rabbit stabbing Elvis to death."

Noemie looked over. "I don't think that's how he dies."

"Well, maybe you didn't see that far."

Noemie shrugged. "Can you do him on the toilet?"

"Ooh, yeah. I actually specialize in toilet pictures."

I finished off a chocolate croissant and leaned in to Dev, whispering. "They look like they're having fun."

"Turk could have fun in an induction oven."

"Fair. Am I sensing some kind of thing between you and the witch?"

"Like something metaphysical and magical?"

"Ha, yes. What's going on here?"

He stared over to the table. "I'm not sure. She did save my life."

"She did. I think that's why doctors shouldn't date their patients, big guy."

"Well, I'm not a patient anymore."

"Tell her that."

Dev paused for a minute. "Do you think Elvis really dies on a toilet?"

I scrunched my face up. "It actually sort of tracks."

Milan stepped back in from his office, in the back of the flat. He still had the little towel he had been washing his hands with all day, since the shooting. I wondered how long that would go on. "Okay, I found three people I trust. We fax them some drawings, boom, somebody tells us what the fuck is in that box. "

I cheered. "Easy peasy."

He walked over to the table and looked over Noemie's shoulder. "Well, not easy. I am paying these people."

I held up a cup of coffee, "A toast to the giant fax machine we never thought we'd use." Dev and Turk cheered.

Milan put his hands up. "Hey, I've used it. And it's a regular-sized fax machine."

I threw a croissant at him. "Intello."

"I am not a nerd. I'm telling you, everyone is buying these. I can send pictures all over the world."

"Ooh, send this one." Turk held up a new picture. "This is Elvis riding a toilet like a spaceship."

Noemie nodded at her. "This one is really close, actually."

Turk smiled. "Nailed it. What do you got?"

Noemie held up a few pictures in a row. They all showed a box with arcane writings all over it. She had shaded it well, showing it from all sides. It seemed very complete.

Milan nodded, looking through the pictures. He realized that taken all together, they presented a complete picture of the box. A 360-degree rotation. "Good job. Nice."

Noemie looked up at him. "Is that enough, you think?"

"I think it's more than enough. I'll fax these out to our people." He collected the drawings and started toward the office.

"Ooh, send this Elvis one, too. Tell them it's for sale."

Milan stepped back in the room and grabbed hers, too.

***

As it got darker, I could feel myself fading. We kept the lights on. I missed the breeze but felt better with the balcony door locked. Turk was hanging on me in a way that felt altogether amazing, testing out the tattoo on my back, which was healed enough to touch now. She tried to tell me jokes and elaborate stories about how she was going to kill Elvis. But I don't remember any of those. What I remember are her deft fingers flitting all over me like tiny hummingbirds, moving in closer, caressing me, trying to communicate.

She tried to tell me a dirty limerick, drawing the letters on my back with her tongue and the goose bumps all over my body rose higher than they ever had before. Her tongue vibrated like a telephone ringing every time she laughed, and if you know Turk, you know that was a lot. That tiny phone rang off the hook.

Across the room, Noemie was telling Dev her life story over coffee and chocolate and, every few minutes, they would laugh. It was an easy laugh, one that was entirely unexpected from someone who had been lying on the floor dying just a few hours ago and the woman who brought him back with a plane of light that I could still see all around me when I half closed my eyes.

My ears were tired, so I stopped trying to make words out of sounds, letting them fall around me like raindrops, playing the marimba on every scattered object, tones shifting and changing with size and composition. I sank into the evening and tried to forget it all.

Until Milan stepped over to the table next to us, rummaging through the contents. "Were you girls using the same pens?"

Noemie got up. "Yes, the pens are right there. Is something wrong?"

"I don't know." He ran his hand through his hair. "All three of the people I faxed just asked me the same question." He took a deep breath.

"Why I had faxed them a picture of Elvis on the toilet. And then a bunch of empty pages. So I looked. When I tried to copy the pictures of the box, I got this."

He held up a series of blank pieces of paper.

4. When mornings pluck petals off dreams

Où les matins effeuillent les rêves
Pour nous donner un monde d'amour

When mornings pluck petals off dreams
To give us a world of love

That night, I dreamed I was with Turk

It was 1966. My dad, Devique, and I had gone to Paris for a show.

A single show.

It was the middle of March and James Brown was playing at L'Olympia Bruno Coquatrix in Paris. It would include The Famous Flames, and everyone we knew wanted to be there. My father, a veteran fan, knew every single song and was ready for an epic event.

And he wanted us to see it.

We had meant to fly into Charles de Gaulle -- the airport, but our flight was delayed. Rather than wait, Milan had pulled out a massive wad of cash, in full view of everyone, and booked three tickets into Orly immediately. He likely paid a fortune for that one hour plus long flight, first class. I was 16 and Dev was nearly 19.

And first class had everything we needed.

That day was the third time I'd ever seen my father cry. Oh, for sure, since then, I'd seen him cry time and time again. Hell, I once saw him cry during a baguette commercial. But this, I remember. It was only the third time.

We sat in a cafe in Orly, having just flown in. We were eating lunch and laughing. I remember Milan training Devique on observing the exits and entrances without looking like you were looking. To me, he was pointing out the men and women all around us who wore their wallets and pocketbooks in full view. He called them "Fresh fruit." and they were everywhere. A slight bulge. A bankroll. A waistbag, purse, change purse stuffed with bills. The fruit was falling off the trees, he would say to us. It was all around. The men would literally drop 20 franc notes while paying, folding their wallets up hastily just to stuff them back in haphazard pockets. I learned that many people kept cash ready, in hand, at the airport. And that very often people forgot what valuables they were even carrying.

The news was playing in the cafe. It seemed like a big deal. The airport security vehicles, usually moving at a casual pace through the wide corridors, had all fled to one side of the building. Milan looked up. A boy of 24 had tried to stowaway in a flight from Moscow, hiding in the wheel well. The plane had arrived on another runway, just as we had.

But while we traveled first class, the young man from Moscow had frozen to death on his trip. The news told us what was happening across the airport right now, where professionals used torches to detach his frozen fingers from the pistons of the chassis, to pry his tiny body from the landing gear of the massive plane. They suggested to us that he was only 24.

"Just a boy," Milan mouthed, along with the newscaster.

And he cried. In a fancy airport cafe, surrounded by his onion soup and bites of steak wrapped in cheese, pockets full of cash, he cried for a stranger frozen to death trying to get...

Where? Was he coming home? Was he escaping? Defecting?

Why was my father crying? In retrospect I can tell you.

That boy had nowhere to go. This must have been the case. Why else steal away in an open hole on a massive plane, hanging on so tightly tens of thousands of feet above ground that his hands merged with the steel of the thing?

And he cried.

Maybe that was why he did what he did. Or maybe it was just him. I don't know.

I didn't know.

But we settled into the hotel and made arrangements for dinner. And a film. We would go to the performance early the next day and listen to the band sound check. This was something Milan adored. To watch them tune up, toss chords back and forth, joke as they marked up song lists he would later surreptitiously swipe from the bottom of the stage, to press in one of his albums back home. This is when he was alive.

But tonight, we finished almost none of dinner and slipped away to the movie hall next door to the restaurant for a showing of Le Deuxième Souffle, with Milan explaining everything the cunning larrons had failed at, the places they got it all wrong. Where these thieves failed. We yelled out each time they showed some odd Marseille backdrop almost as though our city was a fan favorite character in this movie, in on all the heady secrets and equally on the run from Commissaire Blot of the Paris police.

Of course, we rooted for the thieves. As we do.

The main character, Gustave "Gu" Minda, escaped criminal mastermind who never once gave up an accomplice, was played by Lino Ventura and he even looked like Dad, minus the actor's famous Roman nose.

It was a good night.

Our hotel was just a few doors down. I grabbed the leftovers from the seat next to me, wrapped in an elaborate shape by the enthusiastic waiter, and made my way to the room as Milan and Devique set out to find a place to order a few drinks.

I was happy to have some time to myself, honestly. We had been on the move since early in the morning.

I took the lift up to the fourth floor and approached the room. From where I stood, in the hallway, I could see the door was wide open. A girl, close to my age, was standing in the room looking around. I ducked behind the maid's cart for a moment and listened.

She was whistling. And she was very good. I was sure my dad could have made out the tune, but I wasn't so positive. It was French for sure.

And it was beautiful.

I pulled an apron from the cart and slid it over my head. I grabbed a duster and stepped into the room.

"Excuse me. I'm sorry, Miss. I didn't see a card on the door. Do you want me to come back later?"

She turned around. There was no anxiety in her face. There was no artifice. There seemed to be no lie about her at all.

And yet, she lied.

Breathing steadily, she smiled. "If you can. I'm really sorry. I'm trying to get out of here for dinner, but I think I lost something."

I smiled and moved into the room. "Do you want some help looking? What did you lose?"

"Oh, it's fine. I don't want to waste your time because I'm an idiot. I'll put the card on the door when I leave."

"You're going to eat?"

"I was." She looked at me with a smile, cagily challenging the maid, "Do you know a good restaurant nearby?"

I lifted the bag in my hand. It held the remains of all three meals, more than enough for her. "You know, I just happen to have a bag from one. Would you like some?"

She stared straight at me. Her face was a perfect heart shape, with cheekbones that made you silently beg to see her smile. She was about my height, but her hair was huge. It was, even then, beautifully round and fluffy, framing her face, giving her the illusion of being a doll, constructed by some master craftsman, skin flawless and beautifully smooth mahogany.

She wore a pair of red fashionable overalls that threatened to open at the front, exposing her to the world. And her voice seemed to play across the room as though it were something fluid and alive, bright and sonorous. It never fell.

I wanted to hear her laugh.

And she did. Her face opened up and she laughed. "With you?"

I laughed back. "Of course with me."

She cocked her head and whispered, "this is your room, isn't it?"

I slid the apron off and nodded. "It is. But I'll absolutely help you rob it if you want."

By the time Milan and Devique returned, coming from down the hallway, singing "Papa's Got A Brand New Bag" at the top of their lungs in anticipation of the show, I had eaten my second meal of the night and she had eaten the rest. We explained the situation and my dad lectured her on leaving the door open. He showed her where someone like him would hide the valuables. He warned her to be aware of when someone entered. He laughed and pointed to any treasure she might have missed.

And let us finish the wine they had brought.

Turk and I never spent a full day apart since then. Milan bought another ticket for the show that night and another still for the plane ride home.

I dreamt about that first day in Paris with Turk. About how it turned into two days and then three and then a family and then more. In my nightmares I came back to the room just a few minutes later or our room was just one floor up or I had gone to drink with them.

And I missed her.

But on good nights, I didn't.

On good nights, she came back with us. And she told us that the weight of her family disappearing on her was lighter every day, until she one day found herself wishing them well, wherever they were. The mother and father she barely remembered deserved their freedom, in her mind.

And she deserved us.

***

I woke up to Turk shaking me half-heartedly. She was never awake before me. I pulled her back under the covers roughly.

"Okay, it can wait." She giggled.

She kissed me. I kissed her back and took my time, opening my mouth lazily.

"Why are we awake, puffy girl?"

"I was going to surprise you with coffee or something. Captain Bly wants to take the boat to Calanque de la Crine."

Calanque de la Crine was on a tiny island called Pomègues, only a couple of hours away. It was really beautiful. But an odd thing to just decide at six in the morning.

"That sounds pretty." I rolled back over and rubbed myself on her.

"He says there's an antiquities expert there. Apparently our pictures don't fax."

I turned back to her. "Dad tried again?"

"Yep. Sabrina's been drawing pictures all morning with various pens, pencils, even a crayon. It won't fax."

I sat up. "That is really fucking weird."

"He said we can make out on the trip."

I nodded, thinking about the ordeal of putting clothes on.

"Okay. I'm in."

***

We took a shower and met up with everyone else in the living room. I looked over at the balcony and saw the door shut. I wondered if it would ever be open again. Dad sat on the couch, lost in thought. He was wearing a shirt I'd never seen for the second day in a row.

I gave Noemie a hug. She had managed to arrange her black wraithlike dress differently today, so that it only rose over one shoulder. It was flattering and somehow happier looking. She still carried off the brooding gothic wisp look, though.

I squared off, facing my father and took a deep breath.

"You're seeing someone. She cooks. She lives next door."

His face turned to me and he nodded. "That was good. That was very good." He stood up and walked over.

"The balcony was open every day. Not surprising. But it nearly connects next door. You can jump it. Put a chair over it and crawl. You're wearing new shirts. Tea infusers? You drink coffee. That cheesecake was homemade. A sportscar? You're thinking about Mom. You weren't trying to convince me you were loyal to her. You were convincing yourself."

He looked at me and shook his head. "I couldn't have done that."

I patted his chest. "Yes, you could. Ruach, he came from her place. We need to talk to her."

He looked down. "Yes. I tried. She's gone. Out of town. A note."

"Do you believe the note?"

He slowly shook his head and pulled me in for a hug. I held onto him and ran my fingers through his hair like he did to me so many times. "Do you think she's okay?"

"I don't."

We rocked back and forth for a few minutes until Turk came in to hug us both. We could work this out later. From the corner of my eye, I could see the table covered in images of the box.

We needed to work that out.

Dev came in from the back room, smiling. He intentionally bumped into Noemie, making her laugh as he addressed us. The two of them looked, possibly, even more comfortable than last night. It occurred to me that I rarely noticed how tall he had gotten. I compared the Devique in my dream, the shy but kind boy, thin, handsome, to this version, towering over six foot, muscular, confident, and the embodiment of life and vitality, despite what had happened yesterday.

"Okay, people, we can cuddle on the boat. It's island time."

I tugged at Milan's beard and let him go. I could hear everyone distinctly, each person, my brain separating Turk's silky unrestrained laugh from my father's gruff approbation, Noemie's quiet encouragements from Devique's playful captain's orders. And it all became liquid.

I started to tip over, leaning into it and falling onto the couch. Turk stepped over and grabbed at my hand. I took a breath and saw that she wasn't fooled by my efforts to make that look intentional.

We all invent words to describe our experiences. My good or bad days, days when my senses were less than what they could be, these days I called "slips." And, who knows, maybe I would be better tomorrow. Maybe tomorrow would be a good day. But the times when I lost something permanently, when the edges of my vision pulled inward and the shade was pulled for good, or when I lost words and my ears couldn't find them, these were "hits."

And I was acutely aware that I could only take so many of those.

The problem was that, on the day, there was really no way to tell the difference between a slip and a hit. The job was to hang in there. The job was what it was for everyone, all the time.

To live for one more day.

We made our way down to the street, where Turk had pulled around my wheelchair. I shook my head at her and climbed in. It was grey, aluminum, minimal, a modern folding chair with a simple nylon seat and back. Turk had drawn all over it in marker, though, nearly every inch, tiny black thickline drawings of penises, vaginas, and various sex acts. It was not meant for polite company.

Before I could move toward the van, she grabbed the back, rushing me down the street. Milan looked up, raising his hand. I knew what he would say if he could get it out.

"Turkana, don't kill her," or

"Slow down, young lady," or

"Where's the fire?"

But it wouldn't matter.

We ate in the van on the way to the harbor and started toward the boat that would take us to Calanque de la Crine. We would be doubling back a bit, since it was closer to Marseille, really, than Cassis. But it was a good day. Mostly. Devique told us to wait 20 minutes for him to get the boat ready and then to join him.

And he was Captain.

Turk pushed me down the dock, pretending to toss me in the water. Even here, this close to the dock it was impossibly blue and clear. I laughed and breathed in as much of the air as I could, greedily. Right near the water, it was so rich and thick with the sea. And it was all mine.

Noemie was impressed with how modern the boat was as we approached. As we walked around to the back, to climb in, Dev stepped onto the dock.

"Ok, ladies and gentlemen. It is bad luck not to name a ship. So, here we go." he waved us to the back where he had painted, in precise black letters, on the sharp white of the stern "XMAS."

"I give you, the good ship Christmas."

We applauded and cheered. Noemie smiled. "That's so pretty."

Devique took a bow. Milan put his hand on Noemie's arm. "In French, Christmas is Noël. The name."

Her head shot back toward Dev, who was cleaning up his paints and brushes and preparing the boat.

Turk leaned over to her. "This is what happens when you save the captain's life."

Noemie stepped onto the ship. She was surprisingly graceful in situations like this, despite appearing to be a woman who was made to be seen at night. Her dress flowed around her, looking like translucent feathers on a raven, lifting her onto the deck of the ship like a bird, setting her down next to my brother, on his boat.

I let Turk push me around and dump me on the couch. My balance had returned, but she was having fun tossing me around. It was her unbridled physicality like this that made me feel connected to her so much. She seemed to have no physical boundaries when it came to me. If it entertained her to treat me like a delicate beautiful girl, she would. If it moved her to treat me like a sack of flour, throwing me around and laughing, she would, too.

We sank into the couch pit in the back cabin with Turk on top of me. I closed my eyes as she placed both her hands in mine and told me stupid jokes with sign language, her hands flitting across my palms, letting me feel each sign.

Tactile.

Connected.

Some of the jokes were dirty and sexy, flitting back and forth between French and English, whichever made the joke land better:

What's the difference between a French virgin and a unicorn? Nothing, they're both fictional characters.

What's foreplay to a real French woman? She licks butter off your pussy.

But some were complex, word games, forcing me to pay attention.

Did you hear about the woman who jumped into the river in Paris? She was declared in Seine.

And my favorite:

What do you call the ex-president now? Charles de Ghoul.

I laughed out loud to that one, sitting up to kiss her. It was disconcerting how easy it was to just turn off all input except her.

All except her.

I feel like I want to tell you all of these little moments because, to me, they were as important or more than what was about to come. How this little trip meant so much to me, especially given the eventual destination. I feel bad for you that you have to sit through my deflections and diversions, my drunken walk toward the point. I promise you, it's not out of any desire to punish you.

Dev proved to be a pretty good captain. About an hour out from Plage de la Grande Mer, he turned the boat off and we sat on the back deck, listening to the bucking spill of La Méditerranée as it drew itself up into the warm July afternoon, spitting the occasional wave into the matching blue of the gulf sky.

Turk and I peeled off our clothes and slid into the water as Milan stared off toward the islands. I felt the black silk rope that connected us, my right wrist to her left one as the water took us in. I felt like you could see all the way to the bottom.

It was a clear day, but the warm wind from the Calanques had fired up the Lion's gulf, sending thick buckets of blue scattering upward around us, animal-like waves that meant to carry us away from the chalk-white tipped clifftops all around. Tiny up in the distance, I could see the winding road where my dad had directed his stolen blue speedster, with me in the passenger seat.

I could see everything.

Turk yelled out to Devique and Noemie as they stripped off their clothes to join us. Noemie kept on a tiny black thong. That and the silk rope they had tied to connect them screamed out against the impossible whiteness of her skin like letters in a new book, freshly opened, pages perfectly clean except for the rich ink that gave them life.

I shook my head. This was me floating around, making stupid attempts at poetry while floating in the greatest poem of all. I laughed.

Between the port and the island, according to the map, was a limestone reef. As we dipped underwater, we could easily see it, just about 50 meters in front of us. Turk and I swam toward it. As we approached, the water became shallow. The floor of the reef was slick, but it had enough traction to crawl on, and then, eventually, to stand.

The boat was now nearly 100 meters behind us and the port much further behind it. But in front of us was clear water as far as the eye could see, with no obstructions on the horizon line.

I held Turk's hand and stared out toward the island, seeing nothing but a vast expanse of blue. It felt infinite, impossibly large. We were like toys on top of a wedding cake, effigies placed on the bowl of a massive globe, billions of gallons of untouched water between us and anything.

We screamed into all of it.

***

We pulled our underwear back on in the boat, pulling red blankets over ourselves in the cabin while Dev and Noemie played in the water. I looked down at my clothes, pushing the bunch off the couch when a lighter sized piece of black fell off them onto the floor. I reached down to pick it up.

It was the pager that Ruach had thrown at us. The one we were meant to use to contact him once we had the box. Turk looked at me.

"Did you bring that?"

I shook my head. Milan stepped into the cabin and handed us a bottle of wine. I took it and held up the pager.

"Did you see this?"

He looked unfazed."Is that what I think it is?"

I nodded.

"You brought it with you?" He surveyed both our faces.

I shook my head. "No. We should get them back on the boat."

He turned and made his way to the deck while we put our clothes on. Turk was the first one fully dressed. "So he or one of his people were in here."

"Or he made it appear somehow. I'm not ruling anything out."

Devique reached for the device the second he entered, pulling on a pair of linen pants with the other hand. "You are sure you didn't bring it?"

"Yes, Captain."

Milan shook his head. "I don't like this at all."

I took a breath. "I don't love this, either, but at what point do we tell Karras about Ruach." I looked at the dark haired girl pulling on her dress. "Noemie, you know him."

She looked down. "We don't. He's incredibly paranoid. If he thinks for a moment that you kept that pager, he'd kill you."

"I never liked pagers. I would kill me, too." Turk affirmed.

I sighed., "Yeah, well, I can't get rid of it."

Noemie straightened up. "Can I see that?"

For a second I wondered if I could trust her. A moment later, though, that sentiment was washed away. I realized that I wanted to trust her and, ironically, that was the thing that was keeping me from fully trusting her. It's possible that my father's constant lessons on the life of a thief had messed me up a bit emotionally. I made a point to dive into that later.

She held it tightly in her right hand and closed her eyes. At one point, she reached out with her left hand and grabbed my arm.

A few minutes later she opened her eyes and handed it back to me. "It's a tether. A simple version of the spell. It's following you."

"Wait. It's following me?"

"Well. probably the first person besides Ruach to pick it up. It's connected to you. It will follow you until its job is done. Until it's used. If it were a more advanced tether you could control it. This one you can't."

Milan considered that. "So, if she threw it into the sea, right now, it would come back and follow?"

"Yes. Although, I don't know how waterproof it is."

"So you think it's magical, but not waterproof?" Turk lifted it, seemingly weighing it.

Noemie laughed a little. "That's weird, I know."

"No. no. it makes perfect sense. Did anyone here have a magic beeper and a phantom fax machine on their Christmas wish list?"

Dev tried to shake it off. "Anyway, we should get to the island. The guy's name is Talarico. I told him, essentially, what we were looking for. He's probably got it all figured out by now. He doesn't have a fax machine so I didn't bother. "

Milan interjected. "He will, eventually."

Out the windows, we could see the Frioul Islands. There were four of them. Ratonneau, If, Tiboulen, and, right in front of us, Pomègues. The Port de Pomègues was only a few hundred meters away.

I think I'm supposed to use klicks for nautical distance.

At any rate, we were about to dock. The Port de Pomègues was what's called a quarantine port. During the plague, the French government would quarantine newly arriving ships on the island, making sure that the occupants survived the first week or so. If they didn't, obviously, they had the plague. If they lived, they were allowed passage into Marseille. It goes without saying that the Island experienced its share of death and, as a product of that, entertained a number of mystical and mysterious ghost stories. Much of France is haunted, let's be clear. But the area around the Port de Pomègues is particularly haunted, by intemperate and hostile ghosts kept captive while their shipmates died, spreading disease to them.

And that's where Talarico lived.

We stepped off the boat onto a quiet dock. We would have to hike to Talarico's, but that would only take 20 minutes or so. It was a small island.

Devique pointed. "He lives up here with his wife about 10 minutes further. It's a nice place. I tried to explain to him the piece and he said he'd look it up before we got here. I may have led him to think he would get the sale once we got it."

Milan walked quietly next to him. "That's okay, son. We do what we need to. If he can find any information about this, it'll be worth it."

Noemie stopped. Her eyes went wide.

I think I smelled it first. And I wouldn't have if I hadn't been enjoying the day so much. Every smell since we'd left the Depot was exciting and clear, like big color pictures in the center of a page. For most of us, most of the time, smells are like the inscriptions in the margins. But these were all big and colorful, filled with the immensity of the sea and the depths of the forest we were stepping through.

Fire.

Noemie was even paler than before. She closed her eyes. "No. no. no." she turned around and stepped back on the path, toward where we'd come.

I looked at Milan. He nodded and ran up ahead.

Dev stopped and turned to me. "What's going on?"

"Maybe nothing. Do you smell that?"

Just then, the breeze carried it back to us. Milan moved toward us waving his hands. "Stop. Stay here. Don't." He bent over, leaning onto his knees. Then he fell, his legs scraping the ground.

I ran up to grab him, kneeling next to him. "Dad, are you ok?"

He looked up at Dev. "I'm sorry, son."

Devique walked slowly, staring up the path. I reached over and pulled the binoculars from around his neck.

A few hundred meters in front of us, I could see it. The compound was on fire. It was thick, with black clouds billowing from it. I lowered them and could see, not far in front of us, snaking across the hiking trail, a set of ropes framed by the smoke behind it, crisscrossing.

And hanging from that were three bodies. A man and two women. Their throats had been slit and blood had drenched the fronts of their clothes so much that the natural colors of the garments couldn't be determined. One of the women hung close to the man, the other off to one side a few meters.

I saw Milan cry again. He sank into the dirt of the footpath.

"Her name was Selene."

I dropped to the ground and hugged him. Devique pulled the binoculars from my hands and looked. I heard him yell out and throw them.

They careened off a tree and shattered.

Turk joined me holding onto Milan. There were three more ghosts on the Port de Pomègues.

From behind him, Noemie called out, her voice cracking. "Devique. You need to see this."

She was standing on the side of the path. There was a construct, made with stones and sticks, and it held down, in the center, a simple drawing.

A red rectangle.

I saw her eyes, as red as the drawing. She hadn't seen what we had. She didn't look.

She just knew.

Devique walked over to her and bent down. I pulled Milan's arm, nearly carrying him.

We stared at the shape for a few minutes, trying to make sense of it. Noemie pointed to the letters drawn on the red rectangle. "I couldn't see this. In my head. This word here is the same in Aramaic as it is in Hebrew, mostly. It's an old word. Perakh."

I nodded. "What does it mean?"

She sat back in the grass and sighed. "Okay, on one hand, it means 'blossom,' or 'flower.'"

Turk sounded relieved. She was quieter than usual. "That's great. It's a little flower. That's pretty. It's probably dead by now, but that's okay."

Dev crossed his arms. "And is there another hand?"

Noemie looked up at us. "This is strange, because we're talking about eleven thousand years ago. If this is Aramaic, it's in the lowest level. It's from when the tower of Jericho was first built. It's old."

Milan followed. He sighed. "So a very old flower."

Noemie nodded at him. He looked broken, lost. "This is a time when language was just being invented. And humans,we are a predictable people. About five minutes after a language is invented, poetry is invented. Metaphor, simile. Symbolic constructions."

I asked, "So, blossom, flower, this could be metaphorical?"

"Exactly. Blossoms grow. Flowers take over. Plagues have been called by the names of flowers. Mass infections."

"'Ring around the rosie was about the Black Plague, right?" Dev offered.

"Yes. And it gets worse than that. The infections and rashes from plagues are often called by the names of flowers because it's a deeply ingrained metaphor."

Turk put her hands on her head and looked at us. "So, this could be a dead flower in this box, super pretty, maybe dried, harmless..."

Noemie stood up. "Or it's some kind of infectious agent that kills everything."

5. The Bird, It's You

L'amour c'est toi
L'amour c'est moi
L'oiseau c'est toi
L'enfant c'est moi

Love, it's you; love, it's me
The bird, it's you; the child, it's me

When my tattoo had fully healed, it became a large part of how Turk and I communicated. There was a sense that my back was our playground, a place for her to invade my mind.

And I loved it.

At first, she traced the hypertrophic scars that built the spines of letters to simply spell out words. She used her fingers, her toes, her tongue, to plant her pictures while I sank into the pillows and laughed along with her. She typed with alphabetic precision, erasing typos with her face, touching me delicately as long as she could before she couldn't help herself anymore.

And always resting on the 40th character. The heart at the base of my spine. What Milan had called the most important one of all.

And then shorthands evolved. Tactile combinations of letters on my back and in my hands. Elegant skin-to-skin dances all over me that communicated complex ideas, rich elaborate storytelling, with often terse and liquid touches, treating me, in my entirety, as a keyboard that was hundreds of times more receptive and expressive than the one sitting in front of you.

We laid in bed for hours at night and in the early morning, lights off, making meaning out of touch in ways that people who had never considered losing their sight, their hearing would never have contemplated. We laughed as I sang songs she typed across my skin in real time as though I were the most efficient instrument ever made and she was the musician born to play me.

And I liked the sound of me.

But eventually, every time we would lean in and just hold each other. And touch each other in ways that didn't need to mean anything, ways that were better than language.

We had spent the last month or so visiting libraries, Noemie stayed with us, but checked in frequently with Karras, giving us some insight into his comings and goings. He was back now on his island, to his home in Heraklion, on Crete. We didn't reach out to anyone else. We had learned from Ruach that if we valued anyone's life, we would keep them out of this.

And we did.

None of the books we scanned through seemed to have any real idea of what was potentially in the box. And pictures that any of us drew of it, if they approached the accuracy of Noemie's visions, couldn't be photographed or sent over wire. They were either blurry or blown out or just gone. More than anything, it felt like a parlor trick, but we knew it wasn't.

Milan eventually told us more about Selene. She was a kind woman, he said. From the photos, she seemed attractive, a woman in her early 40s. He took complete responsibility for her death and nothing I said could change that. The last he had spoken to her was the morning of Ruach's attack. Which meant that he had kidnapped her at some point during the day and hidden her away, bringing her to the island and killing her there once he discovered our intent to go there the next day.

No part of this made me feel safe or comfortable. He was keeping tabs on us somehow and not just through a magically tethered pager, although that picked away at my brain, too.

But through something else as well.

We made a point to throw away anything not absolutely essential throughout the Depot. This meant paintings on the wall, trophies and prizes, knicknacks, etc. Soon the space was minimal, smooth, expressing a nearly Japanese aesthetic.

Turk, Devique, and I searched next door as well. No one had, as yet, claimed Selene's apartment. We locked the balcony doors and tidied, scouring it for anything that could be sending information to Ruach as well.

"I wish I had a better idea of what I was looking for." Dev was carrying a garbage bag that matched mine, removing anything that wasn't absolutely essential.

"Do you think she had any family? I mean, she was young, right?" Turk picked up an ashtray and put it in the bag. "She, also, didn't smoke, so this I don't get if she didn't have some twisted family member in a pottery class somewhere."

"Yeah, I don't get that, either." I was busy trying to figure out the big thing. I still hadn't. No phonebooks, no journals, no pads...

And no phones.

"Dad said he would call her, right?" I wondered out loud.

"Do you think that Ruach took the phones? That wouldn't make sense." Dev was shaking his head.

I pulled the sidetable away from the wall. "If so, he took the cables, connectors, and plugs, too." The apartment looked as though it had never had a phone installed.

Which wasn't possible.

I knelt down and looked closer.

"Waitaminute."

Turk slid next to me and reached out to the wall. She saw the same thing I did. "There were phone plugs. They're just plastered over. That's a lot to go through to avoid a phone call."

"So, somebody plastered over the telephone outlets in this entire place." Dev looked deep in thought.

I could tell he was thinking what I was. There was no reason Ruach would do that. But what if Selene had discovered that he was using them somehow to spy on her?

What if he had been using her, threatening her? And this was her way of fighting back? Can he listen to what's going on in our place, too, through the phone lines? I stared, thinking.

Turk turned to us, "What are the chances that the evil yellow eyed magical murdering guy who bewitches pagers also likes to magically enchant other telecom technology?"

I cocked my head. "Well, when you put it like that, pretty good, I think."

Dev took a deep breath and dropped his bag. "Shit. We need a phone. We can't just plug up all the phone connections."

"Well, we can use the phone connections, sure, as long as we know..."

Turk nodded. "That sonofabitch is listening. Got it."

I sighed. "Who wants to go get some coffee, go back home, and rip out all the phone lines?"

We made our way back to the street. There were people all along the strasse and the sounds were amazing. I looked up at the balcony door to Selene's apartment that we had locked and nailed shut. And then at ours, the nearly hidden balcony doorway into the depot.

It would be nice to open it. We grabbed some things and went home.

There was a note on the table from Dad. It was a warm night and Milan and Noemie met us up on the roof. After work hours, no one else in the building used the roof but us and we were up there commonly enough that we'd placed a few large cafe tables and some seating up there. The light from the streetlights made it nearly clear as midday up there, even after midnight. There was a common joke that most of your tax dollars in Marseille went to making sure drunk people didn't fall in the dark.

I believed it.

The sounds from the street were just a slight buzz. I wondered how much of that was distance and how much was my own ears sundowning this late at night.

Dad looked like he might have been winning at cards and I hated to interrupt. Turk, however, was eager to.

She walked up to the table and slammed down a newspaper. "Full house, chumps." On the front page of Le Provençal was the lead story. Elvis Presley, dead at 42. "I didn't mean to call you chumps. I just got excited. You're not chumps."

Milan nodded and picked up the paper. "You killed him on the toilet. You monster."

Turk looked serious. "He had it coming. You have to admit."

I looked at Dad. "We actually have important things to talk about, too, but it can wait."

Dev tipped his head to one side and looked at Noemie. "How did you..."

She shook her head. "I honestly don't know. I don't know how it works. Some things just let me know they're going to happen."

She fingered the paper. You could tell that she wasn't surprised, but she was something.

Was she sad?

I thought back to the things that she had predicted. I sat down next to her and pulled her hair over her ear. "Do you see death a lot?"

She looked down, arranging her cards. She nodded quickly, without looking up.

I looked at her.

Me, I was a stereotype growing up. A little French girl mourning the loss of her mother, bouncing all over the world with my sophisticated father and his cosmopolitan friends, musicians, artists, architects, thieves...

And poets.

I filled hundreds of books with poetic pictures of the people around me. Sometimes I felt like it was the only thing I was actually good at. I could see people. I could hear them. I could paint a picture of the hero in them. And then I wrote.

It's high irony.

And this one would have been the subject of notebooks full of poems if she'd been around when I was a kid. This dark, stark black and white wisp of a girl with five slots in her head for spells, ways to change the world magically, who filled one always, permanently with a healing spell because when she closed her eyes at night, the future that she saw was all black.

All death and nothing else.

This was no thief, like us, not a woman of the world, not some criminal looking for a score. This was a girl.

I looked up at Devique and nodded.

He put his hand on her neck. "We need a night out. Oh, and then we'll come back and rip out all the phone lines.

Milan scowled. "Wait. Why are we doing that?"

***

"So, it's called a glamour, right?" I whispered to Noemie outside the Mistral in Le Panier.

She nodded. "Yes. It's simple. I try to keep this spell because it's always useful. Just make something look like something else for a few minutes. It's easy if it's small." She looked up. "Is this place even open?"

Milan shook his head. "No. It was closed by the police last week. But it's not the place." He raised his head, pointing to the warehouse looking building next door.

We stood there, trying to look as though we were deciding where to go. The La Panier neighborhood was only a few blocks from port and the area often smelled like fish.

Since I was a child it had been wasting away, lost in the rush to leave for sparklier places like Paris. Here, on Rue San Antoine, you could believe that no one had stepped here for days.

If you didn't know what was where.

"This would not be my first choice, trust me." Milan winked at her.

Devique was looking out. I sometimes felt bad that this was him, always. Forever looking out for us.

Turk was trying the door of the Mistral. There really wasn't a door she couldn't get through if she wanted. The door gave and she slid inside halfway. "I'll meet you guys next door."

Milan nodded and went on. "Okay, once we're out here long enough, they're going to invite us to fuck off. I'll tell them I'm here for the woodworking workshop."

Noemie nodded. She stared at the warehouse with a strange look, turning her head. "Shush."

"I'm sorry." I didn't understand what she was saying.

She whispered to me. "A spell. It stops people from listening."

I dismissed this. Did the underground card house have a spell of protection around it?

Milan moved near and put his hands on her arms. "It's poker, just like we were playing, except this is a little different. I'll stake you. Blow it all if you need to. The money isn't the thing."

"I have money of my own."

I leaned in. "No, save your money. You need it. This is... I'm not sure if there is a word in English."

Milan laughed. "It's frais de scolarité. Literally, I guess it's tuition. Money you need to spend to learn something."

Dev looked over. "If you're going to be a master thief..."

Her eyes widened. "Okay. I appreciate this."

"Keep that look. Innocent American girl visiting France for the nightlife. Keep them guessing who you are. Poker is people, not cards."

She nodded at him. "Got it."

Milan kept one eye on the workshop door. "This is just poker, like we were playing. Except it's an American version called Texas Hold 'Em."

"You are a pretty girl, like me. So they won't see you coming. It's ok to take advantage of that." I dug in. They give you two private cards of your own."

Milan interjected. "Called hole cards."

"Right. Now they put five shared cards on the table. Your job is to make a winning hand out of three of them, plus your two cards."

She looked up, "Sounds simple."

At that moment, a man stepped out of the door of the workshop. He was big and red-faced and there was no world in which he didn't have a gun in the back of his waistband, tucked into the workshirt. "Hey, the bar's closed. You guys can't be here. Scoot."

Devique stepped over. "Oh, we're here for the woodworking workshop. We have the enrollment fee." He pulled out a row of notes and handed them to the man between two fingers.

The man stood there. "You're sure that's tonight?"

Milan looked around Noemie. "Oh, yeah, I took off work for it."

The reddish man slowly nodded his head and ushered us in.

We stepped through a series of doors to a medium sized warehouse space. It smelled musty and was filled with a patina of cigarette smoke and lights, sprayed out over the large red table in the center of the room. The rest of the room fell away, unimportant,

Dark.

I committed the room to memory as best I could and then closed my eyes. I didn't need them here and they wouldn't do a huge amount of good. I heard Turk call from a small round table in the far left corner of the room. We made our way over and I felt her slide a bottle in my hands the minute I sat down. She pulled my chair close. "This place is kind of BYO."

Milan went on, whispering just loud enough to hear. The room was not noisy despite the 30 or so people milling around.

"Don't look at anyone, don't ask for names, don't smile when you win. Don't frown when you lose. And don't look, but the reason everyone is playing Texas Hold 'Em is sitting at the head of the main table. He's the person you're here to play against."

I didn't need to look. I knew why we were here. "Doyle Brunson is an American. He's won the grand prize at the World Series of Poker for the last two years straight. He's from Texas and it's his game."

"Right. His game." I could hear her breathing just a little harder.

"We're going to pick our moment and you're going to play three hands. Only three."

"Why only three?" She whispered back.

Dev broke in. "Well. it won't be easy. If anyone thinks anything is out of place, you're going to be healing tiny pieces of us for weeks."

"Ooh, remember how my pieces go together."

I slid my hand into Turk's. She started using her fingers to explain the room to me. I felt her turn to me, her legs framing me. I listened to Milan and Devique explain the game to Noemie but in my head I explored the room with Turk.

There were seven tables in the room, spread out widely enough that no one could hear the others. In rooms like this, people whispered. No one wanted to be heard. In poker, all information you give someone about yourself is information they can use.

The table closest to ours contained four French men in dark suits. They were all drinking, suggesting none were going to play. We pegged them as poker fans, harmless, possibly businessmen who dreamed of one day stepping up to the table and taking a massive pot home. Possibly they worked in finance and fancied themselves hunters of men, warriors in the boardroom, taking down the biggest prey, bringing the carcass home to their families.

In front of that one was a table with a man and two women. They were working him, neither one drinking much, pouring alcohol down his silk shirt-clad gullet and convincing him that they knew this place.

That he belonged in this place.

They tried to make him feel dangerous, alive. But they might take him home tonight once he could no longer remember the way. They would be gone, along with everything he had, in the morning. Weeks later, he would still smile thinking about it, though.

Next to them, if you can say it was close, was a table of women. They were pooling their money under the table. One of them was there to take a pot for all of them. Was this the regular excursion of a book club or a gathering of suburban wives, a league of sorority sisters, aged out of school, looking to score in solidarity. Turk thought they were cute.

Behind them was a table that sat two couples and a single man. Had the man brought his friends to show off? He would play tonight. He wasn't drinking, just swirling a glass around, contents pulled from a single bottle in the center of the table. He might sit for a hand. He held chips in his hand, two of them. They were lucky pieces, silly giveaways in a room that used rolled up banknotes for entry. He was suspicious. That meant uncertain of his own abilities. I hoped he'd be at the table.

Next to them was a table with a single man, sitting, watching, trying to pretend he was reading a letter. This was a bit of business to prevent people from watching you watch them. This was something Milan had perfected. Read a letter, thumb a book, fix your glasses, even darn a sock. Something you've done so much that your own muscles could carry it to completion while your eyes and mind scoured the room.

And the table in front of that one was security, seated, each forward in their seats, suggesting that they all carried their guns in their waistbands, the worst place possible to keep a gun, excepting your hand. I laughed as she signed that, kissing my hand as she played the word "hand" across it.

And there were a few other people, scattered around the room, moving in and out. But the big event was at the table in front of them all. It was wide, big enough for 10 people. Five men sat in it, with Doyle Brunson at the head. He wore a cowboy hat – an affectation that was designed to make him look simple. And next to him was a crutch - another affectation meant to make him appear feeble. The truth was that he was a vibrant man with a master's degree and that a knee injury damaged his chances at a promising basketball career.

He was here in France to satisfy his goal of playing all over the world, something he would detail in a book.

The game was his, but he played by the rules of the workshop Twenty thousand franc bet limit. Cash, no chips. Last bettor shows first. If there is no bet on the final round, players show in clockwise order starting at left of dealer. And one rule that would help us most of all.

No mucking.

Usually, anyone can muck -- not show their cards -- if they fold. If they know they've lost. In Brunson's game, all cards would eventually be shown. So, if Noemie were going to play, if she was going to win a hand by glamouring her cards, she would have to sit to the right of the dealer and never bet in the last round. If any of her glamoured cards were identical to a card on the table, we would all be outed.

Milan walked her through what her best course of attack was. "Do you think you can see card hands?"

I heard her answer quickly, "No. It's one of the first things I tried. I don't see things like card hands or mistakes when the waiter brings your order."

Dev tried to lighten the table. "Okay. So, we'll play 99% of this straight, right?"

"Exactly." Milan took a beat. "Okay. You're in for three hands. Tell them that up front. You only have three hands before you have to be home. Set the money down. Sit to the right of the dealer. Make up a reason for that. First hand. If you have something big, push it. Bet it. If not, fold early. Don't waste money and look stupid."

Dev broke in, "but don't look calculating and smart."

She laughed. "Okayk. Look somewhere between smart and stupid."

I could hear the smile in Milan's voice. "See, she's already a master."

"Now, second hand. Bet modestly. Lose and lay your cards down last. Change one card so the hand was better than it would have been but don't win. If anyone sees it, they will think you aren't aggressive unless you really have it." Dev was really enjoying this. It had been a while since we could show someone else the ropes like we'd been shown.

“This is important. You’re telling them who you are. If you don’t think you have it, you sit or fold.” Milan continued, “Now. Last hand, Bet twice. No more. If you’re the last bettor on the river, fold and we go home. Otherwise, call.”

“Don’t raise.” Turk sounded like she’d had a drink or two. She was about to get very silly.

“Be confident,” Dev finished. “Be the last one to lay your cards down. You want the most boring hand possible that ekes out a win.”

Milan counted out, “no flushes, no quads, no straights with exact board cards, no full houses with paired boards, nothing flashy. Nothing to make people go ‘wow’.”

I thought, something boring but winning. Two pair. High top pair if you need. But not if you don’t.

“I didn’t realize this would be so complicated.” I could tell she was nervous.

Dev whispered, “don’t be scared. The big thing about being a master is that anyone else in the room could be a master, too. Anything you can do, someone else might be able to. You have a bit of an advantage.

Turk took a breath. “Here is the last thing. If anyone reaches to check the deck. I’m going to cause a scene. A big one. Go with it, no matter what happens, find us and leave with us as fast as possible. Don’t grab for money, don’t do anything but end it.”

“Open hands, walk away.” Milan had this phrase drilled into us since we were kids.

We waited until the two working girls took the man home from the front left table. We relocated and sat down. Up here, closer to the light, I could open my eyes. I was used to my vision sundowning by this time, but it felt good to see the tableau that Turk had described so accurately.

Noemie started over to the table. I gave her a hug. “You are the bird. The blackbird. If you need, you fly.”

She nodded and hugged me back. I slipped six rolls of banknotes in her hand. And she stepped over to the table.

We saw her negotiating, standing to the right of the dealer who was just left of Brunson. I couldn't make out what she said to him. If it had been me, I would have made the case that I could only play with my right hand and this was the only seat that would let me play without elbowing him.

The dealer was a short man with a middling French moustache. I was willing to bet he was the owner, waiting to tell the world how he had sat with Doyle Brunson. He motioned to a thin player next to him to move over and she sat. This maneuver would never have worked if she weren't an attractive woman. I'm aware enough to mention that out loud if I have to.

The dealer sat up a bit straighter. Noemie's scent was working. He made a big deal about establishing the rules.

No splashing the pot.

No Hollywood piles.

No mucking.

This last was our salvation. But in a real game it would be a dealbreaker for a lot of regular players. You learn everything from someone by what they lay down. Every hand they won't follow through with is a biography.

And no one wants you reading them in poker.

The center table was lower than the others and it gave us all a chance to see the play in front of us. The first hand was dealt. Noemie lifted her cards and stared at the five community cards on the table. There were two aces represented, which suggested to me that a new deck hadn't been shuffled enough. Brunson shook his head.

Amateurs.

They played through. I was glad this was the hand for her to fold. Pulling out another ace or, Buddha forbid, two of them would be insanely risky. Turk took a drink and put her hand on my lower back. She sat up on the edge of her seat and tapped on my back, using me to keep track of bets. I felt each movement across the numbers like I was her personal notebook.

Two rounds later, the pot sat at 24,000 francs. One more round and final bets. Like clockwork, Noemie let her shoulders sink as she folded, letting a couple thousand francs sleep on the table.

This was good.

Brunson won the hand. He reached over and cut the deck, challenging the dealer to shuffle again. The smaller man looked sheepish, his cheeks reddening as he did it. Noemie took the opportunity to bump her shoulder against his slightly, asserting her attractiveness.

She apologized shyly.

This was working. She seemed to understand the table dynamics well. The one thing she needed to remember was who was at the head of the table.

Doyle Frank Brunson.

She said something across the table and Brunson smiled. He had heard her American accent.

Now, to all of us, every American sounds like a Texan. They're all cowboys. But Brunson placed her as a New Yorker immediately.

Looking smart.

I secretly cheered for her. Master thief.

The second hand was dealt, with a runaway card across the table. You could tell Brunson was nearly done with the owner/dealer. Turk tapped out on my back:

"Dealer's getting his ass kicked."

I laughed a little too loudly. No one had a clue what I was laughing at.

The pot rose to over 30,000 francs. Three rounds of betting and the thin man took it with a royal flush. Brunson had a flush, too, but a smaller run. Noemie laid her hand down last. Two pair, fives high. Possibly a playable hand. But a losing one. I wondered what she'd changed.

This was going well, just like we'd laid out. If she won, it would be a modest pot, but it would prove something. Any other scenario, we were ready for.

The dealer laughed at a joke Noemie told. It was quiet enough that I wasn't the only one who missed it. But it seemed to elicit a chuckle out of Brunson, too. As long as he was happy, the table was healthy.

First cards went out. Noemie made a big deal out of looking slightly happier. She bet the cap.

Twice she bet the cap.

Then she called.

She was going to have to think fast. Brunson started laying down his hand. A relatively low card diamond flush.

But a flush all the same.

Next to him, an aging Frenchman shook his head, putting down three of a kind. He had Doyle's missing diamond for a straight flush, causing him to purse his lips. Next to him was a younger man, handsome, muscular. He had three of a kind. It seemed like the cards were all over the place. Noemie had to beat a flush, which meant a full house. Anything more than that would cause suspicion. I tried the permutations in my head, reading the community cards. A two and an eight

Honestly it would have all been too fast for me.

I breathed easier when I saw the tall man throw down a pair. He was embarrassed for himself. And he should have been. But I didn't care.

Noemie looked around shyly. Then she smiled widely.

Full house twos and eights. Missing was the two of diamonds that Brunson had in his hand. He looked at her hand and good naturedly lifted his two, pointing at her. She would have had four of a kind, he laughed.

It was a wow hand, but it was the only thing to do, except to lay it down. She stood up and apologized. It was three rounds. For this one she took in 48,000 francs. Minus what she'd lost, she was still over 40k up.

She shook Brunson's hand and gave the dealer a quick kiss on the cheek. She walked to the door and we got up to follow. If you've ever sauntered out of a room where you've stolen something you knew how we felt. You move with a bounce, but not one that draws attention. You're quick, but not fast. You breathe, but not very much.

She was standing on the street in front of the bar when we walked out. Dev lifted her up in a hug.

I was right behind him, walking with Milan, while Turk trailed us.

We stood there, laughing, breathing in the fishy air when the security guard came quickly out the door. "Hey. You can't leave yet."

Milan stepped in front of us. "We can. And we will. She was clear that she only had three hands in her tonight."

The reddish man shook his head. "You don't win a pot like that and walk right out."

Turk stepped over by Dad. "Yes you do, people do it all the time. It's like a 45k pot. How poor are you?"

He started to move toward her and I took a step to the right to make sure he was covered on all sides. I didn't need to bother.

Turk pulled out a gun and kept talking. "Look, I get it. Rent is a lot. I mean, not for me, I don't pay rent, but for you, maybe."

She pointed the gun at him as he reached behind him, his face dropping as he realized it was his gun she had lifted.

She went on, "Also, I just learned that sensitivity decreases on the lower back a little so you have to..." She turned to Devique, still waving the gun around as she spoke.

He finished, "accommodate that. Is that the word you were looking for?"

"Yes. Thank you. You have to. You know. Accommodate. But tomorrow, because we have to go home tonight."

We started walking down the street. Turk held up the gun and yelled back, "I'll mail this back to you. I promise."

Milan put my hand on his arm. I pulled him aside as the laughter faded. His hands were warm and inviting and I hated what I had to say. "I know what's in the box."

He looked at me. I think he'd put it together, too. But we just didn't want to admit it. He looked down. I went on.

"It's the only thing that Noemie can see, in the future. The only thing she can predict. Not cards or even attacks from bouncers."

He took my hand. "I know, sweetheart. It's death."

6.The Girl of the Shadows

Moi je ne suis qu'une fille de l'ombre
Qui vois briller l'étoile du soir

Me, I'm a girl – a girl of the shadows
Who watches the evening star shine.

Turk twirled that gun around for a bit until she made it seem to magically disappear somewhere, a sort of parlor trick. We applauded and marched home, making some decisions between us.

First of all, we were united in our understanding that, if this box contained some deadly infectious death, neither of these men could have it. Karras was, at best, an opportunistic sociopath and, while we had no problem helping him potentially get a little richer, we had to draw the line and helping him do mass murder.

And Ruach was... well, we were sure he was a monster. Potentially a real monster.

So, in this decision was born what we were calling, among ourselves, the Jericho Dance. By the time we made it back to the Depot we had established the six positions of that dance:

1. If we bailed on this job, it was likely that Karras would kill us and almost certain that Ruach would. Which would result in us being dead.

2. If we tried to just disappear, we would spend our lives running. Eventually we would be caught. Which would result in us being dead.

3. It needed to look to our fellow thieves like we were honestly making the effort to finish the job. If Aggie or Rialtos or Nikola -- especially the Nikola -- suspected we were being dishonest, they would out us to Karras. Which would, again, result in us being dead.

There is a theme here.

4. For all that, we needed this money. Milan was set on us having a nest properly feathered for us when I could no longer work. I might object, but I also recognize, not being a complete idiot, that it was possible my career as a larron was coming to an end soon. Millions of dollars of Rhodium, gold, etc. would not be a bad idea.

5. Under no circumstances could either of these men be handed a box that contained some kind of spreadable death. And that was non-negotiable. And 6.

6. We could only trust ourselves with this. Ruach had made it clear he had no problem killing people. Karras himself had a verifiable and legendary killing streak. Anyone we confided in would almost definitely die.

We had three months and three days.

Despite all that, we were in a pretty good mood. Noemie had become a bit of a card shark and was on her way to master thief. She laughed and joked with us that she was ready for the next step.

Ready to rob a bank.

Turk assured her that this would happen, racing her home, looking like a kind of exotic bird in her brightly colored flower print peasant top, sun bleached afro and bright yellow bellbottoms, next to the eerie frame of Noemie's gothic shape, dark and nebulous, shadowy, like some spectral raven.

If that seems like too much, you're right. I shook my head. I can force you to sit through my endless material digressions but I probably should tamp down my girlish 10-year-old poetic fervor. I want you to understand this, all of it.

You're going to need, at some point down the line, to understand why I did what I did.

By the time the sun came up, we had ripped out and plastered over all the phone lines in the Depot. A small pile of plastic phones in a black garbage bag sat right outside the black wooden front door of the depot while we slept Wednesday away and part of Thursday.

Turk and I made plans to take Noemie out shopping for clothes on the weekend before we did anything else.

The total budget was about 40k. I figured if we couldn't spend that along Rue Paradis, we weren't really trying.

But we had something we needed to do first.

***

So, first thing Saturday morning, we sat at the kitchen table, the balcony thrown open wide, writing a letter to Marc Bolan, from the band T-Rex.

Turk grabbed the page from a bare-chested Devique. "Let me see what you've got."

"Hey, I'm not finished."

"Do we want to call him Mr. Bolan?"

I sat back and watched her. She was convinced that this was something she needed to do.

"What?" Turk looked at me.

"Nothing. I've just rarely seen you so dedicated." I reached for her foot under the table with mine.

"I don't know how much time we have. He's 29."

Noemie sat crosslegged next to her in a black t-shirt. She looked like she wanted to climb under the table herself. "I can't really see when. It's soon."

"See? Marc Bolan is going to die soon and Ddad is going to freak out." She finished writing her sentence as I grabbed it from her and read.

"Dear Mr. Bolan. Our witch says you're going to die soon. We don't know how, so please stop doing stuff. Yours, Turk."

"It doesn't sound great out loud."

Dev looked up. "How do most young men like that die? I mean, he's my age. If I died, how would it be?"

I handed the letter back to Turk. "Well, aspirating vomit from an overdose. Fancy rock star airplane crash..."

"Auto-erotic asphyxiation..." Turk added.

I nodded. "Killed by a jealous fan."

Noemie spoke up softly. "Car."

"Excuse me?"

"It's a car accident. A crash. A car crash."

There was a moment where we all had nothing to say. It got quiet enough for me to hear Dad in the shower. The sounds from the street rose up.

A car crash.

Turk asked first. "Let me ask you a question. This is a shitty question, but why do you think you can see some deaths so well, so easily, but some people, like the Talaricos, you can't see until you're almost right there."

Dev looked at her and shook his head. He addressed Noemie. "You don't have to talk about it."

"No, it's okay. This is going to sound nuts."

Turk leaned in. "Try us."

"It has to do with ascension. With godhood."

I looked into her face, trying to figure out if she was telling the truth. None of this made sense to me.

Noemie continued. "Okay, what I do -- this magic -- is not my power. It's ambient power. It's power that exists. I have to learn how to move it around. But it mostly goes where it wants. It does what it wants. And it focuses around belief."

Turk jumped in. "Like belief in yourself?"

"That's a big part of it. Belief that it's real. Belief that you can do it. Belief, in... things. Belief is really powerful."

That made some sense. I understood that, I think.

"The early gods, at the beginning of mankind, were just people, bigger than life. They made people trust them."

"Confidence men." Turk understood that.

"Well, I guess. They built belief." She looked around the table. Turk had pulled out her set of tiny colored pencils to write this letter. Noemie grabbed two croissants from the middle of the table and stabbed a tiny pencil in the first one. "Here. A normal person. A person or two or three believes in them. Believes that they can do things, maybe."

She set the croissant down in front of her.

"Now, this one. Someone famous, maybe, a celebrity, a person who is wel-known." She placed about 20 tiny pencils into this croissant and set it next to the other one.

"Okay, so ordinarily, in a day-to-day sense, they are the same. No different. But once the power of the universe, that ambient power, starts to flow." She raised her hands and whispered "burn," and the tiny pencils started smoldering. Their bases, sticking out of the tiny pastries, started to catch fire. One looking like an office party birthday offering, small and controlled. The other, like a runaway flame.

With 20 tiny wooden sticks all on fire.

I leaned back into my seat. She had set them on fire without touching them.

"Even then, both are visible, both are part of the world. Now, when things all around us become chaotic, complex."

She raised her hand again, mouthing something under her breath, and the light in the room seemed to lift upward. I can't explain that any better. The room sank into darkness, but not normally, not how it might if the light source simply extinguished.

What happened was more like the light and dark were separated, with the light rising to the ceiling above us and the dark swirling below, at our level.

It got dark.

I felt a kick as my balance shifted. I held the chair under me and my peripheral vision closed in, as though I had turned the knob on an old kaleidoscope and let the edges in. It was even harder to see through this magical darkness than an ordinary one.

But, as I looked down, I realized that I could still see one of the croissants, as bright as day. The one pierced by many flaming pencils was still visible. And bright.

"You can see it. You can't look away. That person. All that belief is like a beacon. It makes them into something we can't miss, we can't look away from."

Dev whispered, "who is 'we?'"

She had become so intense. She whispered back. "The Universe. The people in it. The powers in it. All of it. Enough belief, you become ascendant. You become legendary. More than that?"

Turk looked on in wonder. "You become a god. If you believe that."

Suddenly, the light switched back. The flames disappeared as though they had never been. My head danced as everything snapped back to what it was, making it look like it had never changed.

Like none of it was real. Like a scene had changed in a movie.

Noemie nodded. "If you believe that."

I closed my eyes. My head was spinning and my arms on the table were the only things keeping me from tipping over. I reached for the croissant to her right, the one with only one pencil stabbed into it. I released the pencil and lifted the pastry to my mouth. Demonstration over.

When I opened my eyes again, Noemie had stood up and was hugging Devique from behind. Turk had gone back to writing. Dad stepped into the kitchen. I wasn't looking forward to the conversation about the future of T-Rex, one of his favorite bands. In my head, I could hear "Get it on."

Well, you're dirty and sweet
Clad in black, don't look back, and I love you

I looked over at Noemie. "What's your fifth?"

She looked up, her arms still around Devique.

"A healing spell. A glamour. The flames. The darkness." I counted off the spells she had shown us, remembering back to when she had said she always kept five spells ready.

"What's your fifth?"

Milan sat down where Noemie had been sitting. "What's going on?"

Turk was still hypnotized. I could tell her mind was moving a million kilometers an hour. "We were just asking Noemie what five spells she had prepared."

Milan looked up at Noemie. For a moment, we all were. Devique put his hand up, touching her arm.

"What if I said I couldn't tell you?" She kissed Dev's head. How far had their relationship advanced? I realized I didn't know. I didn't know where she slept. Ordinarily, that might have set off an alarm in my head. But as much as I listened for one...

There was no alarm.

"Is there a magical reason you can't"

She paused for a moment and nodded slowly. It was almost imperceptible -- the gesture.

Dad had grabbed on to Turk's hand. He kissed it and looked up. "What could happen?"

A strange look washed across her face – something I couldn't place. Her voice became thin, tinny.

"What if you stopped believing in me?"

I put my hand into Milan's other one.

Well, you're an untamed youth

That's the truth with your cloak full of eagles

You're dirty sweet, and you're my girl

I listened for the alarm.

Still nothing. No alarm.

But there was a knock. Milan looked over at me. The Depot wasn't a place people casually visited. From the outside, it was meant to look like a storage area -- a warehouse for the stores below. Devique stood up and pulled on a red shirt he had sitting over the back of the chair next to him.

We stood up. The knock returned, louder this time.

Turk took a breath. "Hey. At least they're knocking this time."

Milan nodded ambivalently as we watched Dev open the door.

It was Karras's son, Nikola.

He was nearly the same height as Devique, and nearly as wide. In fact, Dev was probably the only person that could make Nik not look imposing.

And Nikola knew that.

He stepped inside, waving his hand, speaking in English. His hair bounced as though he had just come from a hair conditioner commercial. Which was actually on the table as possible. "Don't get up. No big deal. I'm here to drop a few things off."

Milan leaned in to shake his hand. "How are you, son?"

Nik was clearly doing his best to seem likable and friendly. This was business as usual. This was a casual visit. "I'm good, sir. My father sends his best. And a few things." He looked around, specifically staring at Noemie. "And his best to you, too, Ms. Mason. He says your company is missed. But it seems like you're in good hands here."

Turk broke in, "we're turning her into a card shark."

Nik looked slightly surprised. Then laughed. "Hm. That could come in handy in the next job, for sure."

I cocked my head. "Next job?"

It wasn't clear how much of Nik's affability was real and how much was just meant to keep us off balance. "Well, you know, if this one goes well, there's no reason we can't do more jobs together. I mean, everyone needs money." He turned his head. "Is anyone else here?"

Devique shook his head. "No, it's clear."

"Excellent. He pulled out a satchel he had been holding close to him. Opening it, he placed some items on the table. "Well. Firstly, your tickets. We're going to meet up Wednesday, October 5th. We'll have accommodations for you on the island. We'll stay there and plan until the big event.

Milan reached down and spread the tickets. Five first-class airline tickets. "Good. Well done."

Nik pointed at the tickets, "There should be meals on those flights. Sorry about the commercial plane, but we're trying to make this seem as normal as possible."

I agreed. "No. It makes sense. Under the radar."

He placed six bundles of francs next to them. "Some walking-around money, cash to take care of what is needed. There is a list in the bag of a few things to bring."

Turk picked up a bundle of cash and made a point to slip it into her shirt over the collar, into her bra. I smiled. I grabbed the list from the bag.

"Okay. I think you'll be pretty happy with the view and the amenities on the island. After the job is over, you will be welcome to come back and stay as long as you like, decompress, swim, whatever."

Milan put his hand on his shoulder, "That's very kind of you." We had agreed at the start that Milan would play the part of the elderly father fading off and I would assert leadership. This put him in the place he was the most good. Out of the immediate line of sight.

Underestimated.

"Well, my father is grateful for your help. And I have a good feeling about all of this." He looked at Devique. "Right?"

Devique nodded. We'd been family for long enough that I felt like I could read his mind. Flashing across his forehead, His thoughts were like a beacon: I think I like it better when they shoot me.

I smiled. Turk put her hands on her hips. "Well. We're about to take her shopping. Clothes. Black. Stat."

Nik held up his hands. "Great. Why don't you let me give you a ride?" He scanned the room. "Better than a taxi."

***

For us, clothes shopping works like this. You begin at the top. We would start with Rue Paradis. This is up-market – this is where you find signature pieces –the one piece that everyone asks about. It may cost money, but it's the center of your wardrobe so it's worth it. You find a couple you like. Remember, you can always return.

The next step is to hit Rue de Rome or Saint-Ferréal. These are second-level stores, still worth it. Here you find pieces to pair with your signature pieces. The next thing someone looks at. Shoes, pants that accent that perfect shirt. You know.

Then, we go to Rue du Tapis-Vert. Thrift stores, second-hand stores, small family stores, local designers. Here is where you inexpensively bulk out your wardrobe, with the rest of what you will wear. You know the signature pieces by now, so you want to match them. By this time, you may know which of the more expensive pieces you will use and which get returned.

When you are a larron, your clothes have two mutually exclusive jobs. You have to either look expected...

Or you have to look unexpected.

If that seems counterintuitive, imagine that a job is a river front scene. The people working to make it happen are the river. The distraction?

That's the boat.

So, you may be the river. You may be the boat. We dress to direct where people's eyes go. Simple.

Noemie and I sat in the back of Nikola's car as he drove us downtown. Turk braved the brunt of his incessant conversation, sitting to his right in the front seat.

“I might do some shopping while I’m in town, too.”

“Well, I’ve got some tops I don’t wear if you need any color.”

Nikola looked at her and laughed. I remembered him a bit from when he was younger, when they had lived here. He seemed to have developed a sense of humor.

Not a great one, but still.

I felt in my pocket for the little rectangular piece of plastic. I had come to expect it, anywhere I went. It just appeared. I felt its heft. It was always a bit more substantial than I thought.

A little heavier.

I wondered if Noemie could turn off the enchantment. That was a conversation to be had later.

“I need to show you around on Crete. I think you guys will fall in love.”

I knew Turk well enough to know that about 30 percent of her enthusiasm was a misdirection. The rest could have been real. “I always wanted my own Minotaur.” Turk looked back at us and made a face, waving in our direction. “All these other girls wanted a pony.”

“Well. Let’s make it happen.” Nik laughed awkwardly. It was always hard to know exactly what he took away from conversations like this. I found myself secretly grateful that Agnes hadn’t come with.

He stopped the car in front of Le Placard Sinueux. This was going to be my first stop. My heart dropped a bit when I realized that he’d sussed that out. You don’t want to be a book any idiot can read. I opened the door to step out and so did Turk. Nikola reached back and stopped Noemie from leaving for a second.

“If you don’t mind. Just a quick private word with Miss. Mason.”

I looked back at her. She nodded quietly and Turk and I stepped out onto the curb.

“What do you think that’s about?” She tried to overhear as Nikola spoke. Noemie listened.

"Well. My bet is that she's being yelled at. If it goes on for too long, we'll rescue her." I looked at Noemie's face. Something I'd been rolling around in my brain made sense.

She opened the door and walked out of the car right as I was about to extricate her. Turk took her hand in pretend disapproval, "What was that about, Le Fay?"

Noemie laughed. "He wanted to give me more money." She held up another wad of cash. "And make sure that if I needed anything I would reach out to him directly."

I narrowed my eyes. "Does that seem normal to you?"

She shook her head. "That was literally the most words we'd ever spoken."

Turk crossed her arms. "I think the magic part of this thing is bigger than we thought. He's afraid she's going to bail."

I looked at Noemie, "Do you think that's it?"

"It could be. I was the only one from my coven willing to do this."

It hit me. "So you weren't his first choice?"

She slowly shook her head. This needed unpacking.

We walked through the door at Le Placard Sinueux. In America, we would have looked like an odd group of poverty-stricken hipster kids. Here, they were used to serving actresses and models, rock star girlfriends and wives. It was reasonable that Turk might have been wealthy.

Famous, even.

Salesgirls came over and complimented her on her outfit. She was decked out in rich purples today and she definitely looked like she belonged. While the salesgirls tried to charm Turk, I grabbed Noemie's hand and looked for something she might like.

We needed something that was her. Something dark and gothic, but still a signature piece. Something she could wear a few different ways. I let myself sort of sink into the energy of the store. The truth is shopping like this was always more fun than it should be.

It wasn't that different from poker. It was about people and connections.

Turk returned with a Latin-looking woman in tow. Long hair and sparkly makeup. She wore a flowing black suit that honestly wasn't far from what we were looking for.

"Ladies, this is Lis. She's the hottest one. She's going to help us but don't stare directly at her."

Lis laughed. "I could listen to that some more, honestly."

I smiled at her. "She's a charmer, but she's not a liar."

Lis took my hand. "Oh, wow. That was sweet. I only get a 10 percent discount, but it's all yours."

Noemie was looking at her outfit approvingly.

I shot back at her, "I also think you have the exact right style to help my friend here."

Turk stage-whispered, "we can talk about her like she's not here."

"Oh. She's got a great shape. My instinct is to play up her neck. Let people find her tits on their own.

Turk pretended to grab Noemie's tits. "Funny, I already found them."

Any woman who says she hates being adoringly dressed up by pretty girls is probably lying about other stuff, too. Noemie's face lit up.

Lis ran around and earned her commission. She picked out the best pieces they had, nearly all of them in stark black, the occasional deep maroon or dense forest green. Pieces that would sit next to black well.

I considered Nikola Karras's visit. On its face it was harmless. It was even something we might expect from a partner on a big upcoming job. He seemed kind, affable, friendly. He bore gifts and promises of future jobs.

And none of it felt right. Even the fact that he had dropped us off at the very store we had planned to visit first. It felt invasive. He was, in essence, no different than this pager I held in my pocket.

Uncontrollable.

He would be there when he wanted.

His visit said, "don't think you are in control."

I watched Turk flirt with Lis. I shook my head. I don't think the poor girl had any more discount to share with us. I got the sense she would give us what we wanted, with or without a commission. I made a point to tip her well. I put my hand in my pocket

And the pager vibrated.

I looked around. It wasn't supposed to go off. This was meant to alert Ruach to when we had the box for him.

Not before that.

It buzzed again.

The room was bright and I could see into pretty much all of it. It was daylight outside. Everything felt familiar.

It felt safe.

I pulled the pager out. As I looked at the tiny screen on top, it buzzed in a new way.

It was continuous.

No one seemed able to hear the vibration in my hand. When it stopped, a number appeared on the screen. It was one I didn't recognize. But it was local. Same exchange.

No matter what direction she was facing, Turk always seemed to have one eye on me. I flashed her the sign for telephone and showed her the pager. There were no visible phones in the store but right outside was a phone booth.

I pointed to the booth. She nodded and followed me out with her eyes. I settled into the phone booth and positioned myself so that I could see inside the store. It looked like Noemie and Turk were keeping Lis laughing all the way to the cash register. The pager buzzed again, continuously. It stopped and the number flashed again.

I picked up the phone and fished a 10-franc coin out of my pocket, listening to it fall. I gave thanks for the buttons. The last thing I needed right now was a rotary phone.

"You need to take me seriously."

The line clicked. The tone was about twice as loud as it should have been. It was jarring. Violent. I looked out of the glass of the phone booth. The lights in the clothing store flickered and three black shapes appeared out of nowhere. My heart dropped and I yelled out, trying to back out the door of the booth.

It wouldn't open. I yelled louder, slamming myself into the door.

That's when I heard the shots. Three shots. They rang out in a row. I couldn't see anything inside the shop anymore. The figures seemed to swim in darkness. It was as if someone had poured ink into the water of an aquarium and stirred. I rocked the phone booth back and forth, over and over, letting it fall backward, finally, onto the curb, spilling glass into the street. I pulled myself out and ran to the door, shards of glass biting into my palms, as I tried to open the door to the store. It was locked.

Ruach had used the beeper to get me out of the store. To trap me in a phone booth while he...

I thought for a second as I pounded on the door of the shop, leaving bloody streaks across it. Without warning, it fell open, propelling me onto the floor in the middle of the front foyer of the store. I dragged my foot and pulled myself up. There were sirens coming closer, digging into my ears, jamming their fingers deeper and deeper, pulling out what was left of my hearing. Suddenly the air seemed to drop, to thin, and my ears clogged, as though there were two shells placed over them.

Nothing.

I couldn't see Turk. People were running everywhere. Finally, I saw Noemie hunched over a body. I pulled myself over next to the checkout counter and saw her with her hands on Lis's chest. The younger girl lay there in a pool of blood.

With a hole where her face was.

Noemie was rocking back and forth, she was pressing her hands against the salesgirl's chest.

And nothing was happening.

Turk slammed into me, holding me.

Her face was wet and her hands were full of blood. I made a quick hand motion to explain that I couldn't hear. But I could see the lights of the police cars. I pulled myself up. Turk stood up, holding me. We helped each other to the counter and turned. The police were standing outside, advancing, batons out. I looked around the room. The black figures were gone. There was no sign of them. But the after effects were everywhere. Salespeople and shoppers scattered the floor. Blood and glass was everywhere. It smelled like death.

But it looked like Noemie and Turk had been unharmed. Noemie leaned back. There wasn't anything left of Lis. There was nothing alive to save. Black eyeliner ran down her face. I grabbed a salespad and a pencil and wrote four words on it. Taking a deep breath, I pulled myself along the counter until I reached her. She was still trying to protect Lis' body. My hand stained the note with blood as I let it slip into her hand. She read it and looked up at me, nodding frantically.

I saw her fold the note up and make a move to slip it in her pocket.

That's when I felt the man behind me push me back down onto the counter, pressing my hands together. I let my nose rest against the glass of the counter and waited, deaf to all the activity behind me. I saw a blue-clad figure line Turk up next to me and another kneel down to talk to Noemie.

Noemie pushed him away, stood and screamed.

This was the scream of someone who had just watched someone die and couldn't stop it. One of the lights flickered again. Suddenly, the bracket holding the light fixture fell, sending broken pieces of plastic and metal down all over the floor. Noemie protected her head and face. As the police led us out, I saw the bloody note I'd passed to Noemie on the floor. I kicked it into the pile of blood. Noemie had read it already. I didn't need anyone else seeing it. Blood started seeping into the surface of it, obscuring the words.

"Make Them Trust You."

7. My Sun so Dark

Toi mon étoile qui tisse ma ronde
Viens allumer mon soleil noir

You, my star, who weaves my circle,
Come and light my sun so dark.

It was summer, 1974, at the Théâtre de Verdure, in Jardin Albert 1er, outside Nice and the world was safe from us.

Thick, plaintive horns painted the air, dotted with seagulls, winding through the scent of clove cigarettes, mixed with jasmine and the sharp brine of the sea next door. A row of pine trees lined up like soldiers, torched by psychedelic stage lighting, violets, reds, oranges, leading from where we stood on a thick grass hill that Turk and I owned as much as we owned anything, anywhere. Bubbling guitars and the quick staccato skeletons of drums paced her while she danced over me.

She was wearing the thinnest mottled white and blue jean shorts, nearly dissolving with every movement, a billowy crochet top more defined by its lattice of holes than by any thread or yarn used to make it, and silver bangles and bracelets that seemed to clink effortlessly in rhythm.

The song was "Darkest Light," played on stage by the Lafayette Afro Funk Band at the Night of Fire and Saltwater Jazz and Funk Festival, and wheatpaste posters rimmed the space, drawing a line between us and reality, showcasing the journey of the band. They read "Afro Funk - New York - Barbés - Nice."

And I couldn't turn away. Turk and I had been together for eight years and there seemed to be something building every day. Every morning I would wake up and wonder if I could find the bottom of this hole, the place where I'd stop falling and finally gain a foothold.

And it never came.

Milan and Devique moved around the grass like cartoon cats chasing the scent of fish. Their lips moved to every song, just as Turk's hips did to this one. We laughed earlier, thinking about the thieves arrayed in that grass, weeds scattered across it in clumps, mingling with the Algerian drummers and their white sandaled girlfriends, replete with toe rings and bellychains; the Parisian art students arguing over genres in a tinny whisper as bands mounted the stage, their power muting the argument forever; overly-tanned German hippies with sun-blotted wineskins around their barrel chests; and tiny clumps of Black American GIs wondering why they ever considered going home again.

And maybe they wouldn't.

Just like the band itself, the Lafayette Afro Funk Band, who played in Paris in 1971 and then, surrounded by the city lights that had hypnotized Nina Simone and James Baldwin, stayed, rejecting the thick centered whiteness of America in favor of a welcoming French collusion of color. Spread out in between all of it were pickpockets, bodymen, low-level thugs, robbers, burglars, con men, grifters, romance artists, relay phonemen, and more. Each aware of every wallet, every pocketbook, every clump of cash, they instead chose to let them all stay home safe in their owners' pockets. We weren't thieves here. We were fans.

The song seemed to call down the sun, steamy syncopations lulling it to sleep. It was the bold line between day and night, as the electric-red Nice sun fell over black waters of the Bay of Angels, sliding toward the Cap d'Antibes, we danced.

And then it happened. As the dark fell, for the first time, up and down seemed to reverse themselves. The college boys who had been trying to catch our attention as possible dates for their debauched afterparty in Villefranch-sur-mer rushed up to catch me as I fell down the hill and hit my head on a stone.

Devique pushed them away and carried me to a tent on the other side of the field, away from the stage, while Turk held my hand. A bangle wearing volunteer bandaged my head and suggested I go to the doctor the next day. It would be my 24th birthday, although I was in the habit of calling myself 24 already, something people in their 20s do and no one else.

My preliminary diagnosis was in the minimalist office of a strange doctor from Nice, Dr. Archiquette, who, once he realized how familiar we were with Usher's syndrome, had no problem predicting my next few years.

Milan held on to my hand and we cried. Everything was going to change.

I don't know if I can explain how it feels to be at the beginning of a life you love, just as it is, to wake up as something you are grateful for, and then be told that you are a caterpillar-like thing with no control over your eventual form. I'm sure that sounds hyperbolic, but to me, it was real.

Few people know that, in the cocoon, caterpillars dissolve completely. They become a kind of ooze, a liquid. And that is what the butterfly is born from. It's no easy transition.

I was leaving something, abandoning something.

And it felt like this.

***

We spent the night of the store shooting in a holding cell in jail. It was also the first night I spent completely deaf. My condition is exacerbated by stress and that night was enough to push it. Luckily, it was just a slip. The next morning I opened my eyes lying on a bench in a shared cell, the sounds of the prison invading my brain. My hand hung over the edge, resting across Turk's belly, as she laid on the floor next to me. Noemie was sitting up stroking my hair.

I wasn't sure how long she'd been doing that.

"Are you ok?" I asked.

"Yes. They aren't charging us. I told them we may have been the targets. They wanted to keep us until morning to protect us."

"That was kind." I shifted to look up. From this position, I could see part of her face.

She paused. "How did you know?"

I sighed. "How did I know your last prepared spell was to make people trust you?" I shifted, making sure to keep contact with Turk, sleeping below. "I suspected it for a while. And it was the only thing I could think of that you would be afraid to tell us."

"I never used it on you. I promise. I promise so hard. I never did."

"I know. I believe you."

Her voice dropped. "I promise I never used it on Devique."

"My brother can handle himself." I smiled. Of all the things I knew to be true in the world, that one was near the top.

She breathed out as if in relief. Sometimes you could feel the last secret in the air when it came out. It was always warm from being held so tightly. It was like a thick current in the wash of space between you, grateful to be free. "I want to learn how to do what you do."

At this point, in my head, that could have been referring to a million things. What I do. I was a pickpocket. Not something I wanted to admit in a jail cell.

She whispered. "With people. Knowing people."

I laughed. "Do you know who Arsène Lupin is?"

She thought. "I don't."

"Oh, I have so many books for you, little girl."

I told her about LeBlanc's Lupin, the gentleman thief. How he stole from the corrupt wealthy. I told her about Pierre Alexis Ponson du Terrail's Rocambole. About Hornung's A. J. Raffles, the other side of Doyle's Holmes. About Charteris's Saint and Vance's Lone Wolf. All of them, thieves, all of them.

And what they all had in common. They loved people, each in their own way. They knew people.

I chuckled. "You are the God Stone."

"What does that mean?"

"In L'Île aux Trente Cercueils, Lupin encounters the God Stone. It's a radioactive stone that cures people."

"I should read that."

A thin cop who couldn't have been much older than 20 appeared at the gate to the cell. "Good morning, ladies. If you feel safe, you're free to leave. Your family is here."

I sat up and nudged Turk. "Thank you, Officer."

Milan was asleep with his arm draped around Devique when we left holding. I gently woke him up and we made our way out. The station was on Canebière, a mostly empty street this morning. We walked slowly toward the ports until we found the green van.

Devique slid into the driver's seat while Milan took my arm.

"You know, the cafe below the Depot, l'Heure de la Fête, has been there, in the same spot, since you were a little girl."

I nodded slowly. "I know, Dad."

"Lana, the daughter, used to work there when she was 13. She's coming back from college. She'll be there again."

"I'm sure she will." I stared over to where Turk and Noemi were standing, talking to Dev. I suspected that he was having the same conversation with them. But Milan was making it my decision.

I looked into his face. He looked tired. "I told Noemie all about Arsène Lupin."

His eyes lit up. Somewhere in the back of his mind, Milan was always Lupin. When other parents were reading to their kids from children's books, Milan was reading to me The Gentleman Burglar, The Crystal Stopper, The Eight Strokes Of The Clock, The Golden Triangle... stories that he would sometimes act out.

"Oh, yeah? We'll have to get her the books."

"We know what Lupin would do."

He looked out into the street, around his beloved Marseille. "Yes, we do."

Open hands. Walk away.

We couldn't be around anyone anymore. Ruach was afraid. He thought that on our own we were controllable. But other people were wildcards. When Nikola came, when we got close to the salesgirl whose name I tried not to think about.

We needed to limit our contact with other people. This meant leaving. It meant staying away from the things and people we cared about until after this job was over.

We wouldn't go back home.

I sat next to Dev in the front seat. "What do we have in the van?"

"Well. We have go-bags for everyone but Noemie. We have cash. We have about a week of dry food. The boat is another story. It's stocked for weeks now."

"You have a chart?"

He smiled at me. He had a chart.

***

I pulled Turk aside on the dock, while everyone piled into the boat.

"Are you ok with this?"

She took my hands. "What choice do we have, huh?" She stared into my eyes. "We don't have a chair for you for bad days."

I shook my head. "We'll get one." I tried to open my eyes as widely as possible to take her in. This woman who slept on the floor of a jail cell just so she could be touching me. I started to cry.

"What am I going to do when I can't see this anymore? This is literally the only thing I need to see in the world."

She pulled me in. "I'm just afraid you'll finally notice I have a terrible personality."

I felt myself laughing into her neck. Her hands slid down to the shape at the bottom of my spine. She outlined the heart. It was beginning to feel so familiar.

"And when I can't hear this voice." I broke down.

Her breath was all around me. She put her lips on the nape of my neck and slowly blew until it felt hot. She whispered, "you know, this is for the best, probably. I plan on really letting myself go."

"Oh, yeah?"

"I never have to wear makeup again."

"Never?"

"I'll never wear a matching color."

"Promise?"

"Oh, my god. Everyone but you will think I'm insane. I'm going to be such a fucking eyesore. I'll be like Medusa."

"And everyone will turn to stone."

"Everyone. Immediately. There'll be rows of statues, just because I look like shit."

She wouldn't though. I knew what she looked like. I held on tightly until I couldn't laugh anymore.

I think I just needed to be reminded of what I wasn't leaving behind.

In the table of the aft cabin of the boat, Milan had placed some of the things we knew we had. He always had money with him. A number of brown satchels full of large-denomination franc notes sat there. The airplane tickets were still back at the Depot, but he had paperwork for all of us, including Noemie. Entry visas for various countries, fake birth certificates. We all had additional passports in our go-bags. These were all tied together in color-coordinated rubber bands.

Money and documents related to money in red bands. Identity documents wrapped in green rubber bands. Properties, maps, and locations in black rubber bands. Everything else in beige. Another methodology that made it easy to see at a glance what we had.

We still needed to find more clothes for Noemie. Luckily there were now a number of bathing suits stored on the boat. The weather was warm and would stay that way for another month or so.

Milan looked around the room, "Anything else anyone has?"

I pulled the pager out of my pocket and dropped it on the table. Noemie picked it up and reached for a blanket. She wrapped it over and over again in the blanket and handed it to Dev. He reached into a drawer and pulled out some duct tape, taping the blanket.

She looked over at me. "Unfortunately, you will need to keep it close, or else it will just show up. But this way, if he's listening through it..."

"Don't tell me it's that easy." I put the blanket wad down and sat on it. Listen to this, Ruach.

"Well. It'll be muffled. It's the best I can do until I can prepare a spell."

Turk pulled out a gun and placed it on the table. Then another and another. Three guns. I was just hugging her and had no idea where she was hiding three guns.

Milan looked down. "Good, We'll hold onto these."

She reached into the pockets of her bellbottoms and grabbed a few handfuls of ammunition. And two badges.

Noemie looked confused. "Did you steal all that from the police station?"

Turk nodded. "Cops always trust the little lock thing on their holster way too much."

Dev picked up a gold badge and held it up. "I think I'm going to hold onto this." He slid it into his pocket. Lupin had badges from every city he ever worked.

They came in handy.

He motioned us all to the back of the room.

"Here's my overview. All right, crew. If you need more information just address me as Captain and I'll try to slow down."

Milan nodded. "Yes, my captain."

"Okay. We don't need a plane. We can take our time and get to Crete. And this is better, because we can pick up things we need on the way. We won't put anyone else in danger. We relax and consider this a little vacation. We leave port here, pass Corsica and land in Sardinia. We end up in this port, Cagliari."

Turk interjected, "we can get a wheelchair."

"Right. And we can stock more dry food. And fill the containers in the hold up with potable water."

I nodded. "We'll need to fuel up?"

"Yes. Every stop. Last stop we will also grab portable fuel cans. I don't want to have those around unless we absolutely need them."

"To blow shit up."

Dev continued. "Next, it's Sardinia to Palermo, Sicily. This is Sicily. We get anything we want here."

Noemie looked up. "Books? Mystical books?"

I laughed. "Anything. Seriously. You'll see. If there is a book you need..."

"Next up is Malta. Every boat in the world stops at Malta. We get repairs if we need, but provisions, fuel, upgrades, this is the place. We can stay here docked for a while, away from everyone. We might want to do that."

Milan seemed more comfortable. "Then it's just one more stop, Captain."

"Well, yes. We can make Heraklion in Crete from there. That's easy. It's a long trip and we need to take it slow to conserve fuel, but it's reasonable. But I'm going to suggest something else."

I tried to remember if Devique had always been fascinated by boats and sailing. For the life of me, until he'd bought this thing, I couldn't remember a single time.

Not one.

"What if we take our time? We stop here in Chania instead of Heraklion. We fuel up, we look around, we avoid Karras. Remember, we'll still have lots of time. And we go here."

He pointed to a place that looked like water on the map.

Turk shrugged. "Cool. We drown."

"Well, it's not on this map. It's too small. But right here, it's visible off the coast of Cyprus. A tiny island called Yeronisos."

Milan shook his head. "I've never heard of that."

"No one has. It's a rock. It's tiny. No beaches. No permanent structures. Rocks and caves. You have to bring your own food and water. But it's a perfect staging area. It's right between the ports in Israel and Karras's island area in Crete."

I saw it. "Our home base."

"Exactly. We can set up there. It's uninhabited. You need a skiff to even land there. And the natives in Cyprus stay away."

Noemie turned her head. "Why do the natives stay away?"

"Well, you have to time a landing with the tides and waves. No beaches. Just a cliff to climb when you reach it. But the big deal is that it contains a series of altars. Sacred, maybe sacrificial. Definitely ceremonial."

Turk smiled, "So it's a do-it-yourself ritual human sacrifice center?"

Dev thought for a second. He stood up straight and nodded. "Well, yes."

It was right in between the two most important locations. It was virtually unknown. And people were scared of it.

I shifted on the blanket. "We have a home base."

There was a little light applause.

Noemie took a deep breath. "I wanted to say something."

I pulled my legs up under me. I figured this was coming.

"You asked me yesterday. The fifth spell I had prepared."

Turk crossed her arms. "Trusting. To make people trust you."

Noemie's eyes widened. "Did you all figure it out?"

Devique smiled. "It wasn't that hard."

She looked at him plaintively. "I promise, I didn't use it on you."

Milan leaned against the counter and watched. I knew he wouldn't interject himself unless he needed to.

Dev countered. "I know. Because I don't trust you."

She looked like someone had punched her in the chest.

"I don't distrust you. I just… well, I don't trust anyone."

I spoke up. "You used it against Brunson."

"I did. How could you tell?"

Milan laughed. "You're a New Yorker. He's a Texan. Your American accent should have made him like you less."

Turk raised her hand. "Yeah, you Americans hate each other. You should look into that."

I thought for a second. "When we get books for you in Sicily, we need to figure out which of your spells to keep and which to replace."

Milan nodded. "Healing you should definitely keep."

"Agreed. Bringing the dark could come in handy. But it needs to be faster. How big a space can you do?" I asked.

"Size is actually not an issue. I can work on faster, though." I could tell she'd never had a conversation like this.

Devique considered. "On the job, you probably won't need trust."

"Fire can come in handy." I thought out loud.

"Unless we have matches." Turk wasn't wrong. And the glamour would always be useful.

We could figure out what to replace two of her spells with. This was something I obviously hadn't ever had to think too much about.

What would we need on this job.

Turk motioned to me. "And can you heal her?"

I wasn't looking forward to this conversation. And I didn't really know why.

Noemie breathed in slowly. "It doesn't really work that way." She looked at me. "Healing, this spell, it's like fixing. Using the energy of the universe to connect to someone's energy and return them to their functioning state. You aren't really broken. You were born like this. For me, healing can't take the place of surgery. It won't make me... ...look like a biological woman. I'm not broken."

"Can you slow it down?" If I had more time, maybe.

She shook her head. "There's not really... I can't."

Quiet washed across the room. I realized they were waiting for me. I clapped my hands. "Okay. Who wants to go do Italy?"

***

We would have to get used to just floating at night. If we left now, for example, we'd be in the middle of the Balearic Sea by nightfall. At that point, the sea bed was either thousands of feet down or we would be over underground fields of flowering Posidonia -- sea grass. Anchoring would be hard and actually environmentally unsound. These fields provided oxygen for seas and oceans all across the hemisphere.

But if the winds were low, floating wouldn't take us far off course. And, in all honesty, we had time. Even if I didn't.

Every day I checked my field of vision. The raw edges of my peripheral were constantly there now, organic, reddish-black, closing in like the sides of a cave. Even in bright sunlight, I felt as though I were looking through a cardboard tube, obscuring the world to either side of me.

And my hearing was failing more and more every day. Notwithstanding the scare at the police station, I felt like I needed to actively work to make out sounds. I often felt like I needed to "turn on" my ears.

The combination created a sort of stickiness to the world around me. Almost as though my head required effort to move back and forth. I was moving through a viscous honey all the time now.

To make matters worse, over the last year, I had been dealing with Charles Bonnet syndrome. In CBS, when your vision is delivering less and less information, your brain begins to make up artifacts – hallucinations – to fill in the blanks. In some cases, it's a simple visual bridge over the space you don't see. In others it's an elaborate light show or even a fantasy animal -- something that can fill the space your brain feels like you are missing.

I'd begun hallucinating.

And as much as I trusted Turk, my brother, my dad, I couldn't tell them. I couldn't let them know that I was becoming even less worthy of their trust, even less reliable.

Even less believable.

So I kept my tiny hallucinations to myself. I tried to take my time to determine what was real and what wasn't. I tried to avoid situations when I felt out of control, when my brain began to work harder to take over for my failing eyes. I was asserting control. I needed control.

And floating in the dark in the Balearic Sea was not it.

I sat, that evening, on the aft deck, my sundowning night vision having seen Marseille recede behind us hours ago. A part of me knew I'd never step foot into the front door of the Depot ever again, never sit in the cafe downstairs drinking the tiny cups of coffee with powdered mushrooms Milan loved so much, smiling through the sensations, even as his eyes welled up with tears.

So beautiful. Everything.

A part of me, the biggest part, knew that Marseille would never be mine again like it had been.

And I squinted to see the last of it, until the darkness stole the rest of my sight like a deft larron slipping wallets from open pockets.

The engine shut down, taking a moment for all vibrations to thin and then go silent. I thought about the pager under me, still wrapped in a blanket, duct taped, hidden from the world and I felt the same way. Hidden away from the sensations around me. This is where the world came to end, it seemed like.

Turk had joked earlier about dragons, about floating off the edges of the flat earth and I felt both of those now. The flashing lights that signaled an episode of Charles Bonnet syndrome could easily be the night's wash of flame from the mouth of a descending dragon. And this feeling churning in my gut might have been the curl of gravity's release as we fell away from the world, falling through the nothingness, thick and wild all around us.

I could hear the lap of the night's waves on the side of the boat. I tried to sense if they were pushing us port or starboard, but I couldn't. I couldn't even remember the word for forward on a ship. I smiled, thinking that I might die on a boat not knowing what part of it I had died on and that would certainly make me haunt someone.

The air tasted like copper and brine. The sea seemed to carry the same qualities -- the same components – as blood. And it was the blood of the whole planet. This was the gash in the earth. In this part of the Mediterranean Sea, the waters from the Atlantic breached the mountain ranges connecting Europe and Africa like a massive inhuman fist. They say the waters flowed for two years at a speed of 100 km per hour, driving the sea level up by over 10 metres daily until the sea was formed.

Through violence.

Tonight was my reminder that the world is mostly ocean, mostly sea, mostly unfeeling water, always willing to carry the unwilling to where it wanted us. It would never sit still in patience waiting for us to decide our own fate.

It was more alive than we were.

I felt a hand on my neck just as I smelled her. Turk wrapped her arms around me, holding my chest while she kissed my neck.

And a strange inversion of perspective happened. The sea went from being some strange monstrous adversary to a carnival ride, a perfectly constructed device meant to spirit us away, a magic carpet, a wide ferry committed to carrying us away with all our secrets intact.

She pressed her bare breasts against my back, trying to communicate on the letterboard of me and I laughed. So much faith she had in me that I would be composed enough to read this way when I was drunk from every time she touched me. The lithe perfect sound of her laugh followed mine.

"Come on. I want to show you something."

She pulled me up and into the aft cabin. It was empty and dark and I could still see nothing. I felt her lips open up mine and I experimented with a kiss that could really slow time. My lips and tongue lapped along the bottoms of hers. Her hands played along the bottoms of my bathing suit and I leaned into it.

"Here." She pulled me toward the front of the boat. I still couldn't remember what it was called. I stopped for a moment.

"Hold on." I reached out and grabbed the blanket ball that contained the pager. I liked it hidden away. I had no interest in it escaping this cage and following me around, listening in.

Telling all our secrets.

We made our way to the forward deck, then up to the top deck, wider and more open. Seats were scattered around and I could smell Milan sitting on the edge, watching out, more than I could see him. mMore than see. He always smelled like some combination of leather and bergamot, vanilla, licorice, and vetiver. This was the smell of my father.

Turk called out. "You got it?"

I heard Dev adjusting something. He stepped down next to me. "Yes. Clear. It's ready."

Suddenly there was a light, bright enough to pierce my vision. At first I thought it might be a hallucination, but it spread horizontally like a piece of paper in the wind, floating, flapping. It grew thicker and I could see it rise up over an equal size block of darkness.

The two grew at the same rate, with the light beginning right about at my waist and the dark descending from there to the deck and below it. The light block rose, foggy and rich white in the sea air as I looked up.

Now I could see what Dev had been setting. Above us about a meter was a disco ball, floating from a wire, moving easily in the wind, spinning. The light rose, inching upward until it touched it.

Then it happened. An explosion of luminous color shot out, flickering in the dark all around it, sending shards of crystal light all around us in a circle.

Noemie stood there, smiling, waving her hands and watching the show. Milan pressed the button on the boombox in front of him.

Highhats and horns opened the space around it. The boat seemed to widen up.

Sunny, yesterday my life was filled with rain
Sunny, you smiled at me and really eased the pain
The dark days are gone and the bright days are here
My sunny one shines so sincere
Sunny one so true, I love you

Boney M's version of "Sunny" blasted out and in it, I could see Turk, her hair round and wild, wearing the bottoms of an old bikini and a transparent wrap around her waist, pulling me in next to her to dance. We spun around and slammed into each other without a single other boat or plot of land for hundreds of kilometers in any direction.

And it's still so (sunny)
Not a cloud in the sky (nah)
Don't go, I don't like the sound of goodbyes
Last chance, I'm in town for the night
Take my hand, show me 'round to the sights
Cellphones off, need a reset
Good vibes, any bad ones, deflected to the side (yeah)
Pinky finger out
Aimed it to the sky (whoa)
Show you what I'm about

You ain't ready for the shine (nah)
Anything you want
You don't have to decide
You can have it all

I would never live with Turk, or Dev, or Milan, ever again in Marseille. I knew that as though I were a witch, leaning forward to look at the future. But I was here now.

And I would live forever tonight.

8. Dark are the misery, the men, and the war

Noir la misère,les hommes et la guerre
Qui croient tenir les rènes du temps

Dark are the misery, the men, and the war
Who believe they hold the reins of time

Turk and I grew up as Yé-yé girls for sure, minus the unsustainable affectation of innocence, with her pointing to me at parties and telling all the boys I was France Gall and weren't my eyes so much greener than they were on television.

They would cluster around us and sing "Laisse tomber les filles" ironically, never knowing HOW ironically.

Stop messing with the girls.

The week we had met, at that parisian hotel, Gall had discovered that her top-ten hit, "Lollipops," written for her by Serge Gainsbourg, was actually about oral sex, something she sussed out from watching a music video on the show Au Risque de Vous Plaire where the background dancers were dressed as giant penises.

She put two and two together.

And found out why the men all stared.

There are secrets all over. You figure them out and things fall into place.

It took us five days to reach Sardinia, only 340 or so nautical miles away. I was getting used to using nautical miles, the standard for mariners, but it still felt strange.

We had gone some 600 or so kilometers, but we took our time. We kept our speed to about five knots, paused often to swim or take in the view, and didn't travel at night.

So far, it was a vacation.

That afternoon, as we moved toward the port at Cagliari, we got our first view of Sardinia. It was mostly light before detail. A line of yellow and white, stretched out across the sea of black water. The first figure we could see was the Bastione de Saint Remy, like a massive white cut stone god on a hill, lit from below, calling us into the past.

In Sardinia, the last 50 years or so hadn't happened yet. This was the border between the past and now. The port itself was playful and familiar with its sweeping rows of arcades and ancient palm trees, men playing checkers on the same boards their grandfathers played.

The smell of fish was thick and unappetizing, but it fell away quickly when you stepped inward, away from the water. We had decked out the XMAS to mirror the fishing trawlers and schooners all around us.

We were just fishermen. It gave us an excuse to keep to ourselves. We were determined to limit the time we spent next to anyone until we got to Sicily. I felt strong today and pronouncements like that were easy to make.

Despite that, I found myself leaning on Milan a little more than I wanted as we made our way to a small bank of payphones. My vision worked well with the Cagliari roads, narrow and intentional. A lot of unnecessary detail was gone and maybe today that was ok. But my balance was shaky. It made every road seem uphill both ways.

I slid into the nearest payphone and put my foot out to block the wood and glass door from folding shut. Milan leaned in the doorway and took a deep breath. Ordinarily, I would have made this as a collect call, but that's not what this relationship looked like. Milan pulled a handful of gettone telefonicos - little metallic telephone tokens representing lira. No one really knew how much they were worth. You just poured them into the slot until the phone connected.

Welcome to Italy.

I sighed at the rotary dial, entering the number from memory. A young woman's voice answered curtly.

"Ela."

"I'm calling on behalf of the Eurovision Awards Committee. We'd like to speak to Anton Karras. How's he sounding today?"

Was I upset that didn't get a laugh? Maybe. Any response would have worked for me, though. About a minute later, Karras's voice came through the tinny receiver.

"Miss Mäkelä. It's very nice to hear from you. Is there a problem?"

I would work out later exactly how he knew it was me, not a different one of us. "Milan and I are here. And, no, the opposite, really. We wanted to let you know we are on our way to you already, taking a bit of a vacation along the way."

"That sounds lovely. And I hope our Miss Mason is well."

"She's fine. Very excited. We are in Italy, making our way over. We'll pick up some things and maybe show her the ropes a bit."

"Ah. That sounds exciting."

"We got the idea from Nikola's visit. Let's get out more, right? You must thank him for us?"

"Of course. We're a team, right?"

"A team. Yes. We will check in."

He paused. Then responded, matter-of-factly, "see that you do."

I heard the click. That wasn't ominous. Milan shrugged at me and fished out the remaining tokens in his pocket.

"We've checked in."

We switched places and he began dialing. We kept at it until we were out of tokens. A few of the calls were about supplies we needed delivered to the port. These were simple, businesslike, perfunctory. But some were longer. Many had to do with managing our arrival in Sicily. For these I was grateful that the wadded up ball of blanket, so crudely taped shut, was wrapped up again in the sack I carried.

Another layer.

We changed some money while looking out in every direction. I had a mental image of Ruach and his people destroying an Italian open air marketplace because we had talked to the apple seller for a minute too long. If his goal was to keep us isolated and on our toes, it was working. But the more people he hurt, the more we were determined not to let him put a win in this column or any other.

We listened to old world Italian guitar music from tiny boomboxes walking through the port. As we got further inland, however, the oddness of Sardinia surfaced. Years ago, Adriano Celentano had recorded a song mocking the appeal of American music on European charts. It was a nonsense song, meant to mimic the cowboy rhythms of English. It played everywhere, constantly, across port cities in Italy, mixing with Italian standards and nameless local music, every other song another Adriano Celentano.

As we stepped back on the boat, we heard Celentano and Lola Falana's "L'Unica Chance" reminding us about our situation, a fuzzy, liquid bassline rolling up into the truth.

Our health goes away with the criminal

who steals our food for some lire

She, she goes away

she, she goes away

It's pointless by now that you set the table

cause I know that like a lurking hawk

you'll find the enemy on the plate

Here you go, gentlemen, that's the situation

anyone of you who wants to commit suicide, can just enter the store

At what point does a song know more than you do?

We didn't have time or patience for Sardinian secrets right now, This sleepy village watching with a half opened eye, marking you, making you every chance it got.

This was the home of Graziano Mesina, the famous Scarlet Pimpernel of Sardinia who handed cash to children to get out of the line of fire.

"Here, kid. Get outta here. Go buy some candy."

Back on the boat, Turk was in the salon with Noemie, two guns on the table, her Lola Falana hair a perfect disc. I pulled out the two I'd managed to lift from the Italian police wandering around the port.

"Thank you. A lot of teachers have to pay for their own supplies." She lifted one, made sure the safety was on and it wasn't loaded. She handed it to Noemie.

"Now, make that shit disappear."

Noemie held it awkwardly. "Can I cheat?"

"Hell, yes, you can cheat. That's a crazy question. Use anything you got. What can you make it look like?"

"Well..." she thought.

I sat down and put my feet under me. "Think about something no one would be surprised to see you carrying."

"I wanted to see how you guys can hide these in your clothing so well. Even when you aren't wearing much."

Turk was insistent, "We do what we do. You have to do what YOU do. You can do things we can't. You can hold that out in broad daylight and make it look like something else."

"Imagine what you might be holding in front of you." I winked at her.

She slid the gun into her right hand and suddenly, where it was, there was an apple.

"I like it. It's healthy." Turk nodded. "Fuck the doctor."

"That is amazing."

"Can that work?" She looked back and forth between us.

Turk nodded her head to the weapon. "You're still holding it like a gun, though. Hold it like an apple."

She held it up and slid her fingers under it.

"Nice. Let's try this. Think of something you'd be holding out. Something breakable, maybe. So no one tries to grab at it before you get a shot off. Something interesting and realistic. Maybe something you can make a point of giving them?"

I wasn't sure if I'd broken her. She looked confused. And then I looked from her face into her hand. She was holding a bottle of lemonade. It looked ice cold, droplets streaming down the outside. It was remarkable.

Turk stared. "Damn. I'm kind of thirsty."

"Right?"

Dev stepped in from the aft. He and Dad had been putting boxes away. On this next leg, we would have to build more storage. I had plans already for false walls in the dual engine rooms on either side of the stairs. My trick? Place convincing rats' nests and droppings on fake walls.

Everybody hates a rat.

He reached out to Noemie, one hand on her waist. "Okay, give me your list. Last one."

"Oh." I handed him a couple more items. All things we couldn't get here, we needed to get in Sicily.

Noemie let the gun slide back to the table. "I don't know how we're going to find this stuff."

Milan came in behind Dev, moving to the sink to wash his hands. "Where we're going, we can get anything. But we need to move. We're meeting in three days."

Turk had already grabbed up the guns and was looking around. We'd hide them all over the boat. I could tell Noemie felt a little in the dark.

"Wait, who are we meeting?"

I took a breath. "We have an appointment with the Corleonesi family."

Noemie's eyes went wide. "Like, from the Godfather?"

"I want to get a cat first." Turk smiled.

***

If you're going to ask the next question, I understand. Do all criminals know each other? The short answer is no. The long answer is, 'what kind of an idiot wouldn't want to keep up on what's going on in their world?" And what was going on in our world was criminals. Good ones, bad ones, little ones, big ones.

There is a fictional Corleone family, the ones from the book by Mario Puzo, made into a movie in 1972. And the real one. The one run by Salvatore Riina and Bernardo Provenzano. They were working hard then, in Sicily, to consolidate the different crime families. To do that, they didn't need money. All of them -- they had their own boatloads of that.

They needed leverage. They needed a sign that they were the people to follow. So, not to fall too deeply into this adage, we offered them real leverage.

And, yes, made them an offer they couldn't refuse.

We climbed back on the boat and rode out as far as we could, spending the night watching the brash hot lights of Sardinia abrade the sky. You could hear music, but we had our own. If you squinted, you could see dancing.

But we had work to do.

Devique and I threw everything we didn't need overboard, making room for supplies. We filled in holes in the walls with secret areas, added hidden cabinets, made sure that what was accessible was needed. Turk and Milan hid weapons all over. And, finally, when that was done, they blacked the knives in the knife block.

Knife-blacking was a common thing among larrons. You take the knives sitting around your home and you drill holes in them, bending them slightly. You want to make it so that only you knew the proper code to throw that knife. Everyone had their own blacking. We had a very specific blacking for our family, meaning that only Milan, Devique, Turk or myself could ever properly throw a knife found in our home.

The little things count.

Noemie learned. She practiced. She got good at misdirection.

The first two nights we were under engine all night. We didn't want to be late. We had made up enough time so that, on the final travel day, we could relax a little – swim, wait for night, and sleep. On the second night, it was bright on the fly deck, so lit by stars that I could see. And I saw Noemi sitting on Devique's lap in a bikini, black of course, her arm thrown around his neck, barely reaching all the way around his massive shoulders, laughing.

And she leaned in so slowly to kiss him. It was slow enough that any movement could have stopped it. Slow enough that you could tell if someone was waiting. Or if they were just being polite.

And he kissed her back.

My brother looked happy. That night, he wasn't looking after his impossible sisters or working overtime to impress the father that had placed him on such an interminably high pedestal that the thought of falling off itself was deadly.

He was just a guy, maybe falling in love. I couldn't see his eyes.

But the look in hers was unmistakable.

We would land in Palermo at noon, with plenty of time to spare. Well-rested.

La Cala Marina had a wide ring of fishing boats, most pulling in from the first catch of the day. The hope was no one would think otherwise of us. I was resting my eyes until the approach, but the looming shapes of the Norman Palace and Monte Pelligrino were worth staring at.

The port was alive, but filled with what we all called "the Sicilian stare." Which was commonplace here. Look down, look at your box, your work, your hands. Look anywhere but up.

There is no value in knowing what anyone else is doing in Sicily.

Milan tested his earpiece transmitter with Dev. My hearing was too unstable to trust with one. But Milan could sign to me anything we needed to know. Besides, here in Palermo, he would need to be in charge.

The crime families were possibly the most patriarchal systems in the world.

And that wasn't about to change for us.

Turk and I flanked him as we walked inland.

A black van was waiting for us at the end of the walkway, with two men in black suits standing next to it. Milan spoke in a whisper to Devique, below my threshold.

Turk laughed. I sighed, trying to make sure I didn't slip. This would be a bad time to lose my balance.

Milan stepped right up to the first man and grabbed his hand, pulling him into a burly hug. "Carlo. It's good to see you."

"Old man must be in a good mood. Wanted you to see a familiar face. This is Paul."

The other man reached out a hand. "It's nice to meet you, Mr. Mäkelä. Ladies."

"My daughters, René and Turkana."

Carlo shook our hands and joked. "Well, I'd put hoods on you guys but It's not going to fit on her."

We pretended to laugh and climbed into the van. Dad sat in front with Carlo and we sat in the back. It was only a five-minute drive to Vucciria Market and we saw exactly none of it. But the smell of pizza everywhere was hypnotic. We parked next to the market and, as soon as we stepped out, the smell intensified. We ignored it and walked about half a block down, past vendors and milling market patrons, to the castle-like entrance of Riina's apartment.

As we stepped in the door, Carlo marched us past security. Turk handed me half of an arancini she had lifted from a vendor and I inhaled it. It was soft and hot and brilliant. The elevator was slow and massive and it opened on the top floor directly into a wide open den area. The Corleonesi owned the entire building and no one Rinna hadn't vetted would make it up here. As we moved toward the inner area, Turk asked Paul to escort her to the bathroom. I knew she wanted to look around.

I followed Dad into the back of the room where Riina sat on the edge of his desk, waiting.

He was not a large man. Short, balding, with a stony face. He crossed his arms in a stark white shirt, the sleeves rolled up, and a pair of black suit pants. He was a working man, he liked to remind the family members.

Like them.

Behind him was the flag. Corleonesi was a bastardization of Cour de Leon. Lionheart. The flag showed the lion, reared up, open heart large and beating, crown on the lion's head. It was set against a black field of stars.

Death, all of it.

My father approached him, shaking his hand. "El Corleonesi, Don Riina. It's gracious of you to meet with us."

He shook his hand and motioned for us to sit.

I sat in the chair next to Milan and scanned the room. His men milled around the room. But behind the desk was Provenzano, a thin man in his early 40s with a shock of black hair. Beside him was a woman, near my age. She was thin with short black hair and a scowl on her face.

"This is Bernardo Provenzano, my partner. And my daughter Guilia."

The two of them nodded. At that moment, Turk came back in with Paul. The two of them were laughing. Paul abruptly stopped as Turk moved to one side of us and leaned against the thin table next to the wall. Riina tried not to look. I guessed that this was the first black woman ever in his den.

"These are my daughters, René and Turkana."

We nodded. Riina made a quick gutteral noise and continued. "So we are to take the Lucchesiana?"

Milan nodded.

"And you have five?" Riina held up five fingers.

My father nodded again. "I do."

Riina looked around. "We will have five as well." He reached around and his daughter handed him a piece of paper.

"We will need only these books."

Turk looked up. "You don't have a library card, or...?"

Riina handed the paper to Milan and stared at Turk, taking her in. "This one is going?"

Milan sighed. "Turkana, what time is it?"

She shook her head and walked over to the desk. She pulled a watch out of her pocket and placed it next to Riina, returning to where she had been leaning.

The Don looked down. He palmed the watch. "It's not valuable. The reason I keep it locked up is that it belonged to my father. Fathers are, well, important." This last he directed at Turk.

She nodded.

He slipped it in his pocket and tilted his head. "You understand."

Guilia interjected, "Sunday night, we thought. The least people will be around."

I spoke up. "Actually, we were thinking that Sunday during the day would make sense."

Bernardo shook his head, "We don't want to hurt people, do we?"

I responded, "No, sir. But the clergy members will be in the rectory in the building at night. And we definitely don't want to hurt them." Every person in that room was a Catholic. This was the one thing they would all agree on.

Milan looked around the room. "We have a way to clear the whole building."

Riina scowled. "To clear out the entire Bibliotecha Lucchesiana?"

Turk raised her hand. "It's.. actually, it's... magic."

That seemed to close out the meeting. A woman walked in to occupy Riina. She had probably been given a number.

And we had already outstayed it.

He excused himself.

We were on our own to walk back to the boat. I desperately wanted to visit one of the restaurants or cafes on the way, but the last thing we needed to do was get too close to anyone. These men helping us get the books we needed, they could protect themselves. They were literally the only people we were willing to risk. As we walked two doors down, Turk turned around and drew our attention to the guards watching the front of the building.

"Watch this." We saw them light cigarettes and begin to smoke. It looked like they were in a heated conversation. I tried to read their lips, unsuccessfully. Turk was looking elsewhere.

"See the hands?"

There was a rumor that all of the men who worked for Riina had to prove they could shoot equally well with both hands.

They were all ambidextrous.

And what we saw in front of us was consistent with that. These men were ambidextrous. I thought back to the den upstairs. They were all ambidextrous.

Milan shrugged. "Never ignore a good rumor."

Riina's people were unimpressed with magic or the idea that we were thieving magic books to help a witch prepare some new spells. These were not men who were primed for that.

I held on to Milan's arm and breathed in the smells. "So what books do they want?"

He laughed. "Let's talk when we get back to the boat."

And that was the end of our talking business. We watched the people winding through the streets, holding their overflowing bags, spilling thick Italian sauces over the front of their slick Italian shirts. Everyone felt related, everyone felt attached to the pavement with tiny exposed wires, moving where they needed to be without crashing, intersecting, like some sort of clock, precise and beautiful.

Except us.

Milan stopped at a newspaper stand for a moment, staring at the paper hanging from a rope strung across the front. "Son of a bitch."

He stepped closer.

"Marc Bolan died."

***

Back at the port, Milan signed to us before we stepped onto the boat. I have to admit that I was expecting this visit, but the visitor itself wasn't clear to me. We had essentially dared Karras to show he knew where we were.

That he could find us anywhere.

And he had his ways of demonstrating that.

I stepped onto the swim deck in back as Milan and Turk came into the Salon through the starboard doors. I didn't think anything would go wrong, but there is no point being reckless.

It took me a minute and, when I walked through the aft door, they were standing around him.

"Ah. René. It's good to see you." Rialtos stepped over to shake my hand. He was dressed as a priest.

I laughed. "I see you're in a new line of work."

He modeled, spinning around. "Yes, well, I've been briefed on my part. I am ready."

I looked at Dev quizzically.

He nodded. "Rialtos is going to help us with the Lucchesiana."

Rialtos smiled. "We need to get some books for our witch, so I am in."

It was hard to tell how Noemie was feeling about this. She seemed embarrassed. It took me a second to realize that she and Dev might have been unprepared for this visit. Unprepared and busy.

Milan tried to break up the discomfort. "Ray lives here, I suppose."

"Well. Near here. Close."

"If he's going to stay, his dish night is tonight."

Dev patted him on the back. "Okay, the front bedroom is free. There are bunk beds, pick one. It's small but comfortable. Milan has been sleeping in the Salon, We've been in the VIP and René and Turk are messing up the Master in front. You'll have your own bathroom up there."

He pulled the collar off, now looking just like a suave Latin man in a dress. "Thank you. I'll bring my bag down there."

Milan shook his hand again. "You'll excuse us if we talk for a second."

We sat in the salon, the five of us. Noemie looked up. "Do you want me to wait downstairs, too?"

Dev patted her arm. "No, you stay. We're just going to try to figure some things out."

Milan looked around the room, "First of all, has he been in communication with Karras yet?"

Dev shook his head. "Not that I've seen."

Dad went on. "Okay. He will be. Let's make sure we have explanations for everything."

"I told him that there might be a supernatural mob of demons attacking the Corleonesi because of what they are stealing. He buys it."

I was impressed. "That's good. I believe that. It covers that base."

"And that we needed a vacation. Too much work."

Turk spoke up. "I actually do need a vacation so that is not a lie."

Milan shrugged. "See?"

I thought. "We need to let Riina know we're six."

Milan waved it off. "He'll probably add a man."

Devique added, "if we're meeting here tomorrow, we're locked up tight. The place is very secure right now.

“Except for random priests walking up.” Turk pulled out another arancini and handed me half.

“Yes, except for that.” Dev put his hand over Noemie’s

Milan looked over at the dark-haired girl. “We’re going to get what you need. We know what we’re doing, right?”

The rice ball was still somehow kind of warm. I took a bite. “Now, can we know what books they want?”

Noemie laughed at me eating. “I can’t believe you guys can just call up the most famous mobsters in the world.”

Milan equivocated. “It depends on what you say when they answer.”

At this time, the Corleonesi was the most brutal of the Sicilian mob families. In fact, they were the most dangerous one that had ever existed. They were pulling people from other families together and were only a few months away from fully consolidating the stragglers and taking over all of it.

Killing whoever said no.

Once that happened, there would be no other house to stand in their way. Sicily would fall to them, Corsica, Sardinia, all of Italy. And, right now, all the major urban crime families in the U.S. were controlled by their Italian counterparts. If Riina had his way, America was facing a bloodbath of its own.

Milan lifted his hands. “They want us to steal the Interventions.”

I was kind of aware. I think I knew one. But Dev seemed more so. He sat back in his chair.

Noemie looked around. “I have no idea. What kind of a book is that?”

Milan went on. “It’s actually three books. They sit in the Lucchesiana in an impenetrable vault. But they belong to the Vatican. They detail every single time the Catholic Church intervened in secular history.”

“That’s bad?” Noemie was imagining.

She just wasn't imagining big enough.

I looked at Dad. He tried to get her to see it. "Imagine this. For centuries, the Church is the most important and powerful institution in the world. During that time, it interferes, secretly, in the politics of other nations. And every single instance of that is documented in one book."

Dev held up a finger. "It's called the Concordant Leonus. Or just the Regis Creatio. The book of the making of kings."

Milan nodded. "As well, the Church is incredibly wealthy. It intercedes all over the world by funding, paying, supporting, using its vast wealth to change the world. And all of that is documented. Son..."

"That is the Letura Covenantum Umbrae, or the Shadow Covenant. All payments. All investments. Every one."

I raised my hand. "I do know the next one. The church has also killed, taken out hits, murdered people so as to change events in their favor."

Milan smiled. "That's right. That's the third book of interventions. It's probably the most dangerous one."

Devique followed up, "the Evangeliary Tenebarum. The Gospel of Darkness. Just this one book would turn the world on its head."

We heard a knock. Rialtos was at the door. I motioned for him to come in. "Is it okay for me to be here?"

Turk handed him the bottle of Moscato she had opened and was drinking. "Come on in. We're talking about the Mafia Book Club entries for September."

He smiled, grabbing the bottle. "I like it. Did you all hear that Marc Bolan died?"

Milan shook his head. "It's a damn shame."

Rialtos raised the bottle. "'Children of the Revolution.'"

My dad nodded. "Damn right."

I took the bottle. "'Bang a gong...'"

Everyone dropped their faces. I handed it to Turk. She held it up. "20th. Century. Fucking. Boy." And took a deep swig.

Rialtos tried to perk up. "What did our Mafiosa friends want?"

Milan took another drink. He looked sad. "The Interventions."

Rialtos nodded. "They are in the Lucchesiana?"

Devique grabbed the bottle from Dad. "Two years ago, there was a flood in the Vatican basement. It nearly destroyed the Interventions. So they moved them temporarily to the Lucchesiana vault. They will be moved back after renovations."

Milan looked thoughtful., "Ironically, having the Interventions in their possession might be the thing to stop the bloodbath. It will show the other families not to fight. They can't win. Corleonesi has the cards."

Noemi called out, "okay, I don't want to sound like an idiot, but why do they keep these? The Church. Aren't they like, incredibly incriminating?"

I laughed. "Yes. But the story is that, at the Judgment Day, God will judge the Church based off of these. And that destroying them or losing them, et cetera. is an affront to God."

Dev continued, "So, now they are sitting in a vault that is protected every way possible, a vault probably only the best safecrackers could even hope to open."

Noemie looked around. Turk took a big swig, finishing the bottle. "Oh, that's me." She put the bottle down next to her.

"I'm going to steal from God."

9. The Land of Love has no Borders

Pays d'amour n'a pas de frontières
Pour ceux qui ont un coeur d'enfant

The land of love has no borders
For those who have the heart of a child

We slept that night under anchor, in sight of shore. We had all day tomorrow to work out specifics before Sunday. We said goodbye to Rialtos, who left to play his part.

Turk and I went to bed early, laying in the dark, my left hand in hers, signing. Requin, the small black cat, curled up in front of her belly, and I drifted in and out of sleep.

In the middle of the night, I panicked. My eyes snapped open and everything was lost in the void in front of them. My brain forgot it was dark. It forgot much of my vision still worked, mostly, in the light.

I forgot all of it. All I could think was I wasn't ready.

I wasn't ready to never see Turk's face again. I wasn't ready to forget the colors of her. I had time. I thought I had time. I tried to breathe. The stress from planning for this job was drawing me closer and I felt a hit, a real one, nearly every day.

I tried to stand up and I fell over. The boat tipped all the way to one side and gravity went sideways. I landed on the floor, but it wasn't the bottom of the room. In my head, there was still more to fall. I could fall forever.

I curled up. I was sweaty and my breathing was quick. I tried to slow it down.

I felt Requin next to me. Then Turk flipped on the lights. She pulled a blanket over us and slid into the narrow passage next to the bed with me.

"I'm sorry." I whispered at her.

She shushed me and rocked. I waited for what she would say next. I needed it to be something only Turk would say. Out of everyone and everything in the world, I needed her to be her. Just one sentence.

She took a breath.

"I think Isabelle Adjani should get a blonde wig and play you in Godfather Three. Or is that too fake?"

I laughed into her neck. "Tamara Dobson for you."

"I forgot to mention I'm changing my name to Cleopatra Jones."

I pulled her closer. There was no air between us. I whispered. "I like it."

She paused. "I know you're a little freaked out about forever joining the syndicated crime families."

"I really am."

"But I'll be there to help you eat the pasta. We'll get so fat."

My breathing slowed. Requin stepped onto my face. She was tiny. Clearly the runt of the litter. She was warm. She vibrated.

I missed being strong for Turk. I missed being a rock for her.

We fell asleep on the floor, braced by the bed on one side and the wall on the other, protecting us from the harsh liquid tongue of the sea waves. I remembered what water did to rocks. All of them, eventually.

***

Requin was French for "shark.". Turk thought this was a good name for a cat who lived on a boat. We didn't go into detail about where she came from. Turk said she wanted a cat. So, a cat. Unsurprisingly, Noemie took to little Shark quickly and was in the galley Saturday morning testing what foods she liked with a series of small bowls on the table in front of her.

Turk slid into the seat in front of her and pretended to eat the cat's head as I made coffee. "So what's the verdict, Chef Witchie?"

"Well, no surprise but the tuna is in the lead. Eggs are a big hit. Cream with sardines..."

"Which are not on my list." Turk took a coffee from me. I slid in next to her. Requin looked like she needed to sleep off the food. With the three of us huddled around the table, it seemed like a good place for it.

"She's a good girl, though. She just likes it when you make it pretty in the little bowl." Noemie actually looked happy. I suppose having a black cat around, while a bit of a predictable trope, was an iconic choice. And one more person who liked her.

I thought. "Presentation is everything. I think you're turning French."

She laughed. "I wish. Watch. I've been practicing."

She motioned to the cat and petted her. Her fur seemed to swim and dance, resolving into beautiful tiny leopard spots. Requin looked up, the world's tiniest leopard.

Turk took a sip. "Aww. I have a bag like you."

Another pet and she returned to her silky black coat. Now, after seeing her as the leopard, I couldn't help but see the tiny black panther in her. I thought for a second.

"Wait. The glamour can work on living things?"

She nodded. "I've practiced it. I can do about a square meter of something alive."

"A face?" This opened a lot of doors.

"I think so."

"And what we talked about?" I was still a little nervous about tomorrow.

She nodded and closed her eyes. She lifted her hand and the room shifted, filling with rats, rushing all over every surface. There must have been hundreds. One shot across the table and Requin lifted her head, tearing off after it. She dove onto the floor and chased them like a tiny black tornado, whipping around the room.

Noemie lifted her hand again and the room fell still.

Shark looked around confused for a moment before jumping up on my lap.

"I didn't hear them. The rats."

I can't do the sound or smell. It's a visual glamour."

It would have to be good enough.

We finished breakfast and had time to swim, the port ahead of us on one side and the clear Mediterranean spread out flat and motionless on the other. Milan sat on the skybridge petting the cat, thinking about the meet later as the four of us splashed around. The black silk rope connecting me and Turk was just a way for her to spin me around and make me into her puppet. I never minded. I looked at Dev and Noemie with a similar cord tied around their wrists. Neither one of them seemed to pull at it, to force the other. But they stayed close regardless.

For the first time Noemie had removed her tiny black thong to swim, nude like the rest of us. While she had clearly had some surgery on her chest, resulting in a near-perfect set of china-white breasts, fuller and thicker than you'd expect from her thin frame, she hadn't had any work done below. The fact that she felt comfortable exposing herself like this today suggested to me that she and Dev had been intimate – that he wasn't just aware that she was born a man but had been physically close to her independent of that.

I thought back to her mood earlier. Maybe it wasn't just the cat.

I swam closer to them. "Dev...Noemie..."

He splashed me. I laughed and dug in, addressing both of them. "What's your take on Rialtos?"

Devique looked thoughtful. "I like him. He seems smart, but he's not acting deceptively. He answered every question I asked him. He honestly thinks we're on the same team and all is good. I think."

I looked over at Noemie, "That's probably true. He seems to see the good in Karras. And Karras, he treats him differently."

"What do you mean?"

"Karras is a man's man. His son is a man's man. Agnes is lesbian, black, a woman. She's an employee. I'm transgender, a woman, American, I'm a means to an end."

I treaded water as Turk jumped in. "But Rialtos is gay, right? Doesn't that matter to Karras?"

Noemie smiled. "He doesn't see it. Rialtos -- Ray -- he's slick. Karras thinks he is a ladies' man. Handsome, charming. He's the smart, likable, always-on confidence man that Anton wished Nikola was."

Dev interjected. "Nik is a thug. He's like hired help."

I nodded. "You think Anton is embarrassed of Nik?"

"I do. And Nik will do anything for his father's approval. If one of us gets in the way of his father's plans..."

I understood that.

Milan yelled out to us, petting the cat in his lap. "Hey, who do I look like?"

Turk jumped up like a porpoise, screaming out, "GODFATHER. WOOT."

We needed to get this out of our system before the Italian mob showed up. I was worried about them being here too long. We'd had short phone calls, a blisteringly short meeting, nothing long enough to attract Ruach.

But what about today? What about the job?

Let's find out.

By 3 PM we had gotten dressed and cleaned up and were sitting together in the salon.

The Italians would be here in an hour or so, so we wanted to run through any last-minute contingencies.

Dev started. "Rialtos reached out on his earpiece. He's got his room in the rectory and has charmed the priests. He thinks they'll listen to him tomorrow when it all comes down."

Milan nodded, "Good. I have the book list and the uniforms for you and me and the Italians"

I looked over. "They're bringing the right trucks?"

He nodded. "Very showy. So we want to wait in the staging area until there are at least 20 or so people in the library. We need people to witness. Connect the dots."

Turk sat on the floor between my legs. "The Interventions are in the vault below?"

"I'll be with her, getting down there and back up." I played with her hair.

"Ok. Last words before they get here? Confessions?" Milan looked around.

Noemie looked confused. "Confessions?"

Dev leaned in to her. "We have a family tradition before big jobs that we get in a circle and admit things that we are keeping secret. Confessions."

Turk went first. "I confess that stealing from God is making me horny."

I smiled. "I confess that Italy still sucks, but arancini might be better than gougères."

Milan made a noise with his face and shook his head. "I confess that pisses me off a bit."

Dev took a deep breath. "I confess I'm fooling around with a witch."

Noemie looked embarrassed but she went. "I confess that I wish this were over so we could do that again." She put her head in her hands. Turk laughed.

By 4:30, Riina's men had arrived.

Carlo was accompanied by Paul, who wanted to be called Paulie. They brought with them three younger men named Rossi, Bianco, and Bruno. I looked at Milan. My assumption was that these were code names. Rossi meant "red," Bianco meant "white," and Bruno was "brown." In the Corleonesi family, killers had code names.

These were assassins, not thieves.

I started playing scenarios in my head. Why were they here? Milan nodded at me and continued. "Gentlemen. Thank you for being here. I understand Don Riina has placed a man inside, just as we have one now. So, they will keep us informed and help us cycle people out. I want to be clear. This is God's library, under the eye of the Archbishop, and we can't hurt or kill anyone."

Carlo nodded. "Agreed. This is important." Carlo may have really meant it. As for my dad, he wasn't religious in any way. But he was passionate about not hurting anyone. He didn't care about faking the reason.

Rossi was a tall tan man who looked like he belonged outdoors. Bianco was shaped like a brick, with a thick mop of black hair. And Bruno had a reddish face, muscular and quiet. The three of them kept to themselves.

They stayed for an hour, laying out plans, looking through schematics of the library, and talking about timing. And still, no Ruach.

Had he given up stalking us? Was he not concerned anymore about us amassing allies against him?

I had gotten comfortable sitting on the balled up blanket that contained the pager. I had almost forgotten about it. It would have to come with me in a small backpack tomorrow.

But besides that, it was inert.

Nothing.

***

They left a black van at the port for us. By 6 AM we had climbed in it and were on our way to Agrigento. The trip would be two hours in traffic and we'd pull around the back of the flat we'd rented off the Via Duomo. The two other vans were parked there already. One tug on the false side finishing would reveal the garish logos on the vans. By 8:30 AM we were settled into the dilapidated flat facing the street, with binoculars trained on the library entrance. We had decided to wait until there were 20 people in the library.

Not including me and Turk.

We were both dressed in nondescript sundresses with multiple pockets, looking like college students visiting the book stacks. We both wore backpacks, mine holding the pager, which needed to stay close to me. If not, the tether would automatically return it to my pocket. Without the padding.

The Biblioteca Lucchesiana was part of an ecclesiastical block -- a kind of compound clustered around the main cathedral square. It was flanked by the Palazzio Vescoville where the archbishop lived, along with a rectory where many priests stayed, and the Diocesan Museum, which would be closed today. More than two-thirds of the priests would be working on delivering mass somewhere or serving somehow. The Palazzio would be near empty.

We entered on the main floor of the library.

The buildings were impressive on the outside, wide, sweeping natural stone, carved as if by giants, finished with ancient brick and wood from thousand-year-old trees. The peaks rose up into the sky like tips of mountains, pretending to acts of creation outside human capabilities.

But the inside? There was a sense that this construction had some sort of angelic help. The magnitude was skewed. It wasn't just wide-open and massive, but literally geological in scope. The ceiling of the room rose up as though participating in its own indoor heaven, with ranging curves of wood curling inward to brace the arc on top like massive roots to an eternal tree.

While we waited, we tried to find the books Noemie needed. The smell of books was warm and thick, inviting, familiar and exotic at the same time. Unfortunately, nearly all the ones we really needed were behind the main barricade, in collections only accessible to the librarian. We stepped over to the librarian. A thin dark haired woman turned around.

It was Guilia, Riina's daughter.

My stomach dropped. She was his person inside. His daughter. She winked at me. As much as it was good to see another thief on our side in here, I wished it wasn't this one. If we did anything to get Don Riina's daughter hurt or killed, we'd be on the run for the rest of our lives. Unfortunately, she couldn't just walk out with the books. Not the ones we needed.

I smiled at her and handed her our list. "Disculpe, señora..." She'd seen the books on the list, and hopefully had begun to collect them. But we were playing all this as though people were watching. She nodded and slipped behind the barricade.

I told Dev over the earpiece that Guilia was there. He seemed less surprised than me but I could tell he understood the issue.

We didn't have room in our backpacks for these books, but if we managed to get them arrayed on the counter, Dev and Milan could carry them out while Turk and I got the Interventions.

If everything went according to plan.

I scanned the room. There was a paternoster in back that led down to the ancient stairs that would deliver us to the vault. In front of it was a barrier. If you've never seen one, a paternoster is an open-faced dual elevator that never stopped moving. You stepped into it and it cycled around, moving up on one side and down on the other. It was maddeningly slow. And it never slowed or stopped.

Dev came through on my earpiece. "Are you near the back? We're almost at 20 people inside. I'm sending her in."

Guilia was piling books up on the counter. They were bigger than I thought.

We inched toward the paternoster and tried to keep an eye on the front entrance. So far, this was easy.

I tried not to think that.

We waited forever for the front door to open and Noemie to walk in. She wore a red wig and was in a dark red dress. It was a good color for her. I subconsciously started counting. Most of the people were gathered in the row of tables in the center of the room. A few stragglers were upstairs on the second level. They would be trouble.

The first screams came about a minute later. The bright lights illuminated every corner of the library. And running loose all over were rats. Large, black rats. Turk and I screamed along, happily raising the volume of the room. We needed people to not notice that they made no noise.

And panic.

As if summoned, Devique and Milan were the first ones through the front door, trying to get people's attention, ushering them out. They were in exterminator uniforms, faces obscured with masks.

Devique stood on a table as Riina's men poured in, dressed similarly, arms filled with cages and special devices. He began in Italian.

"Ladies and Gentlemen, as you can see, we have a rat problem. We believe that these may be rabid and we need everyone to file out in an orderly way. Thank you for your quick action."

People streamed toward the doors. Carlo and Paulie took the stairs leading to the second level and began moving people out, people afraid to step on the main floor. Noemie raised her hand and rats fell from the roof onto the second level.

The screams intensified.

Turk and I grabbed the barriers around the paternoster and spun them, facing outward, obscuring the entry. We dove into the box as it moved downward, making sure to pull arms and legs inside. It sank slowly but with determination. We kept our heads down, in case other levels were occupied and those people might see us.

They weren't.

Paternosters have no doors and they don't stop. If you miss your floor you must stay aboard and wait for it to make an entire circuit, delivering you back where you wanted to be. We weren't sure exactly how many levels down the Vault was since it wasn't an original part of the building. At the third lower level we could no longer hear the commotion above.

The fifth lower level was a limestone cavern -- a sub-basement. Across the room you could see a door. We jumped out. The light was lower here and my vision was seriously challenged. But I could make it to the far door. If our information was right, through that door we would find stairs to the Vault.

We slid to the right and grabbed the wall. Running toward the door with our right shoulders rubbing up against the limestone walls allowed us to make our way to the door by feel. I hated the fact that we were unable to hear what was going on upstairs but I had the next best thing.

I had my brother in my ear.

"Devique, what's our status?"

"The main room is nearly cleared out. Rialtos is here. He cleared out everyone but the deputy archbishop. We're talking him into leaving now."

"How much time do we have?"

"I give it seven minutes before authorities are here. We alerted animal control to leave a record and the vans in front are all flagged."

"Got it. Give us a few, we're almost to the Vault room."

"Good luck."

We hit the door as he said that. Behind it was a winding limestone stairway. We couldn't see the bottom, but we could see that by the seventh stair or so it was pitch black.

"Goddamnit." I breathed out.

"Hey, language. This is God's hook-up pad." Turk grabbed my hand. I closed my eyes and followed her, my right arm against the wall. The stairs were even and rhythmic and I was grateful for that.

We kept descending.

After about 40 meters, the stairs ended. The ground was uneven and wet in places. I struggled not to slip. I tried opening my eyes but there wasn't enough light to activate my vision. I wished for a moment that Noemie had come with us, giving us light.

Suddenly, I saw a flash. The hallucinatory light trails resolved, giving way to Turk's face. She had found a torch and lit it, filling the space.

"See. Matches work. Fire good."

To my right I could see it. The Vault. It was massive and seemingly constructed of rusty metal. In front of it was a brighter metal front piece. It seemed slightly more modern, at least. Turk stepped toward it.

"Yes. Hi, baby."

"Are you familiar with it?" We had been given almost no information on the Vault itself. No one had any.

"In a way. The frontspiece is an attivatore. If I solve it, it will open the inner Vault."

"Can you?"

"She reached into the backpack and pulled out a small vial of water. "God willing. Holy water."

"Holy water?"

"Psych. It's just regular water." She put the tiny vial on top of the attivatore and began to turn the silver knob. "The tumblers are so tight in this thing that when they slip, when I hit the number, they click. A tiny bit. The front is padded so I can't hear the click..."

"But the meniscus of the water will shake."

She whispered, "right." She stared at the vial, turning the knob. I took a deep breath. I could see the edges of the room only if I turned my head in every direction. There was no other way out than the way we came in. I made a mental note to talk about fire safety with the Roman Catholic Church.

Turk had pulled out a white grease pencil. She had 3 numbers written on the front of the Vault. There could only be one or two more.

Then we'd need to find the Interventions and get back up to file out. I lifted the face of my watch and read the number. Four more minutes to get back up.

The Vault made a thick clanging noise. Turk reached behind the frontspiece and turned it. She had always had a kind of sense of what vaults wanted. She had told me years ago that it was like a mental cheat sheet, something in her brain. She sympathized with safe inventors and developers. She thought like them.

Vaults just made sense to her.

"Here we go." She pulled forward and down and the entire Vault door slid open to our right, exposing a large space, about twenty meters long and ten wide. It held a number of books, gold bars, cash, a few urns, and more.

"God's junk drawer." She slapped her hands together. I smiled. The Interventions would be sitting together – three books. Turk saw them first. They were wrapped in a band, sitting together. The band was red with one word scrawled across it in calligraphy:

"Interventi"

"This feels not really secret to me." Turk winked.

She wasn't wrong. I pulled the books out. Turk turned around and let me slide them into her backpack. She nearly tipped over but I steadied her. I reached in to grab a gold bar.

Why not? It couldn't hurt. A gold bar could buy our way out of a lot. As I pulled it out, I leaned onto the book it sat on.

And I felt it.

It's such a common shape, but I knew that was it. I grabbed the smaller book.

"I have to close this and get out."

I turned around and let Turk put the book and gold bar in my backpack, right next to the rolled up blanket enclosing the pager. She turned back to the vault and began closing it. I felt my watch.

Two minutes.

The torch was dying out and I knew it would leave me totally blind when it did. I tried to remember the steps back to the stairs and then up, back to the paternoster.

Turk grabbed my hand and we slid along the wall. The torch died out by the time we got to the limestone spiral of stairs. I tried to remember with my body the height of each stair and hit them exactly. As we approached the paternoster, an alarm snapped on and a row of knives shot out of the wall on my left.

The wall I was leaning on. The knives were silver, sharp, each about seven centimeters long, just long enough to slice into my arm and cut the straps of the backpack. I pulled back, ripping off the backpack and holding it in my right arm. Turk pulled me into the box as it passed us and we sank into the back of it

I was bleeding down my arm. But I was more concerned about what made the alarm go off

We watched the floors go by until the light of the library burrowed into the open box. The lift seemed to move so slowly. Turk jumped out before the two floors even aligned. I looked up and the arcing visual of the floor rising in front of me seemed to dig into me, slicing away my sense of balance. I lurched onto the library floor from the paternoster platform and the backpack opened.

The knives had cut through the bag as well as the strap.

The blanket ball, gold bar and book fell into the red velvet box of the lift as I knelt in front of it reaching in. The floor rose. I jumped up to grab them, my hand wrapping around the book. I panicked. I needed the blanket ball.

Or else.

The lift rose to the ceiling with me climbing to meet it. Suddenly, Turk pulled me back. I fell backward, nearly on top of her, the book hitting the floor next to me. The paternoster box containing the blanket and gold bar moved upward, out of sight, to be replaced by another.

An empty one.

I looked up at Turk. "No, no."

The alarm had filled the library as I got to my feet. I bent over to grab the book and felt a weight in my front pocket. I reached in.

The slight plastic heft of the pager pulled downward.

I turned to see Milan and Devique at the door, backpacks full, Noemie not far behind. They had gotten their books, as well. Rialtos was next to them, in full priest's attire. Bruno and Rossi were on the second floor, at the far wall. I couldn't see what they were doing. Bianco was moving down the stairs and Carlo and Paulie were spreading around rat droppings and a tiny carcass or two

We needed to get out before the authorities came. Once we were out, we could disappear.

The pager in my pocket began to buzz.

The buzzing got louder. I turned to Turk and handed her the book in my hand.

"Run."

I watched her move toward the door as a black wave began to fill the room, like ink in an aquarium cage. A shape, masked, dressed in a black coat, stepped down from the swirl of ink on the second floor balcony. I yelled, but not before he pulled out a gun and one after another shot Bruno and Rossi at close range in the forehead.

The room fell into chaos. Devique pushed Milan and Turk out the door. Noemie dove toward the bookshelves next to her. He reached for her, one big step left, when another shape appeared, seemingly dissolving in reverse, coalescing from the ink, raising a gun toward his head. I started running toward my brother, but I knew I would never make it. I let out a scream, as Rialtos jumped in front of him, taking a bullet in his chest. The gunman in black spun around and aimed at me. I slammed into him and he dissolved again, leaving me sprawled out on the floor next to Rialtos. Noemi crawled over to him as Devique grabbed my hand.

The black ink filled the room, darkening it, obscuring my vision. Devique held onto me while covering Noemie, who was invoking the plane of light on the floor. She was healing Rialtos. His chest rose.

Her stark white plane of light was the only light I could see as the dark infected the library, men appearing out of nowhere and shooting. The light showed me Guilia under a table to my right, waiting for her moment to make a break. I looked up at Devique and crawled over to her, pulling her into me and covering her. I lifted her and ran toward the door, pushing through it with my right shoulder.

The one not bleeding.

Devique was next out of the door, Noemie under his arm, carrying Rialtos. Milan and Turk had the van running already and the doors open. We climbed in and pulled out, five of us in the back, with Milan driving.

By now, the people around the front of the building were panicking, running away from the doorway. Milan wasn't breathing.

"C'mon. Carlo."

Carlo and Paulie plowed out of the front door, each sliding behind the wheel of a different van. We turned down Rue Duomo and tried to get back to the flat as the sirens got closer.

Behind the flat, we pulled the logos off of the vans and moved up the back way. I carried Guilia and Devique carried Rialtos.

Carlo was the first one in the door. "Son of a bitch."

Milan closed the blinds. "Is everyone ok? Who needs immediate attention?"

Rialtos was just waking up. My left shoulder was still pouring blood. Guilia had been hit twice in the leg and Carlo had been shot in the arm. Paulie looked down to see a bullet had passed through his side, narrowly missing his stomach.

We started triage, bandaging what we could. Carlo came up to me and hugged me, whispering, "Thank you. You saved Guilia. No one will forget."

Something was nagging at me. I let him hug me but something wasn't right. The sounds in the room all swarmed together like honey at the bottom of a jar. It was hard to make any sense of it.

The few sirens came and disappeared.

We stayed in the flat for another couple of hours. We laid Guilia and Rialtos in the bedroom. The rest of us were in the living room, trying to dissect what just happened. We all sat there. Sounds dropped away and we fell quiet.

Until I stood up and looked at Carlo. "What were your men doing on the second floor -- the balcony?"

Carlo shrugged and shook his head. I looked over at Milan.

"If they had been together on the main floor, we would have all gotten out." Milan said.

Carlo rubbed the back of his neck. "There's no way to know."

He was lying. "There is a way to know. You know it. And I think you know what they were doing there."

Carlo's face shifted. His eyes lightened. "We're going to need to get our stories straight about tonight."

Milan sat back and crossed his arms. "To Riina?"

Carlo looked at Paulie and nodded.

Turk put her arm around me from behind. "My story is that I didn't see anything at all. I got your books from a fucked up vault."

Carlo nodded. "You did. Good."

"And she saved Guilia."

"She did. No doubt about it." Carlo looked over to Paulie. He stood up and dropped a small metal device on the table.

Milan motioned toward it with his head. "What's that?"

Carlo took a deep breath. "It's a detonator. The other men were there to set an explosive device in the adjoining wall. It could kill the Archbishop any time, from anywhere. More leverage."

Devique looked back and forth between Carlo and Pauli. "If it had a detonator?"

Carlo nodded.

I could see Milan parsing this in his head. He stood up and shook Carlo's hand.

Carlo looked broken. He leaned into the handshake and pressed his other hand over my dad's. "Everything went according to plan. We got your books. We got the books the boss asked for. We set the device. No one was the wiser. Those demons came. They shot your man. They shot ours. You saved Guilia. We escaped."

I whispered. "Mission accomplished."

10. A child with their eyes filled with light

Comme un enfant aux yeux de lumière
Qui voit passer au loin les oiseaux

A child with their eyes filled with light
Who watches the birds fly by in the distance

We left the keys in the black van after we pulled into the port. It was 3 AM before we got back to the boat to find a cardboard box with a little black cat asleep on top of it.

Turk picked up Requin and slid her into her hoodie pocket. "She may not be much of a guard cat."

Rialtos was still leaning on Devique so I tried to lift the box to bring it into the salon.

It was really heavy.

The six of us sat around the salon and sank into our seats. Turk put her feet up on the box. "I really hope this isn't a bomb."

I breathed out. "Well, that's how this night is going."

Noemie stood up and pulled a cardboard flap open, peering into it. "Wow." She sat back down. "Not a bomb."

Devique handed around bottles, starting with Ray. "This is for saving my life. You feeling ok?"

Rialtos took the bottle and smelled it, closing his eyes. "I'm better now. I sing when I'm drunk."

I took a bottle of wine and nodded. Turk grabbed one from Dev without looking. "Does anyone want to tell me what my feet are hanging out with?"

Milan stood up and walked over. "Riina is well liked because he tends to reward his people for a job done. I mean, I wouldn't call this a job well done. " He reached in and pulled out a bar of gold with an elaborate eagle on it holding a familiar symbol. "'Oro De la Fortezza.' Looks like two for each of us."

I thought. "That's about 60,000 francs apiece."

Noemie looked around the room. "Am I missing something? Why do those have the Nazi Symbol?

Milan handed her the bar. "A lot of Italy's gold reserves were looted by the Nazis from the bank of Italy. It was melted down and reformed and hidden in the Franzensfeste fortress in South Tyrol, Italy, before being moved to Germany. It was recovered later. Riina likes to spend Fortezza gold because it auto- launders. No one wants to pass around a bar of Nazi gold."

Dev took a drink and pulled her over. "So they have to melt it down first. Bam. Now it's untraceable"

"You guys lead a very strange life."

I laughed. "Says the magician."

Devique poured some champagne down her throat, getting it all over. She laughed. We all seemed to be feeling the same way. Just not being shot at felt great. Noemie had rewrapped the pager in a tighter, more portable package. And now that she had books, she could prepare a spell to get rid of it.

If that was possible.

I closed my eyes. "It was the gold bar."

Turk nodded. Ray looked up from his bottle. "What do you mean?"

I sighed. "The gold bar I took from the vault. I bet you anything that's what set off the alarm, somehow."

Milan shrugged. "How?"

“I don’t know yet. But it feels like this wasn’t a coincidence.” I pulled out the extra book we’d gotten from the vault. It was handmade, with a carved leather cover. And on the cover, a rectangular box. I handed it to Noemie. “What do you think?”

She sat up and wiped off her face. “It looks like it.” She opened it, looking through. “It’s written in Aramaic. Actually a kind of proto-Aramaic. And the inscription is here. “Perakh”

I nodded. “Flower.”

“Inside, though, it shows the inscriptions on all the sides”

Milan took a drink. “Can you figure out what it is, using that book?”

Noemie leafed through it and finally closed it. “I’ll try. In the morning.”

***

The news from that night at the Biblioteca Lucchesiana was less confusing than the event itself, likely due to Riina’s intervention. The library couldn’t admit what was taken and neither could the church. So a rat infestation had to be taken care of quickly by exterminators, along with animal control sharpshooters. The spokesman for the library expressed his sorrow over the quick dispatching of the tiny animals but reminded people what one rat could do to an indispensable book in the course of a night. The associate archbishop appeared next to the anchor on the news that night laughing about the single day holy war against rats that god had seen fit to let them win. I considered for a second the utility inherent in partnering with powerful people to steal things that shouldn’t exist. There might be a business model in there.

The library was open again by Tuesday.

And while no one was looking for us, we had no reason to remain in Sicily. We still had weeks before we needed to be in Crete. We were so well-stocked, though, we could bypass Malta altogether and go straight there, taking our time.

Except that wasn't what we ended up doing.

We had gotten up the next day already underway. Up on the flybridge, Devique had slowed to just a few knots while Noemie had the book open on the center table, scraps of paper everywhere.

Turk sat next to Requin, with the same goal of sunning herself while I pulled in over Noemie's shoulder.

"So, was this worth stealing?"

She nodded, "It definitely was worth it. It's technically a book of forgotten reliquaries - an early codex of powerful objects. The box is on the front, but only a few pages talk about it. The flowering box.

"That, on its own, doesn't sound ominous. What's in it?"

"That's the thing. The box itself is an object of power. The flowering box. Once you close the top, time itself stops inside it."

Turk perked up. "So it's like Empire?"

I scowled at Turk. She made me sit through four and a half hours of that movie. Warhol.

Noemie smiled. "Exactly. Except it's literal. Time stops. For anything in the box."

"But nothing about what's in it?"

Turk looked around. "And why are we going so slow?"

Dev turned around. "I thought you guys would want to hear this first. Tell them about the other one."

I looked at Noemie. "Other one?"

She turned the page. "Yes. There are two flowering boxes."

My mind raced as she continued. "Okay, so about 14,000 years ago, the Ice Age was ending..."

Turk called out. "Hey, guys, before this 14,000 year old story starts, this is me with cat boobs." She had taken Shark and placed her in her bikini top, balancing carefully. The cat seemed comfortable as she looked around at our faces squinting from the sun.

Dev nodded as if learning a new term. "Cat boobs."

Noemie went on. "It was the end of the Ice Age and the people of the time, the Magdalenians, had lived their whole lives in a brutally cold and unforgiving world. A massive number of them were collected under someone called the Agellid n Wagris, sort of the Ice King. He had massacred his way into their hearts, apparently."

"Got it. Ice King."

"Now, he had about 30 wives and husbands, but he wanted a main wife. Big ceremony. The sorcerers of the time made these two boxes for the ceremony. They filled one with precious fruits and foods, meads, etc. The other with flowers and small beautiful animals. Both of them could be opened and time would pass normally. But once closed, time stopped for everything inside."

Kittyboobs leaned back on the chair, face to the sun. "So, like dual refrigerators. I like it."

"Yes. Except to get the power to make the boxes, they had murdered nine thousand people for each one. That's what it took to make the magic work. The sacrifice."

"Shit. So what's in them now?"

"No one knows. Do you think Karras just wants the box?"

I looked at Devique. He shook his head. I agreed. "No. That's not enough. A box that preserves things. He's about what's in it."

Devique crossed his arms. "That's what I think. That's why we stopped."

I looked at both of them. I tried not to look at Turk, who was letting the stress of the last few days disappear in the sunlight.

Noemie turned another page. "According to this, the other flowering box is nearby. Very nearby."

Dev continued, "in the �al Saflieni Hypogeum."

I suddenly felt stupid. "I'm sorry..."

Noemie showed me a map from the book. It looked like a series of caverns. "The underground in Malta."

This next part was a learning experience for me, too.

The Hypogeum is an underground necropolis, filled with the remains of over 7,000 people sacrificed ritually. It's one of the best preserved examples of the Maltese temple building culture- a culture also responsible for the Megalithic Temples and Xag⍰ra Stone Circle. It's a large, winding, underground miniature city in Paola, Malta.

And, again, a pattern was emerging.

"The underground vault at Jericho, the Lucchesiana, Yeronisos, these boxes, the Hypogeum, even Nazi gold... What do these all have in common?" I mused out loud as Milan stepped onto the flybridge. He looked at me.

"Human sacrifice." He looked around. "Am I right? Do I win?"

Devique nodded. "You win."

Turk sat up. "Or. And this is me being all glass half-fullsie. But dig back in time and everything -- every site, every temple, every thing of value, all require human sacrifice."

I tried to think. That made sense, too. "Death. All of it." I rubbed my forehead.

Rialtos was still drinking as he pulled himself up the stairs to the flybridge and joined us. "What are we talking about?"

I closed my eyes and turned my face up into the sun. I decided to go for it.

"Ray. Does this look familiar?" I turned the book so he could see it.

He paused and then nodded. I could tell this was not information he was meant to be cavalier with.

My brother turned to him. "Why did you save my life last night?"

He looked around at us. He wasn't an idiot.

This was a test.

"I'm not an asshole. I see some... thing shooting... What are you asking?"

I felt like crossing my arms. I ignored the instinct. "Did you save him because he's important?"

Turk broke in. "Or hot?"

Rialtos smiled and looked at Devique. "I mean...He's not hard to look at. But, no, Miss."

"Do you kill? When you steal?"

"What?"

I asked again, "do you kill?"

He looked flustered. He was in a boat at sea with a bunch of people he couldn't have known well.

"I've. I've never had to. I'm actually good at my job."

Milan leaned against the side of the boat. "Why not?"

"You don't think this is a little heavy for me right now? I may still be a little drunk."

I stood up and took a breath. "If the thing that Karras wants us to bring him could kill many people, would you let him have it?"

He laughed. Then stopped. Then he laughed again, looking around suspiciously.

"Hell, no."

He took a drink. "He doesn't want to kill people. He just wants to live forever."

***

Noemie and Dev stayed up top. She could study spells while my brother aimed us at Malta. The rest of us pulled Rialtos down to the salon.

He set the bottle down on the table before falling into a chair. "I should probably sober up before we get there." He shook his head quickly.

"I think we've got some time if you want to level up." Turk sat on the floor in front of me trying on different ways to wear a cat. It had never occurred to me that a cat might aspire to be clothing, but Requin seemed pretty complicit.

I put my leg around her as Milan got comfortable. "So, how do you know that Karras is looking to live forever?"

Rialtos looked around. "I don't want to be that guy, but I think everyone knows. He's been traveling all around the world looking for ways to stay alive. That's why he was in America visiting witches. It's how he met Noël." He pointed up to the flybridge.

I jumped in. "So, he believes that there is a kind of fountain of youth in the flowering box?"

Rialtos nodded. "I think so. He doesn't tell me everything. But it's one of the things he hired me to do."

"To bring the box to him?"

"Yes."

He seemed honest and straightforward. Were we worrying about this for nothing?

Milan still looked concerned. "So, is there some kind of elixir or something in there?"

Rialtos shrugged, "I honestly don't know. He doesn't tell me. It's something he wants to keep him alive. Make him live… longer. Forever."

I thought for a second. "If he wants to live forever, why would he be willing to wait six months to get the elixir. Or whatever it is. He would want it now, right?"

"He's been talking about getting ready, planning, preparing."

That word hit me. "Preparing?" I looked at Milan. That's how Noemie referred to her spells. Having spells prepared.

"Yes. As I say, I don't know too much about it. He likes me, but he doesn't tell me everything."

I paused. "So, Karras wants us to go grab all we can carry and then bring him a box that is probably just an elixir to live forever. Do we have a problem with that?"

Milan shook his head. "I do not."

Turk looked up. "Not me. Someone's got to be here to turn out the lights in a million years."

I thought. "And if it's more than that, we'll have another one we can swap out." I looked at Rialtos.

He scanned the room. "Agreed." He grabbed the bottle again. "I think I'll keep going with this."

We let go again and tried not to think about it as we approached Malta.

Luckily, we had a lot to do. The main bedroom was the only room on the ship that could be made completely dark. I spent a good amount of my time that day identifying objects by feel. I had made the bed in the dark, no assistance from my failing eyes. And now tossed objects, scavenged from the ship, all over it, running my hands lightly over their surface and trying to place them in bags by category. This was a fork, this was a rag. This was a pair of panties, a tiny jar, etc.

I tried to "see" each one as I felt it. We sometimes forget how much pure information our fingers deliver. Size, shape, texture, temperature, incline, all of it available if we pay close attention. In the dark like this I was reduced to my fingertips, my skin, and all the information my surroundings wanted to deliver.

As much as I found purpose in that room, I also mourned. I mourned for the books I hadn't yet read. The ones I now probably never would. I remembered reading The Little Prince with Milan and Dev, and later, years later, The Red and the Black to Turk as we reveled in the idea that we were the revolutionaries. After all, in a war exposing the soft undercarriage of capitalism, who were the grandest generales but thieves?

Who fought the hardest?

And saying goodbye to my ears felt like betraying Milan. My father, the one who introduced me to Bizet, to Berlioz, Poulenc, Satie, and Messiaen, just so he could upend it all with Aretha Franklin, With Patti Labelle, with the greats like Cortex, Daniel Janin, Jean-Claude Petit, and Janko Nilovic. We lived in music as much as we lived in air, and being without either one felt like a quick death. It felt like running away from home.

I assembled my bags full of miscellany over and over again, The other bag held bills. Here is something you may not know. The habit of folding bank bills in a certain way so that people with low visual acuity can feel the denomination in their pocket or in the dark was developed by thieves. They needed ways to feel for their money in the blackness. A 10-franc note was left unfolded. A 20-franc note was folded once, lengthwise, while a 50 was folded twice. Larger denominations were folded crosswise, once, then twice. The creasing was tactile even after the bill was unfolded. I felt the bills in front of me and tried to organize them in a box. At first carefully.

And then quickly.

I don't know what time it was when Turk came in behind me.

"Hey, blondie."

"Hey yourself." I reached over and kissed her neck. I felt her stretch for the light.

"Not yet. I'm going to go one more time."

She seemed to slump a little. She put her hand on my waist. "You don't need to do this now."

"Then when? When it's all gone? I can convince myself I got the right answers?"

She hugged me from behind. "It's okay. Let's do it now."

"I'm sorry. I know you... I'm sorry."

"I thought the cat would be something that would make you smile."

"I know. And I did. I do. I just... Soon you'll be taking care of me the same way. Like you do her."

"And how many times did you take care of me?"

"Turk, this is different. This is forever."

She rocked back and forth. "It was always going to be forever somehow. We choose the forever part. The whole fucking world chooses the how part."

She wasn't wrong. But I needed to get away. I was about to explode.

That's how we were when Noemie knocked.

"Hey, guys. I want to show you something."

The three of us made our way back up to the top. It was a still night, forcing the thick droplets of rain to fall straight down, tiny spears let loose from the clouds directly above.

We stepped toward the edge of the rail and Noemie took the smaller wrapped bag around my neck. It was Ruach's pager. She put her fingers on her lips and unwrapped it.

Once it was unwrapped, she held it in her palm. I had grown to really despise the tiny hateful thing. The black plastic seemed hydrophobic, shrugging off the rain as it fell.

She lifted it to her mouth and whispered, "shush."

I widened my eyes at her and she smiled. "A new spell. Secrets. It's the same as wrapping it. It can't hear anything. It can't tell Ruach anything."

I nodded. That was a big weight off my back.

"Also." Noemie pulled the pager out of my hand and threw it.

"Wait… hHold on." By instinct, I reached for it.

"Close your eyes and call it." Her face was ringed in my peripheral tunnel. She was so close she filled it completely.

I closed my eyes. I mouthed the word. "Here."

And felt it back in my hand.

"I changed the tether spell. It's ours now."

I took a breath. The rain had matted down my hair. I pulled it back off my face. "Good. This is good."

Turk reached out and handed her a tiny box. "Here you go. I know you had to drop a couple of spells."

Noemie held them to her chest. "Thank you." She pulled one out and struck it. The match burned for a few seconds before the rain put it out.

"I really appreciate it." Noemie hugged her.

Turk tried to lift her up and almost fell on the slippery deck. "It's good. I stole them. Now you can still light shit up."

The last she said in English. I laughed. I lifted my face upward. Holding onto the railing was essential. My balance was so poor right now I felt like I could float off the boat.

"Not just that. Thank you for everything."

I slid the pager into my pocket. Her face filled my vision again. Maybe it was the stress, the movement, I caught it first though.

"Your nose is bleeding."

She put her hand up to her nose and wiped it away. "Oops. sorry. It's... it happens. I think I need to just sleep."

We all needed sleep.

It rained all night. Hours later, I snuck out, back up top, to feel the rain. My vision and hearing had sundowned for the day. I couldn't see or hear anything. I think I wanted the independence of stepping onto the flybridge myself, on my own. I knew Dev was in the lower bridge, moving us toward Malta, because I felt the vibrations of the engine in the soles of my feet. My bare toes played over the rough tape we'd applied to the stairs and walkways, in increments of 10 centimeters. By counting them as I dragged my foot over them I could tell exactly where I was.

I lifted an arm and directed my face toward the source of the raindrops. I could feel every drop through my skin, through the thin t-shirt, through the thin cotton shorts. My body tried to analyze them like a bat might, feeling the shapes in the night that might bend their path, redirect the strength of the droplets before they touched me, hundreds of thousands of connections every minute. Each drop held information but I didn't know how to read it yet.

I didn't know how to parse them. There were no visual hallucinations that night, no auditory ghosts, no other stimulus. Just the night's rain and the way it tried to talk to me, convince me.

By the time I woke up in the morning, we had rounded Sliema and were headed into Msida Marina.

***

Luxury yachts dominated the Marina. It was small and clean and relatively modern compared to other docks we could have chosen, but that wasn't the reason we were here. Here, on Malta, where tourists meant income, our best bet to be invisible yet wanted would be to act the tourist. To be wowed at everything. To overpay for everything, tip, and buy at established prices. Doors all over this tiny country would open for us as tourists.

Most everyone in Malta spoke English, which I thought would ease the strain on Noemie a lot. Her French was good but had its limits while Italian was something she clearly wanted nothing to do with. To amplify the sense we were tourists, we all spoke English, with what we hoped was a Canadian accent. Canadians are welcome anywhere.

The second reason we had chosen the Msida was that we were literally less than 10 minutes from the �al Saflieni Hypogeum. And while no one was watching, the shuttle cab route between the two, stopping at a popular cafe and booksellers, would remove all doubt we were tourists.

As we made our way to the large shuttle cabs, Rialtos ran ahead. "I'll meet you there."

I looked at Milan. "Do we trust him?'

He shrugged. "We either do or we don't. There is no benefit to being in the middle."

Turk nodded, pulling me onto her back like a backpack. "Do you think we can keep him afterward?"

Noemie seemed to enjoy talking to the driver in English, asking tourist questions. Mostly about food. If you want to look like a tourist, pretend you're just about to starve if you don't find a restaurant in the next seven minutes.

Turk and Milan and I sat in back. Dev and Noemie sat in front, pretending they didn't know us. There were only one or two other tourists on the shuttle as we finally pulled in front of the Hypogeum.

There was a kind of semi-permanent tent structure set up in front, right in front of the entrance. It was large and seemed to concentrate the heat from the Malta air. Last night's rain had reached this far inland and added to the mugginess. The temperature wasn't high, maybe 30 degrees celsius, but it felt sweaty.

Two groups had lined up by the entrance. Each was about five or six people. That was good. All we needed was to be alone in our own tourist group. I had a couple ways we could pull that off. I thought about it for a second. But then from behind me, I smelled a familiar scent.

"Hej, �abib..." Rialtos patted Dev on the back and took a turn shaking all our hands. His Maltese was perfect, as far as I could tell.

"Ladies and gentlemen, that's how we greet new friends here in Malta. Now, come close. My name is Mikiel and I understand we have Canadians here."

I yelled out and waved my hands. It was nice not to have to be the driver. I could be the passenger. I lifted Turk's hands. "Go Canada."

"We're going to wait a bit until the next two groups have gone through. In the meantime. What brought you here? What are you looking to see in our timeless caverns?"

I looked up, squinting in the room corners. Sure enough, cameras. Ray had likely sussed out all of them. This little modern convenience, strapped onto the ancient artifacts, likely made the people in charge comfortable.

"I like holes in the ground." Turk yelled out.

Ray laughed as Mikiel might. "Well, I'm a little new here. I've only been a guide for two months, but I can tell you right now, you're going to get your wish."

Mikiel passed the time delivering a surprising amount of topical local historical information, a good deal of which, I bet, was made up entirely on the spot. Or maybe it wasn't. Had Michael Jackson been here? I made a point to ask him later.

As we entered, we saw the topmost level. I was surprised at how wide open it was, as an underground structure.

An effort had clearly been made to keep it exactly as it was found. Scattered pottery shards, broken pieces of figurines, even pieces of what might have been bone sat in the corners and edges of the rooms that looked as though they had been burnt from pure limestone over decades with nothing but torches and tiny knives.

We had no choice but to see the tour all the way through. This was a bit frustrating, but the caverns were nothing short of miraculous. I thought for a moment about how we might manage the caverns under Jericho and tried to imagine the curves and doorways, rooms and walls as things with a function. Things that served a purpose.

We stepped down into the second layer. This was the one that went on, winding, for a distance in every direction. The ceilings made you imagine artists' lofts in Germany, large and filled with gravity, adding import to the art below.

Mikiel brought us to a room in the near dead-center of the level. It wasn't large. All of us could barely fit. But something felt unusual.

There was a vibration.

I had almost started to think of Ray as Mikiel. He slipped, for a moment, back into being Ray. "All right. This is the oracle room. No one can place listening devices or cameras in here because of the unique vibrations. According to ancient scrolls, the vibrations are capable of healing. The room itself heals."

Was I becoming more sensitive to vibrations as my other senses disappeared? I could feel how the room cycled. It was almost as though it were a carnival ride, spinning for a minute or so and then dropping, slowing, grinding, and starting again.

I tried to count it off, to time it. Down here, below the earth, what could be causing the circular rhythms? It was accurate enough, to my senses, that it almost felt mechanical.

"While we have the chance," Mikiel continued, "no one here had a clue where the box is. I've been digging."

Milan looked at him and continued, softly, "son, what if they put it together you started today?"

Ray waved him off. "I backdated my documents. I've worked here for two months."

"I hope they're giving you backpay." Turk folded her arms.

Rialtos smiled and went on. "If you do this right, they won't know. No one seems to know anything about it."

Devique spoke up. "She does."

Noemie nodded enthusiastically. "It's right in the middle space one level down. The book even shows the rock it's under."

Milan looked at me. I took a breath. "Okay, you and Turk. One try. If it's not exactly where you say, drop everything, and meet us."

Turk lifted her head. "Open hands, walk away."

"Exactly," Milan amplified.

Another wave of vibrations hit me. I was feeling something. Almost like my ears were popping. I wondered if the pressure in the room were changing. Mikiel ushered us out past the opposite side door.

I turned. The cone around my peripheral vision seemed to recede a tiny bit. If I spent a lot of time in here, would I recover some use of my senses? Or was this an illusion, too, like the swirling lights that had followed me everywhere lately.

It was so hard to tell what was real.

We stepped out the door. Noemi looked up to the camera and whispered, "shush."

She nodded at me and she and Turk faded away, only to seemingly appear a few seconds later. I waved my hand in front of Turk's face.

Nothing.

Mikiel clapped his hands, "All right you crazy Canadians. Let's ascend."

We followed him with Turk and Noemie's illusions pulling up after us like ghosts, quiet, unseeing. This glamour was better than the rats. We took our time to ascend, noting all the cameras until we returned to the entry tent.

"I really want to thank you for being such good passengers on my tour." Mikiel passed out cards. I looked down. We were meant to rate him. I walked over to the counter calmly and gave him five stars with a tiny pencil attached by a string, sliding the card in the box.

Turk and Noemie seemed to have disappeared. I looked out the front of the tent and they stood there, waving at me. I turned to Rialtos. "Are you coming with us?"

He grabbed me by the arm and stepped over by the door, whispering. "I'm going to stay here for about a week and work. I can make sure nothing is off and no one suspects anything. I'll meet you on Crete."

I nodded. "Thanks for pitching in."

He laughed. "It's all practice, right?"

I turned to walk away. He wasn't wrong. He called out in a whisper. "Hey. And so you know. No one dies. Okay?"

I nodded. This meant more to me than the box. This was something I needed.

I heard a noise as I stepped out the door and saw Noemie hit the ground. My balance wavered as I ran, forcing me down on the hard sand in front of the tent. I shook my head and closed my eyes, crawling forward to her location. Devique was holding her head. There was a slight gash on her forehead but she was awake. I looked up. Turk had the box hidden under a nondescript piece of canvas.

What had happened?

"Are you okay?" I whispered to Noemie.

"I'm fine. I'm fine. I just fell. I think I need sleep."

I sat back and wiped sweat off my face...

and tried to believe that was all it was.

11. The blue bird soaring above the Earth

Comme l'oiseau bleu survolant la Terre
Nous trouverons ce monde d'amour

Like the blue bird soaring above the Earth,
We will find this world of love.

I was young when my mother left. Too young to remember much of anything. I carried our similarities with me. Her piercing green eyes. Her messy gold-blonde hair. Her wide smile, I recalled, that she flashed more and more sparingly as time went on.

I remembered her white cane, tipped red at the end to tell the world she still had left some vision. Watch what you do or say in front of her – A message for everyone who knew. I remembered putting my hand in hers and signing as we walked around the block. Not much of the city was hers, but our block, in La Courniche, was a place she was familiar with.

Her disease had progressed quickly, and rather than cling to us for support, to be her senses, she shut us out. She was a pickpocket, like me. My father had told me she was a larron of the highest order when they had met, and they had magnificent times together. But by the time I was five, this version of my mom was gone.

The one who remained was sullen, often confused. She was letting herself fade away. And while she could still see a tiny bit in the light, more often than not I'd find her in rooms that she herself had darkened. Almost as if she had hoped to fade away into that dark.

When she disappeared, Milan and his friends suspected that she had stepped out the back door, walked to the Rade d'Endoume and stepped into the Mediterranean. She would be able to walk for a time, far enough out to maybe commune with the islands directly in her path. And then slip under until she was carried away. Unfortunately, those islands were old and, in every way, as unseeing as she was.

At the end, it must have been only black.

Devique was like my cousin then, a few years older, helping the men look for her, looking so much like his father, my Uncle Christo. So big and dark and handsome, with a voice that rang out everywhere. I didn't know it at the time, but it would be less than two years from that day that Devique would come to live with us, forever, after his father died, falling from a window.

He became my brother.

If I really try, though, I can remember certain events with my mother. I know that some are tricks of memory, meant to fill in gaps, much like the streams of light and objects that plagued my vision now were meant to replace visual information. I know that, but some still seem real. Some even come to me with a strange vibrating intensity.

I had just turned five. The grocer in front of the primeur had made a point to tell me that my mother and I looked identical. "Two dolls from a Russian set," she had said. My mother laughed when I told her that, signing into her palm.

The woman looked away.

That is how people responded, often. And, at times, my mother took advantage of it. Today we stood by the baskets of fruit, the apples, the thick oversized pears, melons, even more exotic fruits. I tried to speak into my mother's hand, to explain to her the vibrancy of the presentation.

The colors.

She pulled her hand away and put it in her pocket. This is how she would choose to shut me out. I leaned my face into her sleeve and she softened. Her hand slipped back into mine. I took it and placed it on a ripe and thick pomegranate.

It was perfect.

She lifted it, holding it up in front of my face. And I will never forget her smile. As I looked up, the pomegranate disappeared, as if by magic. Without being able to see, she knew where I was looking.

At her beautiful face.

The grocer came running, pointing at her and making a scene. She was calling for everyone to look at my mother. She had stolen a piece of fruit, hidden it away. And she was certain of it.

She'd seen it.

I frantically signed into my mother's hand, letting her know what was happening and what they were accusing her of as the manager approached. She signed back at me and I smiled, pulling close to her.

The grocer harangued my mother, arguing to the manager that she had seen the theft. As she finished, I pointed to her pocket. The grocer reached into her own pocket and pulled out the pomegranate.

The story shifted. The manager saw it now. A simple employee accusing a deaf and blind woman of theft in order to cover her own infractions. He grabbed her by the arm and instructed me to apologize to my mother for him. He patted me on the head and led the woman away, still yelling, still confused.

That might be the last memory I have of my mother before she took herself out of the world. And I tell it to you so that you might respect the coincidence,

I do.

***

The five of us stood in the salon staring at a box built before recorded history. It was about a meter long and a half-meter wide, give or take. It was lighter than I had imagined, the wood of it less substantial. Its surface was primarily a reddish-brown, clay-like, with inscriptions carved into it.

It was still closed.

I looked around. "I'm not sure I have the imagination needed to process what might be in this thing."

Turk nodded. "It's definitely not a new bike."

Milan exhaled through his lips, making a faint noise. "We could all offer up what's not in it."

Dev looked thoughtful. "But what if it's bigger on the inside?"

That was a proposition I hadn't considered. "Noemie, is it bigger on the inside?"

"Nope." She placed her finger on the box and said, in a whisper, "Yehoshua"

I looked around to her side. "What is that?"

She leaned into Dev, sadly. "Inscribed into the box. There are 9,000 names here, see? Really tiny, all over it."

I had to put my face right up next to it to see. Sure enough, what looked like grooves in the box were smaller inscriptions, almost microscopic, as if done by a needle.

"Each of these is a person's name. 9,000 names. The people who had to die to create the magic that binds this box. Yehoshua is one of them."

The idea seemed to haunt her. I realized that this was why I had trusted her. It wasn't a spell. It was that she was capable of recognizing the horror here. That she even tried to parse what 9,000 lives meant. Suddenly, I realized something.

"Okay, guys. Before we open this, I feel like we're at a bit of a crossroads. We're walking into a job full of weirdness and magic."

Turk said, in English, "yeah, fuck magic." Her eyes moved to Noemie, "No offense, witchie."

Noemie's eyes went wide as she shook her head. "Hey. Absolutely none taken."

"I'm just saying that once we open this, there might be no going back." I rubbed the back of my neck. A part of me understood that no one would back down. We needed the money.

For me.

My dad looked at me and I could tell he was seeing my mother.

Turk smiled. "Okay, then, before we open it, Confessions, anybody?"

I closed my eyes and thought. I had a million submissions. I chose one. "I confess that I feel totally out of my depth."

Milan sighed. "I confess I ate all the remaining yogurt."

Turk lifted Requin up and waved her front paws. "The cat confesses she wants to learn some magic. And me, too."

Noemie looked up from the box and shook off her sadness. She still looked down, but she was trying. "I confess that I'm enjoying learning how to steal things."

Dev had something on his mind but he seemed unwilling to let us in. He joked. "I confess I'd like it if you all referred to me as Captain just a little more."

Sometimes you have to tear off the bandage.

I reached over and flipped the top up. It rose up, as if greased, and fell backward away from me, exposing the contents of the box. I realized we'd all been looking away, hiding our faces. I turned and looked into it.

A pomegranate.

In the center of the box, a perfectly fresh pomegranate. That's what drew my eye immediately. Surrounded by fruits. There were figs, lemons, quinces, olives, even carob pods. There were dates, grapes, and a lotus fruit. Next to those was a jar of honey. The jar had no top but it hadn't spilled. Everything looked perfectly fresh, as though they were placed there today.

Turk cocked her head. "So, lunch? A lunchbox."

Dev reached over and lifted the edge of the box a millimeter or two. The items inside shifted slightly. "It's heavier now. With the top open."

I shook my head. "And nothing's shifted or spilled. So when you shut the top, it becomes immune to the effects of time or gravity or movement at all?"

Milan nodded. "But with the top open..."

"Right." Noemie was fascinated.

Turk put her hands up. "This is good news, people."

I agreed. "This is the best news. These fruits are ancient. This is plausibly what's in a box like this. This could be thousands of years old. We close this top and hand it to Karras, he won't know the difference."

Dev interjected, "or Ruach. He can't hurt anyone."

Turk flipped her hand. "Well, unless they're watching their sugar."

Milan stepped over and put his arm around me. "This is good. You did good."

I pulled the top closed. Suddenly it was lighter. I could lift it easily. And even set it on its side. The fruits inside didn't shift.

And I remember thinking, we might have just solved this thing.

***

Milan and Dev spent the day melting Nazi gold down into smaller Ingots we could spend. It seemed about 20 degrees hotter right near the crucible but it was satisfying watching the swastikas dissolve. And the smaller ingots let us stock the boat until it rode almost 5 centimeters lower in the water.

Dry food, fuel, potable water, we had more than enough to get to Yeronisos, but we needed more to stock the island itself, which boasted exactly nothing we could use. If we had to hold out for any length of time on the island, we would need to supply anything we required to live.

Devique did the calculations and we decided not to dock in Crete first before we went to Yeronisos. That meant this leg of the trip would be long, but we could take it slowly and conserve fuel.

We were close enough to the equator that the trip itself might have some health benefits. At least, Turk seemed to think so, as she returned to the boat with as many tiny bathing suits for all of us that a 50-gram gold ingot could buy.

We were on our way in a couple of days and it gave me time to think. The stress of the last couple of months had accelerated my disease, so I went out of my way to make the next 10 days of travel as stress-free as possible. I was on a yacht in the Mediterranean with the people I loved. I spent time meditating, trying to eat right, to exercise my senses. I remembered that feeling in the Oracle room.

Maybe I could push back on this.

I tried to maximize the daylight hours when my vision and hearing were at their best. I still used the dark to practice feeling my way around, learning how to use the objects around me. I had a head start on Turk with tactile sign language since I had used it so often with my own mother at the end. But she soon caught up. She was quick and could communicate with me with a casual touch easily. She was getting good at using the alphabet on my back as well, for more complex ideas. Often we'd walk around on the boat at night, her hand on my back, tapping like a hummingbird across its surface, explaining every sight, every sound, every place I needed to lift my leg an inch. We had developed a set of shorthand symbols with the tattoo ridges. A quick up and down swipe over my spine meant we were talking about directions. A wide circle meant she was explaining the room. We learned hundreds of motions that meant nothing to anyone but us.

And Devique made sure that the textured rubber tape perfectly documented every inch of the deck, letting me read my way around easily with the bottoms of my bare feet.

Turk and I finished the last few secret storage locations, artificial walls that let us keep gold, weapons, paperwork and more. Every inch of this boat was doing a job now and a single day didn't go by without Milan slapping my brother on the back and telling him what a good purchase it was.

Forward-thinking.

Slowly, the rush of preparation died down and left us sunning ourselves on the flybridge with a smaller-than-average black cat while Devique piloted us eastward toward an island considerably tinier than the neighborhood I'd grown up in. Milan was reading, listening to music in the Salon.

Turk called out to Dev. "Hey, where's the witchie? She's missing quality sun."

He shook his head. "She's not feeling great right now."

I let the sun play over my face. "Constant movement isn't everyone's best friend."

He laughed a little. "No. It is not. I mean, I have a captain's constitution, so…"

"Yes, Captain." Turk saluted. I looked over at her. She was definitely going to end up with a cat-shaped tan line.

"So, how is that relationship going?" I was curious. I'd never seen Devique really date anyone. He was quiet, usually keeping to himself. I was sometimes afraid he made himself smaller because he was surrounded by us.

"I'm taking it one day at a time. But, honestly, I can't tell you. She's had a lot on her mind since Sicily."

Turk nodded. "Yeah, it was a bit of a fuckfest."

"Do you think she's afraid this job is going to go like that?"

Dev turned to me. "I mean, aren't you?"

He wasn't wrong. The lift in Malta went easily for a number of reasons, the primary one being that no one besides us even knew the box was there. "Oh yeah, I've been trying to figure out how to keep this from going sideways since we got the job."

"Get me to a vault as fast as possible. That's how we make it work."

Turk wasn't wrong. Her ability to manage the vault was the only really reliable part of this job. "That's the plan. Get you down there as fast as possible."

Milan stepped up the side stairs, a nature magazine in his hands. "Did you all know everything is turning into a crab?"

I looked around, wondering what he could be talking about.

"If we're doing that up here, it's happening very slowly," Turk said ambiently up into the air.

"I mean from an evolutionary perspective. Lancelot Alexander Borradaile figured it out in 1916. The form of a crab is so fit, from an evolutionary perspective, that different branches keep evolving into crabs,. Everything's going crab."

Dev was only half listening, it seemed. "Hmm."

"It's called 'carcinisation'. I'm reading about it now."

I heard the impatience in Milan's voice. I asked, "so we better hurry this up or we'll all be crabs?"

He tossed the magazine onto the table. "Exactly."

Turk turned on her side and looked across the deck at me. "Doesn't walking sideways seem super passive-aggressive?"

"Oh, it is." I made some room for Milan to sit down next to me.

"Like, I'm really going over here, but don't look."

Milan reached behind him and pulled out a Luger -- one of the guns we had managed to palm from passing authority. With a quick motion he pulled it apart on the table. "I mean, I suppose we're crabs right now, driving our shell all over, carrying our home with us."

Dev nodded, "That's right."

Dad reached into the pile of gun parts and pulled out the firing pin, tossing it over the side. He cobbled the rest of the pieces back together and affixed a dirty piece of red tape to the barrel haphazardly. "It's not bad, really. It's kind of nice being just a meter or two away from everything we need, but it's not the real world." He lifted the weapon and loaded it, sliding it into the storage box on the skiff hanging next to us.

The skiff was flat and shallow, essentially a small barge with nothing but an engine in the back. We would need it to get to and from the island.

Dad was doing everything he could, though, to prepare for something going wrong. A gun that only we knew couldn't fire could be a very convenient way to psyche out an opponent in close situations.

The opposite of lifting is planting. And, just like in farming, planting is a great way to plan for the future. Milan was right. This boat and everything on it wasn't the real world. It was better.

It was something that we controlled.

The skies were starting to turn orange behind us. Traveling east, we had created the illusion that we were leaving the sun behind, moving into uncharted darker lands where it couldn't help us anymore. The wind had begun to chill a little, dropping just a few degrees as the sun did. The rush of air that met us as the boat moved forward, slicing the space in front of us, was still warm, but there was a secret in it, a kind of added complexity. It was as if it had more to say now, even as my senses sundowned and could interpret less and less.

I thought about my mom and what she might have felt on that last day, leaving a world she used to love so much. Was it like saying goodbye to a lover who just stopped talking to you? Like stepping away from a relationship once so fulfilling but now filled with secrets and messages that weren't meant for you? Did she blame the world for shutting her out?

Or blame herself.

I looked over at Turk, making the cat dance on her belly while it stared her in the eyes – dark black eyes, intense, connected.

I put my feet up on Milan's lap and dared the world to make us crabs.

***

As we approached Yeronisos in the morning, it became instantly clear why it was uninhabited. We came in from the leeward side, to the south. This was the least choppy, but the water was still brutal. You could see to the bottom and that was deceptive. Despite the clarity, the waves were thick and relentless.

We had to anchor and fill the skiff up with boxes and cases, dropping it into the churning water. Dev and Milan took it into the island as the rest of us assembled boxes for the next round.

Timing the approach of the skiff against the waves was a challenge. But we took turns at the helm and managed it. If we were going to land here after, we each had to know how to do it.

There was almost no beach on Yeronisos. Just a few meters of white sand leading to a limestone cliff face all around it, resolving to a wide flat butte, exposed rock bleaching in the sun with the occasional patch of drying grass. We left the boxes and walked around the cliff face. About 150 meters along, and we saw it. A natural cave in the limestone. It was about five meters up, but the rocks below it made nearly a perfect natural staircase. This was what we were looking for.

Milan looked up. "You know I started stealing so that I wouldn't have to lift boxes."

He wasn't wrong. It was nearly evening by the time we'd gotten the cave fully stocked. I didn't want to spend any more time in it than was necessary, as it dipped to near pitch black after about 40 meters inside. The truth is that we didn't know how far it went. It was possible that a cave like this could be connected all across the butte, boring through the island.

I made my way down the steps in front of it. It resembled pictures I'd seen from the American landing on the moon. The sand, the rock, it was all the same. I moved toward the slight beach where Noemie was staring out into the waves. I slipped my hand into hers.

"You seeing anything bad?"

She sighed. "Just the waves. It's going to be rough getting back to the boat."

'You got to trust the captain."

She smiled. I'm guessing she called him that a lot when they were alone. Her skin was so white, almost clear in the failing light. She really was beautiful. I wondered what her life would be like now if she'd never been dragged into this life.

Would she be sitting around a table with the other people in her coven, safely flipping over cards, talking about the future? She seemed ephemeral – as insubstantial as the wispy black see-through tops she loved so much. But here she was, lifting boxes full of supplies on a hidden island, preparing to do one more job with us – a big one.

Not a thief. But not a civilian anymore.

The air felt rarified, like it hadn't spent any time in other people's lungs and this was a new experience for it. It was strange walking on ground that possibly no one else had walked on, ever.

On sand that no one had ever touched.

I felt Turk's hands wrap around me from behind. "You ready to get, Gilligan?"

"Why am I Gilligan, Ginger?"

"You going to turn down top billing? You know what the paychecks look like on American TV."

"Those are the real criminals."

"That's all I'm saying."

Noemie smiled at us. Turk noticed it first. A little blood ran down from her nose.

"Hey, are you okay?"

She wiped it away. "I'm fine. I might just sleep the whole way there." She ran her hands through her hair.

I thought that was a fantastic idea.

We left for Crete in the morning. The plan was to refuel in Karpathos. Rialtos had promised to check in for us with Karras, but we could call from Karpathos. At that point we'd be a day out, if we followed our model of not travelling at night.

There were so many tiny islands in our path that we could almost follow the birds as they lit from one island to another, like needles drawing threads across the warm sea, knitting the land together into a single route, one followed by Jason, by Odysseus, Benjamin of Tudela, Marco Polo…

And now, us.

Noemie nearly followed through with her plan of sleeping all the way to the port at Pigadia, in Karpathos. Dev had woken her up to meet us at the cafe where we would eat for the last time before heading to Crete. Over a table of charred, grilled octopus and dolmades, saganki and the creamiest fava I've ever had, I stared out at the boat docked right outside the window. As we had pulled in, I saw the ageless green of the bay, so clear and emerald that every boat hull was visible to the bottom.

But now, the water was an unending gray. I realized that, at some time today, I'd lost my color vision. At some point, color disappeared for me forever. I wasn't tired, it wasn't dark. This wasn't a slip.

It was a hit.

I stepped over to the open window and put my hands on the rough wooden windowsill. I closed my eyes and opened them again.

It was the same. The dock seemed so dreary. The light rendered it high-contrast and black and white, like a paint-by-numbers painting before you'd filled it in.

I felt like crying, but I knew that it would be hard to stop. How do you say goodbye to things like this? How do you silently thank color for being there for you your whole life, for filling the world in ways you took for granted since you were a child, as it left.

As it walked away.

The food looked dark and unappetizing. The reds of the tomatoes were black now, the thick carmelized onions on top of the makarounes seemed dirty, soiled. I lost my appetite.

We spent the day in Karpathos, making sure to call Karras. Tomorrow he would have us picked up at port. Then we'd be his guests until the job. He made his offer again for us to stay afterward. We had no reason to distrust Karras. Not one.

Except instinct.

The trip to Crete felt muted, stepped on. I leaned over the port side of the boat and tried to adjust. My balance was so poor that I hugged the rail the entire time.

I realized over the last few days, as well, that sounds seemed to be moving away from me. Even my own voice in my head was thin, far away.

It was easy to make my visual hallucinations into something they weren't. Staring up into the sky, watching dragons and spaceships follow us toward Karras's home, wondering which would overtake us first.

What would kill us first?

I held onto one of Dev's handmade ingots of gold. He was in the habit of tapping different random symbols into each one so that they could never be connected. This one had a chip in one corner and the impression of a rabbit on it. I imagined the cartel responsible for its smelting perhaps choosing the rabbit for its speed and efficiency, a silent symbol that no matter your diligence, the cartel would outpace you – would win in the end. Or maybe it represented the fertility of rabbits, constantly birthing new members, growing, becoming legion, unstoppable –, a way to warn the world that they would soon fill it and overtake everyone, a promise never to stop. Or maybe it was a cartel of cuteness, adorable assassins in bunny slippers sliding up next to their targets in wire-and-fabric ears and painted-on whiskers, stabbing them mercilessly even as they laughed and wondered who that cute bunny was.

That last one was a reach.

This was a good size to tip someone to keep their mouth shut. Or to open a door that should be locked. Or to get into a card game that had reached its hypothetical limit. I weighed it in my hand. It was nearly the same size and weight as the pager in my pocket, but infinitely more useful to me.

We pulled into the Venetian port around noon, the sun riding high on the sky, the massive Koules fortress acting like some strange vigilant guard across the harbor base. We debarked carrying nothing but a bag each, a black cat, and the clothes on our back, with pockets full of tiny nondescript gold ingots bearing different inscriptions and markings. Except for Dev, who now carried all our papers in a faded brown satchel. On a small yacht like this it was customary for the captain to be the one to clear the ship's guests with local customs, paperwork processed quickly when weighed down with a small but appropriate gold ingot.

We walked inland to the road through the smell of seafood and coffee, freshly baked bread, and olive tapenade framing the cafes lined up around the tiny parking lot. Past one or two cars, we saw the drab green Mercedes L409 van in the center of the lot, with a familiar face in front of it.

Turk called out "Mikiel!"

Rialtos was leaning against the van, a broad smile on his face, greeting us. "The tour continues."

I laughed a little despite myself, shaking his eagerly outstretched hand. "He sent just you?"

"I volunteered. I have good news. And I hope you are hungry."

Milan looked over at me. "I could use some good news."

Turk gave him a hug. "And I am hungry."

Rialtos pet Shark, seemingly excited to see us all. "I think I need you guys to breathe a little life into this island."

Dev and Noemie started putting bags in the back of the van, grabbing one from each of us and stacking them neatly.

"I'm with him," I said, motioning to dad. "I need good news."

Rialtos raised his hand. "Coming up."

He reached into the van and pulled out a piece of paper. It looked to be a page, carefully cut from a book with a razor blade. It has writing on one side, but, on the other, a set of three drawings. They looked consecutive, much like a cartoon, each enclosed with a box. I looked closely. It was high contrast enough that I could make it out in black and white easily.

"I stole this from one of Karras's books about the box -- the one he is looking for."

Turk looked at him faux-judgmentally. "Wait, are you a thief?"

He smiled and cocked his head, pointing to the first frame. "You see? Here, people are dead, lying there. Box is closed. Now here, in the second frame, we zoom in – see the box opened. Here, third frame, the box is closed back up. But people are alive."

I followed his finger.

He seemed so excited. "See. What I said. Life. It brought them back. It's harmless."

I remembered for a minute when Noemie was fingering the inscriptions on the box we had stolen already. The name on the box.

Yehoshua.

And I remembered the direction her finger went as she traced it. My heart sank. I turned to see her run her hand through her hair.

"Except Aramaic is written right to left. They started out alive. And then they died."

12. The City with Heavy Eyes

Jour d'une vie ou l'aube se lève
Pour réveiller la ville aux yeux lourds

Day in a life where dawn breaks
To awaken the city with heavy eyes

Karras's villa was 15 minutes away and air conditioned, an affectation you would probably not find anywhere else on that island. It was surrounded by palm fronds and cypress trees, wrapped around a wrought iron fence resolving into a simple gate in front. Inside, it felt like a micro-city, with various buildings, stables, storage facilities, even guest homes. Rialtos took us through what could have been a small town square into an open garden with a wide gazebo in the center.

This is where Anton Karras sat with Agnes and Nikola, eating supper. We stood at the border of the space and waited for a moment, until Karras, face full of food, waved us in. He wiped his mouth with a linen napkin and stood up.

"Please, everyone, come in. There is a lot of food here."

We stepped into the gazebo and officially began planning.

And I want to tell you about the planning process, I do. I want to tell you how Karras stood as some sort of stone gatekeeper as we walked through the miscellany of the job, the torturously insignificant moments, the tiny steps that make something like this work seamlessly when you're standing in the middle of it.

I want to tell you how Nikola tried to take control but eventually got comfortable, even there on that first day, listening more than he spoke, aware of how out of his depth he was in a room full of thieves, and how he eventually sank into the background, nodding and taking the occasional note. We watched him try on the strong silent persona and decide that, yes, it fit.

I want to tell you how excited Agnes was to be sitting across from Turk and how her voice lifted in a girlish laugh every time Turk opened her mouth. How, despite all that, she was smart and aware and concerned about doing her part excellently, a part that mostly included sliding into areas that none of us could hope to fit.

We all had our roles to play.

I want to tell you how glad Ray was that we were there, and how he really shined in groups, loving the back and forth, the interplay. He was, and I mean this with all the love in my heart, a classic conman. He enjoyed people and their idiosyncrasies so much. He loved being the guy you wanted to spend time with and reveled in perpetuating that illusion so much that you could imagine his marks – victims who had lost money, gold, possessions to his schemes still missed his company afterward and maybe, just maybe, were willing to write it off as a fair exchange.

He blossomed in the company of people and reveled in each miniature mask he could pull on, being for people, at that moment, what they needed most. Karras trusted him because you couldn't help but trust him. Even Nikola liked him, as he took time to include the larger Greek man into conversations in a way that made him feel respected and even smart.

Rialtos was good.

I seriously want to tell you all of it, but the planning part of all of this bores even me. We'd be living through it soon enough and either the plan would work or it wouldn't. And in that latter case, we'd create a new one, on the fly, with all the urgency you can imagine embedded in it, and some nonzero chance of success. Plan notwithstanding, the goal was to get Turk near that vault – a vault that held unimaginable wealth and something else. Something Karras wanted.

The plan itself was inconsequential.

Plans live and die all the time. It's silly to celebrate or mourn them. It's results that matter.

There is a part of me that is more interested in what happened after dinner. How, as the sun slid down, we were shown to our rooms, in multi-room houses on the grounds of the villa. Turk and I had a beautiful room with a near floor-level balcony facing an elegant moonlit spring.

And on the other side of the house, in a room symmetrical and similar, sharing a single wall, was Milan. And that night, after Turk and I had drifted off to sleep, I woke up, blinded by the dark, and heard a sound from next to us.

From him.

Karras, in his drive to demonstrate that he knew us, had placed a guitar in Milan's room, an old amber wooden classical Kanda Shokai, hanging like so much art from the adjoining wall. I got up and leaned against the plaster, pressing my ear to it as he played the very first song he ever played on any new guitar.

'Romance Anonimo' was the song that he and my mother had chosen for their first dance at their wedding. And it had been transferred to the forever memory of every guitar in France that had been within playing distance of my father since then. I listened to his fingers dance across the strings and imagined the two of them dressed in their tiny iconic wedding clothes, two fingers of one hand, making that decision to stay, affixed, next to each other forever.

It was sad, but I realized that it was too human to be despairing. It was too Milan. This was a man who knew how to keep the good in anything alive, as though those were gardener's hands, planting, nurturing, making sure that this instrument knew how to woo the next woman it encountered without fear, without hesitation. He planted this song into a living thing, one that would be a tool of passion for someone in the future. What was probably a cold, functional purchase for Anton Karras was now primed to make rooms weep.

I turned away from the wall and listened as he played on, filling the air in the Greek villa with stories that were uniquely French, sweeping away the mythological passions of gods and nymphs and replacing them with the viscerally human fixations of people in every kind of love there was, learning to embrace it all.

The visual hallucinations had come more alive as my color vision had deteriorated, inventing new ways to replace the information that had been lost. As I pointed myself toward the balcony, I saw what I thought was a hummingbird made of pure white-gold light. Against my own better judgement, I reached out and waved to it as it flit around my wrist. I couldn't feel anything, but my brain insisted it was there.

Insisted it was real.

I took a step and followed it as it moved forward, toward the balcony. I could still see the occasional light across the miniature city of the Karras's estate, but now it seemed concentrated around the spring in front of me. The spring itself seemed to be glowing, and it was bright enough that, from a few meters away, I could see waves of steam rising from it, framed by the light emanating in all directions. The little light-bird seemed drawn to it, even as it pulled me that way.

Turk was still asleep, wrapped in a white duvet. I thought about waking her but I didn't. And I knew why.

Milan hadn't yet dispelled every Grecian story from the building, sending them scurrying like rats. Some still remained. These Greek morality plays that punished mankind for essential sins of character. And hubris was the leading one.

Pride.

The kind of pride that makes someone like me cling to my independence. The kind that makes me slide down a wrought iron railing a few meters to the ground in an oversized sleep shirt to check out something odd, even when I could barely see, could barely hear. The kind that sent me slinking after some imagined creature, made of light, toward a glowing pool. Independence was the affront to Zeus that night, right? My naked feet padding toward an illuminated hot spring, alone. Following that tiny bright shock of light like a star.

I stepped next to the spring. I could feel the warmth coming from it. I stared into the light that seemed to be focused upward from deep down in the water like a spotlight buried below the surface. If I hadn't, I might have missed it. In front of the spring, an ink seemed to form in the air, curling, flowing, as though the air were liquid. A drop of black that turned into a black doorway, into a shape.

I watched as it became a man. As it resolved and hardened, looking like Ruach.

This time, as I looked into Ruach's face, I could see the deformation. He seemed to have ridges under his eyes, places where the skin was carved in precise tiny lettering, much like the box we had taken. What I had originally seen as a sort of series of waves across his face were more complex than that.

As I tried to focus my eyes, I looked down at his hands and then back to his face.

"No gun?"

He spoke softly but firmly. "I saw what you did."

I took a step back, trying to assess what was around me. "What did I do?"

He moved forward, keeping the space between us consistent. "The modified tether spell, the secrets spell. Shush. The other box."

I moved around him, trying to stay close to the spring, the only source of light. "I did what I had to so you'd stop killing people."

Ruach breathed out, indignantly. "You really think you're the good guys, don't you? Gentlemen thieves. You hurt no one. Right?"

We both stood with our sides to the spring now, my back to the villa. If Turk looked out right now, she'd see him. "Do you want my commentary?"

He continued. "Except when you deliver a weapon that could destroy the world to a madman lusting after power."

"Is that what Karras is?"

He nodded and his voice dropped to a growl. "Yes."

I whispered back. "And what are you?"

His lips raised in a sneer. "I thought we were clear. I'm the stick. Maybe I need to remind you."

I had no idea how to calm him. I wondered if Rialtos could. "Do you need to kill more people? Do you see Karras killing people?"

A condescending smile warped his face. "He can afford the appearance of gentlemanly good conduct. In a few weeks, he'll have it. What he needs."

I tried not to sound as confused as I was. "What's it? What does he need?"

Ruach raised his arms at his side, as though all of this were obvious. "The Bi'uwsh Olam. The eternal evil." He pointed accusingly. "And you're just going to hand it to him."

I shook my head. Was he reasoning with me? "What is that? And why you better than him?"

His voice dropped. "Because he wants to use it. I want to destroy it."

That hit me like a brick. I tried to back up. "Wait. What?"

"I will wipe it from the face of the earth."

I thought for a second. Was this a con? "We can destroy the box. If it's that evil."

He shook his head. "You would just break the box and let it loose." He pointed to his chest. "I can destroy what's in it."

I realized I hadn't considered why Ruach had wanted the box. His behavior told me he was a monster. Did he want to get rid of what was in the box? "How?"

"Do you really still doubt that I'm powerful?"

I took a breath and tried to walk through our experiences with Ruach. Did this make sense? "Why didn't you tell us before?"

He turned toward the spring. "Before you went down this road, would you have believed any of this?"

I thought about the Talaricos. Selene. Lis. "You killed people."

He turned his face to me, angry. "And I would kill a thousand more to destroy it. You think you're the good guy. Until the Bi'uwsh Olam is free. Then it's millions. Millions who will die."

I stared into the spring. The lithe little light ray hummingbirds dipped into it, dissolving, fading into its depth.

"Let's say I believe you."

His sneer returned. It seemed to hurt him even to have to talk to me. I tried to figure out what it was.

It was superiority.

I was an ant, and here he was trying to get me to agree with him that the ant farm needed saving. He turned to me, his face warped and ugly.

"I have one more on your team. I don't care what you believe. One of you will get it for me. The box. The real one. The one who gets it, maybe I cure them. Ah, I finally got your attention."

He turned and grabbed my arm. "Maybe I am the carrot."

With that, the ink seemed to curl around him and suck him in. It pulled at the light, pushing me backwards into the spring. My equilibrium shifted and changed so much that I couldn't even tell you when I fell.

It was dark now, impossibly dark. My vision died as I slipped under the surface of the water. My arms flailed, my balance betrayed me. There was no way to tell what was up or down. My mouth filled with warm water, drilling into my sinuses. I tried to dispel it but there was no air to replace it.

There was nothing but dark.

I felt it pull at me from all directions, the warmth of it. It was so close to my own body temperature that I couldn't tell what was water and what was my own body, my own skin.

And for a moment, it all felt familiar. It wasn't a familiar feeling pulling from the past. This had nothing to do with my experiences and what I'd done or been through. This was a metaphysical familiarity.

A certainty.

This is how I would die.

It wouldn't be today, I decided, as I dug my nails into the bank beside the spring, pulling myself from the heat of the water into the bracing cool of the night air. It wouldn't be now, but it would be real.

This is how I would die.

My arms towed me upward and laid me onto the grass almost automatically, where I sat for about 15 minutes. I tried to parse what I had learned.

I had to count the steps back to the villa.

But this is how I would die.

***

We spent a couple of weeks planning.

Rialtos left first, and I understood why. He had always been the advance man, since he had started working, as a kid. He insinuated himself and the people around him just forgot there was a time he wasn't around. He was exceptional at what he did.

Milan, Devique, Turk and myself left after that, on the boat. Anton had insisted that Noemie travel with him and Nikola and Agnes, by plane to the Marka – the civil airport in Amman, Jordan. Noemie would use her glamours to help them cross the border to Ein al Sultan without a record of who they were. And then, after the job, Karras would meet us at a hotel in Kdumim where we would determine which route was best and make it back to port.

We'd all leave together on the boat.

If it sounds simple, it wasn't. There was a lot in between. But the objective was something we all understood. Get Turk safely to the lower vault as fast as possible while the whole country was focused elsewhere.

And afterward, depending on how the job went, we had the option of landing on Yeronisos and regrouping. We could be there, from the port at Israel, in a day.

We figured that, if we made good time getting to the port, we could stop at the hotel in Kdumim and plot it out.

No sense in being surprised.

Except that once we made port in Israel and pulled off the Ma'ale Shne'ur Street in a rented black van, we found out that the hotel was actually a library.

Dev kept the van running and turned to me in the front seat. "That's probably a red flag."

We still had time to meet everyone at the job site. So we piled out of the van and stood in the parking lot.

Turk took in the little library, probably unchanged in the last 40 years. "You know the beds here will be shit."

I nodded. I had talked to them about what had happened with Ruach, as soon as I convinced myself I hadn't imagined it all. I know all of that was running through people's minds as well.

Milan thought. "Well. Karras may not expect us to meet afterward. He's going to fuck us over first. Before Ruach does."

Dev broke in, "Or he's an idiot and screwed up the address."

I could tell that Milan thought either one of those would be important pieces of information.

I thought out loud, "and Ruach has another plant on the team..."

My dad interjected, "He says..."

"Right. He says. And it's someone who needs a cure, too."

Turk looked at Dev. "Noemie seems like she might be sick. But I'm sorry for thinking that, Dev."

He sighed. "It's okay. I'm thinking it, too. She does seem...unwell... but I just don't see it, you know?"

I shook my head. "I don't either. I don't see her betraying us."

Milan looked right at me. "Maybe she knows something. Look, you didn't want to ask her. But here's a library." He pointed.

We had about two hours so we walked into the library. It was small and dirty and not promising. But given where it was, we actually might get lucky. We stepped over to the counter and looked for the librarian. The lights were bright, but clinical. The entire room was a stark black and white to me, as though drawn in ink and waiting for color.

But I didn't have that time.

A woman who might have been in her 80s appeared behind the counter.

I took a shot. "Do you have anyone here who might know ancient Aramaic? Or a dictionary or something?"

She looked at us as though we'd just asked for a translator who spoke a long-dead ancient language. So, yes, appropriately. She turned and stepped away.

Turk put her hand in mine. She quickly signed to me that it was probably her native language.

I laughed, turning into her. She was getting good at redirecting her insulting commentary into tactile sign language. It had already prevented a number of awkward encounters.

A minute later, a Muslim girl of about twenty came around the counter smiling. "Hi. You need something translated from Aramaic?"

Milan looked at me. She definitely appeared young. For a moment, I panicked, thinking about how Ruach could shoot this place up. Then I remembered the Shush spell and how it had kept that from happening since Noemie had learned it.

"We do. It's just a term I heard. I don't know how to spell it."

"Do you want to come over to my office?"

We followed her over to a long wooden table piledl with books and random pages from periodicals, some scanned or faxed. I sat down across from her.

"Like I said, I don't know how to spell it."

"Well, that wouldn't matter. The language is long dead. Some words made it to Hebrew, some didn't." Her French was fluid, with a passable accent. She was small, with a delicate face under a light-colored shayla that wrapped around her neck intentionally. I wanted to ask Turk what color it was, but it seemed unimportant.

I tried to remember. "'Bi'uwsh Olam.' I don't know if I'm pronouncing it correctly.'"

She nodded and pieced through one of the books in front of her. "'Olam' is easy. It's similar in Hebrew. It means 'world," or "everything.' It can also mean 'forever' or 'enduring.' Eternal."

My heart sank. This was going pretty much where I suspected it would.

She found a page in the book. "And 'Bi'uwsh' comes from a familiar root. 'Bish' or 'Bishta,' all of it. It describes a kind of badness or evil. It's a superlative evil. The big bad evil."

Turk looked at me. "Okay, so everlasting evil. We get it."

We were still about a half an hour away from Ain es-Sultan and the opening to the Jericho vault. We sat in the van in the parking lot. I sighed.

"Does it even make sense to do confessions?"

"Oh, I will." Turk raised her hand. "That girl was kind of hot. A baby, but hot. And I miss my cat on the boat." She put her hand back down. "That's what I've got."

She looked at Dev. He thought for a second. "I don't like Middle Eastern food, so let's get out of here as fast as possible."

I turned my head to Milan. He had a little gold bar in his hand he was rolling around, flipping it over again and again. "Yes, hummus is shit. Garbage."

I considered that. I didn't disagree. But it wasn't where my head was at. "I think I die by drowning."

Milan laughed darkly. "So maybe not today."

I looked out at the wide sweeping miles of sand holding up the city around it.

"Maybe not today."

We pulled up next to the Tell and, unsurprisingly, it was Rialtos moving toward us in a worker's uniform. He was holding some papers and dragging with him a man slightly older than him, one who looked official. We stepped out of the van and he moved toward Milan, shaking his hand earnestly.

"We are so happy you're here. Professor Marakeh, this is Zev, he's the one that found the first water damage. Zev, this is Professor Dohran Marakeh, from the Architects Council. He brought some students to help."

The other man looked confused, shaking our hands half heartedly. "I'm glad you could make it. This is the worst day for this. Everyone is...you know…"

Milan patted him on the shoulder as he shook his hand. "Yes, it's all over near the airport. But good for you that you caught it."

Zev seemed comforted that it could possibly be fixed.

Whatever it was.

Milan looked around. "You have people?"

Ray tried to appear frustrated. "I could only get two more people from the city to help. They're on their way. Zev needs to stand guard."

Zev looked sheepish. "I mean, I could help…"

Ray put his hand on Zev's back. "I don't want you getting in trouble. Honestly, it's only because of you we can fix this thing. We'll be fine." He turned to my dad. "How's the Council?"

He shook his head. "They're worried. I told them not to be."

Ray tried to act relieved. "Good. Let's not get anyone too freaked out. We can solve this thing today. No problem all around."

Zev seemed to like the sound of that.

We all fell into the role-play easily. We were architecture students. We tried to demonstrate how student-like we wore the backpacks we each had wrapped around our chests. We deferred to Milan and listened as he nonsensically described the structure with hand motions as he read from blank pieces of paper out of earshot of Zev.

The Tell itself was unimpressive. This wasn't much of a tower. But the land we stood on was already some 250 meters below sea level. If there was any water pouring in from anywhere, there was a lot it could damage and a long time before it might stop. The Tell was a buried city buried over another city, flattened and buried over another, many times over. It descended another 250 meters from where we stood, and potentially more.

Nikola and Aggie arrived on a city utility vehicle they had likely stolen on the way. They spoke to Ray and pretended to be uninterested in us after quick introductions. But as he shook Dad's hand, Nikola passed him a note. They stepped up to speak to Zev one final time before the descent as Milan slipped me the note.

It was quickly written but legible, on some kind of white cardstock. I recognized it as part of the cover from a book. Could this have been a religious book? Regardless, the writing, in pen was clear.

"Sorry. Got location wrong. Address in Kdumim is a library, not a hotel. But plans remain. —- AK"

I passed it back to Dev and Turk. "He's sorry."

We stood near the topmost entrance. Ray was showing Zev how to use the walkie talkie.

"Now, if there is sewage or drainage involvement, expect a panicked call from us very soon. If it's just water infrastructure from the spring, it's easy and we'll just fix it. Does that make sense?"

Zev was nodding. "Yes, for sure. I'm keeping my fingers crossed."

Ray laughed. "Me, too. My toes are crossed."

Nik and Aggie began to drill the small hole that we would use to descend. It seemed insane to be doing this in broad daylight. I could see Dev looking around.

Still no sign of Noemie.

The hole was only about 20 centimeters in diameter when they stopped. They pushed down on the limestone, cutting lengthwise for a few minutes under the watchful eye of Zev. It expanded to about half a meter and then three quarters, possibly a bit more.

Wide enough to slide in.

Aggie was the first one in, but we all followed quickly afterward. The surface was a kind of compressed limestone and dirt and it was thick. I didn't realize that this topmost layer was nearly a meter and a half thick until I was halfway through the hole, my body panicking at the sense of being buried alive.

Finally I dropped through to the other side. If our maps were accurate, the drop was a good five meters to the ground below. I could barely see anything, so this drop was more an act of faith than anything for me.

The floor of the main level, the Minasa, felt like clay under my feet. It had a little give. Nikola reached into his bag and pulled out a globe shaped-lamp, setting it in the middle of the room and lighting it. I gave my weakening eyes a second to adjust and I could see.

The edges of my vision only extended to the bare edges of the light. I couldn't see the walls of the room. Aggie stepped over by the light and pulled off a ring she wore around her arm. She set the ring on the ground and stepped away from it.

Her mouth moved slightly, and suddenly Noemie appeared, her foot stepping on the metal ring. She wore black leggings and boots with a flowy black top. And as glad as I was to see her, I could tell Dev was even happier.

She reached down and picked up the ring, moving quickly over to Dev to hug him. She slipped the ring into his hand and he pocketed it.

She had somehow tethered herself to the ring. It hadn't occurred to me that a tether could be used on a living thing.

Much less a person. Dev put his hand in his pocket. He could call her with this.

Ray looked around and lifted the walkie-talkie. "Zev. Good news. It looks like the runoff is clean. Yes. Clean water. Huge relief. We're going to take 20 minutes to find the source, 20 to fix, and a few to make it back. But we're in a good place. Yes. Right. I know, me, too." He checked twice to make sure it was off.

Dev had brought the larger case -- the one that was meant to be full of tools for the vault. We had stored the magic box in it, wrapped up so no one would see. And the truth is, Turk never needed a lot of tools. The Minasa was relatively modern, with rebar visible in places, jutting out from the floor. It seemed to be built almost as a staging area for people as they descended into the lower levels, which seemed appropriate.

It was clean and clear of any debris. I realized we would have to clean up the artifacts from the hole we'd drilled above, but it seemed possible if it went well. As we stepped over to one side, though, I could see there was a massive staircase. It reminded me of the staircase from the Biblioteca in Sicily, thick and blockish, but twisting and downwardfacing. Dev and Nikola brought up the rear, carrying the case, with Turk and me out front. Despite the globe lamp that Ray carried, the thick black of the level below us made seeing anything on the stairs impossible. Aggie was right behind Turk, constantly feeling the walls and partitions around us to check for something. Secret passages, doorways? Who knew?

Ray's voice carried across the depth of the stairway as he whispered, "okay, everyone, from here on, we're on borrowed time."

The texture of the walls felt different here. The clay had given way to a thicker limestone, etched with elaborate images. I ran my fingers over the arches dug into the walls, pointed on top. These felt like remnants of the Ottoman Empire, one of the civilizations represented here in this tell.

I stepped around an obelisk as soon as the stairs reached the ground, and tried to make sense of this level. It was time to pull out the map in my pocket. Turk had worked to press metal pieces into it, creating ridges and shapes in it, indents I could read with my hands. The room became more visible once Ray stepped into it with the lantern. The space was modular, squared-off, with wide open areas partitioned like an elaborate maze.

This area was only about 500 years old, but it felt ancient. It felt as though it had seen generations of people lose their way, looking for the stairs that led further down. And this was only the second level. It was a fairly modern construction, compared to the rest.

I felt my way around the maze, keeping my left hand always on a wall. This would be the most effective way of making it through a man-made maze, but not always the fastest. I was aware that we didn't have as much time as we wished we did and there were still a lot of levels to go..

I inhaled and smelled something that didn't belong. Behind me was the musty static unmoving air of the tell, but in front was something different. I breathed in again.

Noemie stepped up next to me and put her hand on my arm. She lifted her other arm and I could hear her this time, under her breath, whispering a single word.

"Bright."

And the small ball of light she controlled lit up and flowed, rising and creating a plane that cut across our chests. Below it, a swampy marsh of darkness, but above it, like frosting on a long flat wedding cake, rose a bright light that filled the room. It went on and on, across a space that suddenly felt larger than the tell had looked from the outside.

The maze was massive and it went out in front of us, becoming tangled in ivy and flowering plants, things that had no business growing here, across these walls in the dark.

I couldn't see the other end.

13. Night changes to day

Pour que la vie s'habille de fête
Et que la nuit se change en jour

So that life gets dressed in feast
And so that night changes to day

She was named after Noel Coward by upright and uptight parents, but it was posters of Anna Karina, Jean Seberg, Barbara Steele, and the already=iconic Juliette Gréco that papered the walls of her tiny Staten Island room in 1960, when she was 13 years old.

She had remembered hearing once that the parts of you that you love the most endure. That made her think of the drawer, positioned just out of view in her closet, one that she had organized and ordered, boy's clothes up top, with her two drawers of girls' clothing below. Black skirts and dresses, deep red tops and hunter green velvet shorts, to be worn around her room when she was alone.

The cut, the fit, the way they lasted, even the colors of boys' and girls' clothing was different. The clothes her parents bought for her were in whites and creams, grey and standard greens, even this yellow shirt, with wide black stripes. The clothes she bought for herself were clingier, softer, more tactile, in colors that had longer names, like deep crimson red and royal rich violet. They hugged to curves she didn't have yet, creating an illusion that she did.

While the top two drawers were the kind of a mess you might expect to see in the closet of a 13-year-old boy, the bottom two were kept perfectly.

And when Noel left home that year, with only a bag big enough for two drawers worth of clothing, it wasn't even a decision.

There was really no language for what she was going through, no words that could be spread around, to come out of other mouths and make her feel less lonely. There was ust the sureness, the inevitability, the precision in her mind that she was a girl. She applied that same precision, same direct truthfulness, when she told the cab driver her name, shifting the accent to the second syllable.

She was Noël, now.

And as she stood in the bathroom of the Metro 7 Diner, putting on eyeshadow for the first time, she practiced what she would say to the women at the Gaia Center, the witches who claimed, in their tiny ad in the back of Caravan, the music magazine she'd found at Izzy Young's Folklore Center on MacDougal Street, that all women were accepted.

Issue 19.

All women.

The women there were different than anyone she'd ever met. They asked who she was and they listened. Her parents, her teachers, the doctors only asked what was wrong with her. These women, these witches, told her that what she was had a place in history. That it was a part of how the universe worked and that the feminine ideal, once invoked, would win, would rise up and conquer.

They made Noël laugh while they dressed her to accent that ideal. And when they tracked down the hormones that let her feel more like herself every day, they brought them to her room, laid out carefully on a stark white cloth, under glossy black images carved in marble, Baphomet, an unnamed goddess of the moon, and more...

Her sisters held her hand after the top surgery, done in a secret doctor's office in Alphabet City, in a room she had to creep out of before morning, held up with their hands on her back.

But what she saw later, in those tarnished ancient mirrors, it was magic of the highest order. The most mystically perfect thing she'd ever seen.

For her, they would cover up the drawing that hung outside her room, shaped like a uterus, like an iconic representation of womanhood, but a chalice, a face, a bestial icon that connected it to the demonic, to the repudiation of authority, to that rejection of maleness.

Until one night, Noël pulled the cover off. She knew who she was. There was no shame in rewriting the world to be something more true.

And her sisters agreed.

She learned the basics of scrying, how to read Tarot, how to read fortunes, how to pay her own way. It was easy. By the time she turned 20, she was Mistress Noemie, behind a lavish table full of iconography and cards, notebooks and sigils, reassuring lost men that they mattered and sad women that there was a place for them somewhere.

And once they believed it, it was true. Once they had proof, they tried.

And yes, it was easy, but not what she was there for.

A week after her 21st birthday, she healed a bird that had slammed into the window of her room. She pushed open the glass and reached down, grabbing the tiny body from the sill and pulling it inside. The window was still open, waves of cool air pouring into the room as she felt for any spark of life in the black and blue feathered thing. Finally, she found it, fanning it until it grew.

Eventually the bird stood up and pulled itself into the air, frantically circling the room until it identified the open window.

It flew so high. And she watched it.

They told her she could hold four more spells. They all kept five spells prepared, ready to use, spells pulled from the arcane books all over the center, spells that helped them move through the world as something different, solving different problems, seeing different things. She grew to be someone older, respected at the center, but still, really, just a young girl inside. A teenager.

She was tethered to the place by her need for medication as much as by fear.

And she'd never traveled.

So when Anton Karras offered the Gaia Center a substantial amount of money for the services of a skilled witch, she volunteered, without even knowing what the job was.

And this time, when she packed her suitcase, she didn't even need to look at what drawer the clothes came from.

Her room at Karras's estate in Marseille was down the hall from a charming Latin man named Rialtos. He had seemingly just arrived as well. He liked to joke and tell stories and she was fascinated by how dapper and clean he was.

For someone like Noël, Rialtos was an unachievable ideal. Everyone seemed to trust him. Everyone seemed to like him. And just as she had applied her natural talents to witchcraft, he had applied his natural talents to confidence work. Rialtos had a way about him. He made you feel like he told you a secret and he trusted you to keep it. He made you feel like he really did want to see you again.

And when she did see him again, in Sicily, it was like they still lived down the hall from each other and nothing had changed.

He was that good.

***

Aggie put her hands on her hips. "There is no reason why a maze has be solvable."

Milan nodded. "The labyrinth around Topkapi palace wasn't a solvable maze. Just a series of accessible courtyards."

I stared into the winding passage in front of me. "Topkapi was more a test of legitimacy than anything else. If you knew, you knew. That's not applicable here, right?"

Nikola leaned forward and tried to punch the wall in frustration. The lights he brought that seemed to work right above us were failing down here. "That makes no sense. Why have a maze at all if you can't get through it?"

Dev whispered thoughtfully, "I think that's the question."

I motioned to Turk who was a few meters ahead of me in the maze, her left hand on the wall. I had stepped back with everyone else. "Here, come back for a second."

As she stepped out of the maze, I felt it. My watch started up again. I had felt it stop as I moved into the maze and couldn't figure out what was happening.

I looked at Dad. "If anyone is in the maze, time stops."

He squinted at Noemi and held his watch up to his face. "Okay, Turkana, move forward again."

"I like this puppet game."

As she did, I felt my watch grow still on my wrist.

Nikola called out. "Sonofabitch."

"That's good. It's going to save us time. We can spend what we need to on this." Rialtos stepped into the maze, too. He pointed at me. "The lovely René tried it three times and came back here each time. If we weren't penalized for that, timewise, we can do this"

Noemie took a breath. "That means being in the maze is activating some kind of magic. I just don't know what."

I realized I was moving my head too much looking around. It had to be clear to the others that I had no peripheral vision. Luckily, Nikola may have been a bit dense and Aggie and Ray a bit preoccupied. I pointed to an eight-sided symbol with text behind Dev. "Eight religious orders. Mevlevi, Bektashi, Naqchbandi, Halveti, Quadiri..."

Milan broke in. "All Sunni orders." I would not have known that.

Noemie added, "not just Sunni. Sufi. All eight."

I nodded. "Eight orders, eight of us. Who thinks that is a coincidence?"

No one took that bet.

Turk was feeling the walls of the maze. "Okay, if this whole thing is made for us, custom – what does that mean?"

Nikola spoke up. "Who cares what it means, it's a maze. On the other side is a hole or a staircase or something?"

Dev seemed unsure about that. "Noemie, what would a maze made by Sufis be trying to do?"

She looked up for a minute. "That's a good question. A maze made by Sufis would not be a test. Not something to solve. It would be something to endure."

I moved closer to Turk. "So that's why time stops. Endurance. Patience. Surrender."

Milan nodded, moving closer. "A willingness to submit to ignorance. Admit that we don't know."

Ray laughed. "I am willing to admit that all day. I do not know any of this."

Dev picked up the case. "So, what do we do to admit that we don't know?"

I thought for a second. We were admitting it out loud. That seemed not good enough. I could see that keeping the artificial light up was draining Noemie. She was beginning to tire.

"Enlightenment." I looked around.

Dev got it. "We admit we're not enlightened. We turn off the light."

"And we die." Nikola said matter of factly.

I stepped over to where he was standing. In Noemie's artificial light I could see a panel on the floor of the maze, right next to where he was standing, had fallen off. And below it was a drop that seemed to open into a deep chasm, lit partially, descending nearly to infinity.

Aggie stepped away from it. "Holy shit."

Ray moved out of the maze. "Okay, so without the light, we step into holes like that and we drop."

Dev shook his head. "But where? Where are we dropping? That's not below us. It's not real."

Nikola kicked a rock into it and it fell. "It seems pretty fucking real."

I considered that. "I don't think it wants to kill us. We don't learn anything that way."

"You think it just wants us to learn?" Aggie seemed more lost than usual. Ordinarily, she was a lot bigger than this.

Devique nodded. "Real enlightenment."

Noemie looked over at him and her light effect disappeared. Almost as quickly as it had arrived, it was gone. As it did, the room fell into pitch blackness. The black swirled around me like a physical thing. I realized that my hearing was sundowning as well in this area. I stopped trying to make sense of the sounds around me. I thought about ignorance for a minute. The connection between these higher order properties, espoused by Sufism, seemed to point in one direction.

And I didn't love it.

Ignorance. Faith. Bravery, To Endure.

I shut everything out and started running as fast as I could. I didn't put my hands in front of me. I didn't prepare for impacts or falling, dropping, or really anything. I just ran. I heard Turk yell out behind me.

But I didn't stop. I ran past where the first wall would be, past where the hole in the floor would be, past the far curve I had experienced with my left hand. And I kept going.

I had been running for nearly two minutes when I was slowed by a wall of rushing air. It felt like wind, but it slowed as I did. Finally, I broke through and stood next to a wall. I reached out and could feel an opening in it, a doorway.

I turned to call out just as Turk closed in next to me, breathing hard. She kissed me. "Okay. Fuck. Tell me we're not doing that again."

I hugged her. I wished I could. "Is everyone else coming?"

She placed her hand at the root of my back. "Big Nik seemed opposed to falling through a giant hole in the floor."

"He can't tell that I made it through?"

"I think that wall of air stops sounds. I can't hear them right now, either."

Dev was the next one through. His arms reached out and wrapped around us. "Hey, not dead people. I'm really glad to be not dead, too."

I sympathized with that. It seemed like every one of us would have to make the same decision, on our own.

Milan and Noemie came through at nearly the same time. I tried to figure out where they were standing, just by their voices. Noemie was standing next to Dev. "We tried to talk them into it."

My dad broke in, "that's where we've been for the last 10 minutes."

I felt my watch pulsing on the back of my wrist. "We haven't been here even 10 minutes. Time is running normally here. "

Noemie responded, "but not over there."

Time was still slowed over by the opening to the Maze, even if the maze itself wasn't real. I thought about that as I heard Rialto's voice. "Guys? Are you here?"

Dev called out, "Ray, we're right here. Where's the rest?"

"We've been talking this through. I told them I'd try to die loudly if I did. I'm not sure how long it's gonna take them."

I asked, "how long did it take you?"

I heard Ray's voice as he connected with all of us, holding on. "I went about a half-hour after Milan."

That made sense. This time displacement made it even more clear. This was about endurance. It wasn't a simple test to see who could figure it out. Each of us had to endure.

Or leave. Or starve. That made sense. I felt Turk's hand on my back, describing what she was seeing. Her vision had been slowly acclimating to the dark. I was keenly aware that mine wasn't. She said the entry to the stairs going down was right next to us, ahead of us, while the rest of the room was empty behind us. No maze, no panels in the floor.

Nothing.

Aggie was the next one through. She stepped over to Turk. "Hey. You bozos are still here."

"How long did you wait before following?" I pointed my ears in her direction.

"About three hours. I was trying to convince Nikola. He's a serious control freak."

I thought about the eight orders on the wall. "Fuck. I think it needs to be all of us. All eight."

A few seconds later, Nikola came through, nearly slamming into the wall ahead. He was sweaty and seemed to have a half-day's growth of beard now. "Eight fucking hours. I waited. No one could say anything?"

"Nothing we say travels to the other side." I tried to reach out and pat him on the back. He was agitated, trying hard not to be claustrophobic, I could tell.

"Let's just try to get downstairs," he breathed. Turk took lead as we approached the limestone stairs to the third level down. Suddenly Nikola collapsed, spitting up blood.

"Shit." I moved toward him, bumping into Aggie. I felt around on the ground. "What's happening?"

Noemie was kneeling next to me. "I don't want to… damn." I could tell she was struggling to figure it out.

"Guys." Aggie called out."I don't feel great, either."

Dev moved toward her. "But not as bad as him."

Noemie called out to Dev. "What are you thinking?"

"His personal timeline is out of sync with the world's – like, 9-plus hours"

Aggie shot back, "and mine is by about four." I heard real concern in her voice. Something deeper than this.

Ray sounded confused. "And that matters?"

"Apparently it does." Turk asked me if I felt okay, her hand on my back.

I whispered back, "I'm good. You? Does anyone else feel bad?"

Dad called out, "I feel fine. Good."

I tried to figure out where Rialtos was standing. "Ray, can you take him back up and we'll keep going?"

"No. Fuck that. I'm okay. I can go." Nikola sounded hoarse but alive.

"Aggie?"

"I'm going. I'm coming with."

Turk led and I followed right behind, moving down the thick, sleek rock stairs to the next level. There seemed to be some ambient light fading in as we descended what felt like 25 meters or so. The stairs ended, opening up into a new space. The lights were bright enough now that I could see a hazy sort of glow and some objects ahead. The air, however, was agitated, almost like a windy day outside. Turk tapped onto my back, telling me the room was huge, with a circular well in the center. Dev started pulling out rope.

Nikola looked around, "Where the fuck is this wind coming from?"

We were underground by now. There was no reasonable excuse for the wind. Dev wrapped a rope around his waist.

Milan grabbed his arm. "What are you doing, son?"

"It's okay. This seems to be the way down. If I can get there, we can get us all there." He put his arm on his father's shoulder. "I'll be okay."

Dad looked over at me. I could barely make out his face but I nodded. Devique was the best choice for this. I hated it too.

Nikola placed the globe lantern back on the floor and turned it on. Suddenly the little lights we held all came alive. He laughed. "Ok, the lights work here."

My eyes slowly widened and the haze cleared. I moved my head back and forth. There were bricks of gold all over.

A fortune.

Turk looked over at me. "Sonofabitch."

Rialtos cocked his head. "Wait, so the gold isn't in the vault?"

Aggie stared, stunned. "It's everywhere."

I tried to remember what I'd learned about the history of this in my research. "The Mamluk Sultanate."

Milan nodded. "From slaves to soldiers to rulers."

Devique looked at Noemie, "What do I need to know before I go down there?"

She looked up. The ceiling seemed far away. Maybe too far. "Military slave caste. They were purchased."

I thought. "So… gold. This is blood gold. Purchasing slaves."

Noemie shook her head. "Maybe not. Gold could buy your freedom, but you had to earn your rank first."

Nikola picked up a gold bar. "This is bullshit. This is all over the place."

Turk tapped on my back. I nodded and looked back at her paraphrasing out loud. "It's a bribe. You can take it and go. Or you can leave it and continue downward."

Rialtos laughed. "I can be bribed."

"Fuck that." Nikola picked up two more pieces and began juggling, unsuccessfully. They clanked to the ground. "We're going to get what we came for. And this too, if we want."

Suddenly the wind died down.

Devique called to us, "hey, guys."

I stepped over. "What's happening?"

Dev smiled for the first time since we'd stepped foot in this tower. "If I move over the well, the wind around us dies, but this -- it's an upwind. Like the wind is all concentrated here, pushing up. It's cushioning the drop."

"What happens if you go down?" Nikola asked.

"Guys, I don't even know if I need this rope. Look..." He started moving slowly down the well.

Milan called out. "Keep talking." He shook his head at Noemie.

"Okay. This is dark but I can see a little. I'm holding the rope but I don't need to. The wind feels like an updraft, like when you're skydiving."

Turk whispered, "so he's just having fun?"

I shook my head and laughed. This definitely seemed too easy.

"The walls are very slippery. They would be no help. And, allright, there are some spikes here along the wall. Around 15 meters down it widens a bit. If I were just falling, there would be nothing to grab onto. There is still some ambient light, but it's darker."

"Son, can you see the ground?"

"Yes, I can. It's altogether about 30 meters down. More spikes at the bottom. The air is like a pillow, though, so I can kick away from them."

I yelled down."How big?"

Devique called back up, "about 20 centimeters. Nothing big."

Without warning, the wind picked back up again as he stepped out of the shaft into the room below.

"You guys can come down."

I breathed in, relieved. Milan was the next one down. Then Aggie.

Rialtos grabbed the rope to wrap it around himself. The rope seemed almost an afterthought at that point. The updraft seemed to want to keep everyone safe. He leaned over, sitting on the edge. "I'll see you guys in the well."

He slid in and, at first, the updraft seemed to push up at him as well. The rope moved steadily downward. I leaned on the well for a moment, to gain my balance. And I heard it. The wind that was pushing upward from below seemed to be alternating.

It was shifting.

"Uh. Guys. Something's wrong." Rialtos called up.

At that moment, I heard the wind shift. I felt it next to me, sucking downward, threatening to pull me in. It screamed through the limestone walls of the well, shrieking into the half-dark.

And Ray screamed along with it.

I heard Devique yell out below. Then, I heard a wet thud.

"Ray! What's going on?" I yelled down the well. Right next to me, I felt Noemie grab my arm. And my balance gave out completely.

I fell into a black hole, a kind of cone that resolved to a singular point. I shut my eyes to find my balance and a second later, the temperature seemed to have gone up 5 five degrees . It was muggy. I opened my eyes to Devique's face. It was bright enough that I could make it out.

Milan was right behind him. I was on the floor at the bottom of the well. As I let my head loll sideways I could see Noemie leaning over Ray's body, trying her best to heal him. But there was no plane of light, no sound, no movement of his body.

Nothing.

I got up on my hands and knees. Dev helped me up. From this angle I could see it. Ray had fallen onto the spikes. They ripped through his face and chest, impaling him on the floor like so much meat on a knife rack. Noemie slid back on her knees and began to cry, silently.

She looked up at Dev and shook her head.

It was the same look I'd seen on her face sitting over the salesgirl, Lis, in that shop. A look of hopelessness.

It tore at me.

I moved over to where the body was.

Milan's voice was hardly more than a whisper. "What happened?"

I lifted Ray's chest from the spikes and pulled off his backpack. Up above, I heard Nikola calling out that he was coming down.

Dev put his hand on my back. He tapped out how glad he was that Noemie was holding on to me when he used that tether ring to call her down. My stomach was still in knots from the trip, but I was glad, as well.

Now I just had to live through the thought of Turk coming down that rope. I showed Dev and Milan what was in my hand.

That's when Aggie punched me. I fell backward against the far wall and dropped the gold brick I'd pulled out of Rialtos' backpack.

My head was spinning as I looked up. Aggie was straddling me, staring down. "I fucking knew it. I could never have landed that punch before. You're sick. Something is fucking wrong with you."

Milan stepped over and grabbed her arm. "Hold on. Cut it out..."

"Or what, daddy? You're going to get me killed? Just like this piece of shit. She's sick and she didn't tell any of us."

Devique looked like he could snap her in two. "And how is that your business?"

"Because I don't want to die, dipshit."

"I didn't get him killed, idiot." I could hear Nikola scraping the wall as he came down the stairs. The updraft continued, just as it had for Devique, Milan, and Aggie.

"I don't care, bitch. If you're sick somehow and you didn't tell us, that's my fucking life on the line."

Milan raised his voice."What about you?"

The room was swirling so I closed my eyes again to try and regain my balance. I leaned back on my elbows, imagining that they were both equidistant and on the same level. I started there.

"Give me that." Aggie was waving her hands at Milan. She stepped over me and slammed into him. "Fucking give me that, old man."

Devique grabbed her arms and pulled them behind her back, lifting her in the air. "Stop it. Let it go."

"Give me my fucking wallet back."

"What about this?" Milan pulled out a card and threw it on the ground.

"Let me go." Aggie kicked and pulled herself out of Devique's arms and dropped to the ground.

Dev stepped over and stood between us, helping me up.

"Agios Savvas Hospital Cancer Treatment Center. Did you tell us about that? What are you hiding?"

"Fuck you. I can take care of myself."

I thought for a second. "You're sick, too?"

"I have cancer, bitch. I can still function. Look at you. I never would have been able to get a punch over the great René Mäkelä. What's wrong with you?"

I pulled myself up on Dev's arm, leaning over and grabbing the brick. As mad as Aggie was at me, I had my own issues. As Nikola floated gently to the ground and sidestepped Ray's body, I stepped over to him and slammed my fist into his neck.

He dropped to his knees as I shoved the brick onto his face. "This is the fucker that's going to get us all killed. Right, Big Nik?"

"Fuck you, bitch."

I brought the brick down hard onto the side of his head and he fell over. He held his face in his hands.

"He planted this in Rialtos' backpack to test if he could take any gold with him down here."

Nikola spit on the ground. "You don't fucking know that."

Milan stared at him, "why didn't you bring any gold with you coming down?"

"It seemed like a bad idea."

Dev rolled up his sleeves. Ray had saved his life back in Sicily and now he was folded up in pieces on the ground, his blood pouring onto the stone. "Why was it a bad idea, Nik?"

There was blood coming from a gash in the side of Nik's face. He screamed, "look at him. Look at what happened to him."

I waved the brick. "How did you know that he had a brick in his backpack?"

Nikola leaned up against the wall, breathing heavily. "Leave... me... alone." This last word he screamed.

I followed the sound of his breathing. I knelt down in front of him. "There are seven of us now, Nik. If anyone else gets hurt, you will become expendable. It's your job now to keep everyone safe, do you understand?"

He looked at me. I stood there until Turk came down the well, then pulled her aside. "A needs a cure,"Il signed into her hand.

She nodded. Noemie did seem sick, but now we knew that Aggie definitely was. And if Ruach was handing out cures, she might jump.

***

We made our way down two more levels, relatively uneventfully. We found a Caananite city, larger than it should have been. We found a massive firepit, somehow still alive, deeply underground. We found levels locked by slight riddles and one kept safe by a vault that needed to be listened to, but, despite all of it, gave up its secrets fairly easily.

Until, finally, we found ourselves on a level that felt ancient, one that was surrounded in shapes and symbols that seemed to predate history. We stepped down the limestone stairwell and found a simple recessed circle set into the wall in front of us, one seemingly organic and not made by people.

I traced a symbol near the center of it and looked at Noemie.

"Maqor." She whispered. "It means 'source.'"

Nikola came up to one side. "That must be it."

I turned to him. "Why? What do you know about this thing that your father wants?"

He smiled creepily. "I know a lot."

Devique shook his head and moved toward him. "That's it. I'm going to kill this motherfucker."

Turk stepped in his path. "Why can't we know? We can do a better job. Look, man, we want your dad to give us a shitload of money and let us swim in his pool. Tell us how to be good munchkins. Tell us what you know."

Dev spoke up louder, "maybe now. Now's a good time."

"Get out of my face." He pushed Dev away. That was a bad idea.

Devique was my brother. And the kindest, most easygoing men I'd ever met. He was tall and thickly muscled, but I'd rarely ever seen him use it to intimidate. This was a man who got on the ground to play with children. This was a man who liked to cook for people. When he fed a tiny black cat on the deck of the boat he always made sure to break the pieces off small enough so that she wouldn't choke.

But today, he'd reached the end. He growled and stepped on Nikola's left foot with enough force to cause a massive thud. He placed his hands on either side of Nik's head and clamped them tightly, pulling upward, threatening to yank off the man's head. Nikola pummeled him with his fists and yelled out.

But Devique kept it up. Nikola's entire body seemed to stretch like a deflated rubber balloon.

"Fuck. Fuck. Fuck. Okay. Let me go."

Devique dropped him and slammed his hand into his chest, forcing him against the wall.

Nikola wiped the sweat from his forehead.

"Fine, fine. I'll tell you everything I know."

14. Love is you

L'amour c'est toi
L'amour c'est moi

Love is you
Love is me

Milan had never thought of himself as a great pickpocket. He wasn't fast enough. And the best pickpockets had an eye for misdirection. They knew people – they knew where they might be looking at any moment. It wasn't something you could learn, maybe, but something that came to you as a gift. He was what they called an architect. He put teams together, drew up plans.

He thought big.

But that didn't mean he couldn't appreciate a great pickpocket. And way back in the summer Of 1948, on the boardwalk at Parc Borély where the clowns pranced around, he watched a truly great one.

He couldn't take his eyes off of her.

Her hair was blonde and pressed perfectly straight, wrapped around a pixie-like face that held the most perfect smile he'd ever seen. But the thing that the tourists couldn't look away from, the thing that drew everyone in and made them forget, for long moments at a time, what her hands were up to, were her eyes. The greenest, deepest eyes he had ever seen.

They were like glass marbles, each filled with a diorama of a forest, of a glade, of a close-to-port depth of beautifully clear Mediterranean sea, aqua leaning toward liquid viridian green in defiance of the sky.

She danced around the Parc, her movements too fast for anyone to see. And husbands stared, until their wives pulled them away, fathers took time from watching their children to lean into her with their eyes. Even wives were fascinated. How to walk like that, to move like that.

So elegantly.

Milan watched from the bridge, inching closer to the body of the boardwalk, toward her. In his head, he wondered what her voice would sound like, what it would feel like if that smile were directed at him. The only thing he didn't wonder about was what Christo might think.

That, he knew.

As he approached, he saw the man in the black coat move toward her. Milan changed direction slightly to intercept them both. The man had grabbed the blonde woman's arm and was speaking into her ear.

Her expression hadn't changed, even as she faced arrest.

The two began walking toward the end of the boardwalk. Milan was suddenly in front of them, lifting his hand.

He flashed the badge at the man and stared him in the eyes. "This is our sting, pretend you just helped her avoid a fall, keep walking until you are off the boardwalk."

The officer glanced quickly at the badge as Milan slid it back in his pocket and started to pretend to talk and laugh with the blonde woman. She put her arm in his and they made their way to the far gazebo, ducking behind it.

"He's gone." She crossed her arms and smiled at him.

"He looked very by-the-book."

"I'm guessing he'll notice his badge is missing at some point." She slid around him and grabbed his hand, pulling him toward the trees.

Milan laughed. "You caught that?"

"It was clumsy."

He moved a hair from in front of her face. "Well, I'm not you."

She tried to figure him out, scanning his face. Milan was young, around the age I am now. He wasn't tall, but he was handsome. He wasn't rich but he never wanted. And he wasn't willing to look away from her for a second, for fear she would disappear.

"You did save me. So you get one wish."

Milan's face opened in a wide smile. The breeze that had raked through the park all summer seemed to have been rehearsing for this moment when it could play in his hair and give the illusion that he was a rogue, a devil sent to make her life a game. The wind built him up into this dashing figure. And then died down so she could hear as he whispered to her.

"Spend the day with me."

That was Suvi Laine, my mother. And that was how they met. I heard the story from both sides over and over again, how they horribly misspent their day in ways that would get them both arrested on any other day. How they stole lunch and then dinner and then coats when the sun went down and those winds across the city grew more playful. How they stole everything in their path, until the day, tired of keeping watch over them, changed over to tomorrow, which proved no better at restraining them.

And neither did the rest of the week.

***

Turk stared at the recessed pit of sand in the wall. It looked like a vault. It felt like a vault. Except it was made out of porous, insubstantial sand.

But it was a vault, nonetheless. And Turk understood vaults.

Since we'd been down here, Turk hadn't spoken out loud very often. Most of her comments had been shared privately with me, either on my back or in my hands.

I think this might have been her way to stay out of the fray and focus on this.

The vault.

Nikola sat against the wall, a light glob in front of him. Everything in the room seemed lit from below with that admittedly eerie flicker that made horror movies work. I couldn't see much in that room but I could see his face.

He started, "When I was a kid, my father told me that vampires were real. Like a lot of kids, I was really into Dracula. So he tells me it's real, all of it."

Devique crossed his arms. "Bullshit."

"No, son. Let him go on. Let him dig his grave."

"Thank you, old man. You see how wise he is?"

Nikola grinned and something inside of me snapped. For all this, for Ray, I would take care of him after this. This was the first time I'd ever had a thought like that.

"So, they're real, right? And not just them. Other monsters. Things we don't have names for. What they all have in common, every group, is that they hate each other. "

Aggie nodded. "Of course. Makes sense."

"And they're all blood monsters. DamShedayya, they are all called."

Milan crossed his arms. "So they live on blood?"

Nikola flashed that creepy smile again. "No. It's metaphorical. They feed on life. That's the metaphor. They drain people of life. That's their food."

"DamShedayya?" I said, looking at Noemie.

She shrugged her shoulders. "It means 'blood demon,' I guess. Aramaic, again."

Turk looked around. "You know what would have been super helpful for this job? An Aramaic dictionary. Right?"

Nikola continued. "The very strong ones can bite and transfer their entire power to a new form. It's called the Demasar."

Dev looked impatient. "This sounds very much like a fairy tale."

I agreed, trying to wrap this back. I snapped my fingers. "So what's in the box?"

Nikola looked at me and the anger washed across his face. He seemed to change, for a moment, into a different person. "Maybe you could listen, BITCH."

Dev shook his head. "Nope. He dies." he started walking toward him.

Nikola cowered. "Whoa. Whoa. I'm telling you the truth, not like your 'Dad.'" He put as much mocking energy as he could into that last word. "Ask him what really happened to your real father."

I pulled some tape out of the backpack and moved toward him. "Ok, I'm done with Dummy the Greek." I'd always thought Nikola's jealousy of Dev was harmless. That he, himself, was harmless.

"ASK HIM!" He yelled.

Dev yelled back, "I don't need to, I know. I've always known. My father committed suicide, okay? Now, what's in the box, asshole."

Milan moved toward Dev and put his arms around him. My brother seemed broken up. Dad looked over at me and Turk. "You were too young. And Turkana wasn't around yet. Christo and I were... we were in love."

Dev pulled Milan in and looked down menacingly at Nikola. "And if you say my father's name one more time, I will fucking cut your tongue out."

Dad went on. "All three of us. He was the most French man I ever knew. He loved us both so hard. And when Suvi died, it ripped him apart."

Devique's eyes grew big as he moved closer to me. "You were too young to see all this at the time. I saw it. It's okay, Dad."

Suddenly, a massive bang rang out to my left. I turned but it was too dark, too far from the light source. Aggie's voice followed up.

"Hey, hey, fucking poetry nerds. I don't care. I'm here to get that thing and get paid and go home. Our time is almost up."

Milan advanced on her. "Put that thing away."

She stepped forward and I could see the tiniest glint of a gun.

"I don't think I will." She stared out coldly. I realized I had taken all these people too lightly. I didn't realize how big a problem they could be. I should have had eyes on Nikola and Agnes all day. And if I had watched out better, maybe Ray would be alive.

"It's a child."

We all turned to Nikola.

"It's a toddler, a child that contains the energy of the DamShedayya. The Demon in charge, who who lives on the other side of that portal, her name is Daivana. When she wanted to keep all the groups in line, she birthed a child. A child that has all the potential of the DamShedayya in one form."

"A child?" I repeated. "In the box?"

Dev looked at him. "What does your father want with it?"

Nikola took a deep breath. "The child has enough energy to feed on the entire hemisphere. It's dangerous. But if my dad grabs it, holds onto it, he can trigger it to bite him. And that bite will release the energy into him."

Milan nodded, "And he'll live forever?"

"Damn right. The thing will live inside him. The Demasar. The blood bind."

I struggled to figure this out. It was pretty far outside my area of expertise, which, to be absolutely honest, was picking pockets. "Then what will keep the other demon groups in line?"

"He will. He'll be strong enough to save this whole planet."

Noemie stood behind me. She whispered, "unlikely."

I realized that this child in the flowering box was leverage. This was a bomb in the wall, meant to keep war between these creatures from breaking out. It kept the various demon "families" from battling.

And it needed to stay there. Right where it was.

I thought out loud. "The Maqor."

Nikola tried to stand up. It seemed like he was still sick from the time differential. "The source. Maqor is like a black liquid ink that lets made things travel through unmade spaces."

Dev looked confused. "What?" I realized that he hadn't seen it. When Ruach disappeared using it at the depot, he was on the floor. And at the store, at the pool. He'd never seen it.

Nikola laughed. "It's the ink that paints the world. It's how all the DamShedayya travel. From here, through the Haqal Dema."

In my head, I knew that this was real. It still felt like nonsense to me. I turned to Aggie. She was pointing the gun at me.

"Fuck this. It's time for your girlfriend to do her job."

Turk called out. "Whoa, Agnes. Point that over here. Calm it down. Point it at me. I think I got it. Here, come here. Look."

Agnes stepped around me. Turk continued. "Look, it's a regular vault. Entirely. Except all the pieces are just shaped sand. Until I do this." She lifted the tiny precision butane flamethrower in her right hand and ran it over the sandy shape of a knob. "Watch. I already ran it over this outside ring. It turned to glass almost immediately. I figured that water and fire were the only ways to harden sand. And fire would be more precise. See this?"

The knob in the center of the sandy vault face began to coalesce and turn transparent. It was turning to glass, matching the ring around it. None of this should work.

But it did.

Nikola reached out to Aggie. "Put the gun down. People can get hurt easily when in the Maqor. It sort of dampens protections." I thought back to Ruach appearing and disappearing in the black ink. I shot a look at Dev.

Aggie waved the gun. "All you all motherfuckers need to stop telling me to drop my gun. Seriously."

That was the moment I felt Dev slip something into my pocket. I couldn't tell what it was. I made a point to feel for it when no one was looking.

Turk blew on the glass dial to cool it and moved it forward. It seemed to spin reluctantly, but it moved. I could tell she was trying to put on a show, to keep Aggie's attention.

And the sand fell away, revealing a thick wall of black viscous ink, floating in the air.

Nikola pushed himself to the front. "I need to go first. I have a vision in my head of where to go."

Aggie looked him up and down. "And that matters?"

"Yes, it's how to travel."

I realized that Nikola was losing it. He wasn't handling the combination of his nine-plus hours offset from the timeline, and having been in the dark for 8 straight hours, and what happened to Ray, all of it. He stood in front of the vault opening and spread his arms. With a grand flourish, he let himself fall backwards into the black. Aggie waved her gun, pushing the rest of us forward. Dev and Noemie grabbed hands and stepped through. Milan followed. I dragged my feet a bit. I realized that a lot of Aggie's rage was born from the fact that she disliked me.

And I was sick, too.

I put my hand in Turk's and spoke to her with my fingers. "Neither of these people can get this box."

She responded. "Ruach wants to destroy it so he can be head monster. Karras wants to suck it up so he can be."

That seemed succinct. The only way this worked was if the status quo were kept. The box had to stay there. I turned and felt the butt of Agnes' gun come down hard on my head. The floor came rushing up and flipped the room around, tuning it all black.

***

I woke up in a bright space, in Devique's arms. I was being carried. Wee were moving forward, stepping slowly. I was facing to the side and it was hard to parse what I was seeing.

Turk leaned in. Her hand had been on mine. She whispered, "you okay?"

I eased myself down from Dev's arms. Noemie and Turk helped me stand up straight.

Turk's hand in mine explained that she got a good punch in after Aggie had knocked me out. For a moment, I was sad I missed it.

I scanned the space. It was huge. It seemed to be a giant cave with an opening ahead that led to broad daylight. All through the cave were jewels, gold, precious metals, ancient pottery, billions of francs worth. I'd never imagined anything like it.

Noemie whispered. "This side of the portal is a place called Haqal Dema. It means "blood field."

I nodded. "Sounds delightful." Did that portal lead to an entirely different planet? Or a different dimension? And why did everything have the word 'blood' in it? I stared forward.

Nikola and Agnes were moving through the space panicked, looking for the box. Assuming that Agnes was working for Ruach, they both had bosses to answer to. But that didn't explain the rush. As we moved toward the opening of the cave, I realized why. Outside of the cave was a massive, rocky world, going on as far as you could see. I squinted into the light and could make out massive figures, crawling on the rocks. In the distance, a figure large enough to block out the sun was approaching. It was as tall as the mountain that housed this cave.

A creature larger than any building I'd ever seen in my life was coming right toward us.

Noemie pointed. "That's Daivana. Or one of her Envoys. We're not sure. But it's huge."

I sighed. "How long until she gets here?"

Dev shook his head, "We don't know. Depends on how big she is. I think she's really huge and it's less than a minute. Oh, and we think Big Nik is losing it."

I looked over at Turk. "Shit."

We moved back in, Turk called out to Nikola. "Did you find it, Champ?"

He shook his head and gave her the middle finger. That seemed very American. Suddenly, I thought. "Turk, how did you and Noemie find the other box, on the lower level, at the Hypogeum?"

Noemie shook her head. "We were just talking about that. We actually don't remember."

Milan looked at me sheepishly, "That's the thing. The information seems to be removed from their brains."

I looked at my dad. I could see something familiar in his eyes. "So bad I want to just go rob a regular bank, Dad."

He smiled and ran his hand through my hair. "You sound so much like your mother. She would have hated all this."

Turk laughed. "She would have been right. I feel like there's a chunk removed. How did we find the box?"

The massive shape outside had gotten closer. It started to darken the sky a bit. I could feel the room dimming. How big was it?

"Why would you forget?" I thought out loud.

"Some kind of memory spell?" Dev offered up.

"But we found it and got out quickly," Noemie said.

She was right. They were already out when we got up. So it didn't take long.

"A strange trauma," Milan looked at me. Trauma can wipe memory. He wasn't wrong. But, again, so quickly?

Noemie suddenly looked past me. It seemed like there were letters and symbols all around us. She focused on one grouping. "There."

I turned. I couldn't make out anything.

She looked up at Dev. "'Mesar.' it means 'submit.'"

I nodded. "That sounds like the theme of this entire job so far." I considered how we had to basically give up at the maze. We had to give up the gold at the well. This whole job was about giving up and submitting. And letting something else take over. What a shitty lesson.

Turk looked thoughtful. "Submit. Fuck." She turned and ran toward the sign. Noemie followed her. I grabbed Dev's arm and we followed. Turk reached the area first, stopping and turning toward us. Her eyes were black and vacant. Noemie stepped over to where she was and the same thing happened to her.

The two of them stepped a few feet away and bent over. They rose up again and began to move toward us.

"Holy shit." Dev called out as he saw the image fill the front of the cave. I called to Turk and Noemie but they were still walking, entranced, slowly. They made their way right in front of us and bent down again and dropped something. I could barely make it out in the shifting light.

It was the box.

I heard Aggie and Nikola call out. Turk shook her head and her eyes returned to normal. I grabbed the box and lifted it. Again it was incredibly light. I put it over my shoulder and moved quickly back toward the portal.

Suddenly, gunshots rang out. Aggie was shooting out the front of the cave. I looked backward for a second. A massive hand and arm rammed its way into the cave, slamming into Nikola. He called out, running to catch up. Aggie was right behind him.

I was unconscious when we had come in. I didn't realize how far back it was to the portal area. We ran. I was holding the box, trying to keep my balance as the giant arm behind us dug deeper into the depths of the cave. It pushed forward, its massive meaty fist and claws ripping the floor of the cavern open. The lights in front of us were thin and barely able to keep the slim cone of my vision alive, but I kept running anyway. Aggie reloaded her gun and was almost snared by the huge hand, collapsing the cave behind us as it pushed deeper into the space. The gold and jewels behind us fell away as the ceiling of the cave threatened to collapse, trapping us. I felt the floor begin to give way.

I pushed, running as fast as I could. I could feel the air heat up behind me and smell the stench of the arm digging its way into the cave.

Finally, we saw the black ink of the portal. Nikola sprinted to get ahead of us. We weren't sure if he still had to go through first. I turned around. I wasn't taking any chances.

The hand that followed us was attached to an impossibly long arm. The fingers were longer than my body, sharp, cracked, with black nails that shot toward me like massive rockets looking to impale me. I felt Dev's hand behind me pulling me into the blackness and my senses died. It was like the tether, dragging me against my will into the space under the well, clouding my brain and throwing me to the floor. This time, though, everyone else was going through it, too. My head slammed on the ground and I struggled to stay awake, pulling the box with me as I crawled across the room.

We were back in front of the vault door.

Aggie was the first one up, marching toward me with her gun up. But all I could think was "we failed."

We failed at everything we needed to do. We hadn't left the box alone, hadn't stopped Nikola or Aggie from getting it, hadn't gotten any gold.

We failed.

Aggie advanced as I reached out and put my hand on the box. I remember Turk grabbing my other hand trying to cover me, while Milan stepped over, hoping to disarm Agnes. She turned to point the gun at him as she kneeled onto the box, pressing against it. "Back off, old man." With her other hand she pulled out a pager, exactly like the one Ruach had given me.

She pressed the button on top.

The room began to churn and flip as she raised the gun and shot my father in the center of his forehead.

I screamed and the world disappeared.

***

The sun was dropping as we fell, rolling down a white sand hill outside. I looked up. We could have been anywhere in the world. I tried to pull myself to my feet. Turk got up first and dug her hands into Aggie's neck.

"What did you do?!"

I crawled over. My brain was scrambled, but I saw it.

She killed Milan.

Turk's voice rose to a screech. "WHAT DID YOU DO?"

"I'm sorry. I'm sorry." Agnes tried to spit out words as Turk ripped the life from her. I reached over and put my hand on Turk's leg. I could feel her shaking while she slammed the other woman's head into the sand and dug her fingernails into her neck.

"YOU FUCKING KILLED HIM." Turk choked out, her face distorted in a way I'd never seen. I squeezed her leg. I tried to give her the strength to squeeze harder.

To kill Agnes.

"Motherfucker, motherfucker!" Agnes's eyes were bulging, her face darkening, as I looked around. I couldn't get any breath. It was like there was a bubble around me.

Nothing could get in.

Suddenly, a gunshot went off. I crawled over Turk, trying to protect her. She let go of Agnes and slid back into the sand. Her arm was bleeding.

It was just her arm.

I tried to make my eyes work, harder than I ever had. I focused over Agnes's head.

A figure resolved from the black ink. His eyes looked grey to me but I knew they were yellow. I felt the gunshot on Turk's arm. It had gone straight through. Why didn't he kill her? I tried to memorize the area around us before my vision sundowned.

This was where the beeper's tether had brought us, face to face with Ruach. It looked like we were still in Israel.

"It looks like one of you wanted to be cured more than the other one. Pity."

Ruach reached down and helped Agnes up. Turk's face darkened even more. I realized why he didn't kill her as he reached down for the box. Turk saw it first.

"We'll come work for you. Both of us."

He turned around. His eyes opened wider. "Oh, yes? Tell me why you would do that?"

Turk glanced at me and then back to Ruach. "Kill her and we'll work for you. Make it hurt and we'll do anything you want."

Agnes spit on the ground in front of Turk. "Fuck you. And fuck your little blonde bitch."

Ruach laughed. "Ladies. This got interesting very fast."

I felt lightheaded but I was getting good at hiding it. All of it. Every part of how I was feeling. My father was dead and I didn't need feelings anymore.

Turk growled. "She shot my father in the fucking head. Kill her and we work for you."

"It was a fucking accident. He should have stood down like I told him. It was a fucking accident."

"You killed their father?"

Agnes started breathing harder. "It was an accident."

Ruach made a big deal out of wiping the dirt from her face. He turned to us and held her hand. "See. It was an accident. There's no reason why we can't all get along."

Agnes looked at us and started to moan. Imperceptibly, at first, her face seemed to thin. Her hair fluttered and a band of gray appeared, washing across the entire thing. Wrinkles sprouted in a wave from her forehead down to her neck as she lost her footing. Ruach grabbed her, supporting her as she slipped into infirmity. "Accidents happen, I suppose."

She looked at him pleading, opening her mouth to beg. As she did, her jaw fell, pulling itself from her skull while the rest of her shriveled up, every bit of energy and life gone.

He had sucked her dry completely.

Her body fell to the ground like a canvas bag of bones.

"When you plan badly. Right, ladies?"

Turk fell to her knees, crying. I felt her lean against my leg as I stared at Ruach. "Absolutely."

He cocked his head. "Is she going to be alright?"

I shrugged. She lost her father. We both did. We failed. We lost. "And now, what? you destroy the child?"

He nodded. "The child. Yes. I make sure no one can ever use her for leverage."

"Her?"

"Oh, I'm surprised no one ever told you. The Bi'uwsh Olam. The eternal evil, the ṭarāf d'perakh, leaf of the flower. She is a girl."

"A little girl."

He stepped closer. "Don't get sentimental. This child was born to house the near infinite energies of all of Haqal Dema. She would grow up to be the new Daivana, the de facto leader of all DamShedayya. You saw her, didn't you? Do you really want this child to grow up into that?"

"Your boss?"

He laughed. "No. Not my boss."

I looked at him with a look I hoped came across pitying. "You're just a vampire, right?"

He leaned back and centered himself on the sand. "Vampire? I am the leader of the Zar Qurbana. We go back to the beginning of recorded history on this planet. We've had no bosses for millennia. And once this is destroyed, we never will again."

I felt the tears running down my face. It was hard to stand. Turk was waiting for me to make my play, breathing heavily, leaning against my leg.

I reached into my pocket and fingered the metal ring, the one that Dev had placed in my pocket. I dropped it and let it roll down the hill. "Here. Where are we? Where did you transport us to?"

His voice became even more soothing. He looked at me and saw a woman on the edge, someone who had just lost her family. Someone who needed guidance. "Tel Yitzhak. It's not far. It's not far at all. No one is looking for us. Let me get your partner some help now." He reached for me.

"Maybe she needs a drink."

I turned in the direction of Dev's voice. He stood with Noemie right behind him, just out of reach of Ruach. He held up a bottle in his hand.

Lemonade.

I yelled out, "Thank you..."

The Maqor swirled around Ruach as he slipped from my location to stand in front of Devique, confronting him. Just as the thick blank ink began to dissipate, three shots rang out. The first hit Ruach in his left eye, the second tore a hole through his right cheek and the third drilled directly into the front of his forehead.

He slumped and hit the ground.

Noemie came running over to us. She shook her head, crying. I sank into the sand next to Turk. I tried to think about what to do next. I tried to remember where Tel Yitzhak was. I tried to conjure up a hundred things in my head that would make sense. What we would do next. None of it did.

Milan was gone.

***

We were closer to port now, so the four of us decided to make our way to the boat rather than try to get back to Kdumim. We knew that would mean Karras would try to kill us.

But it was hard to care anymore. We would get back and regroup, get to the island that Karras didn't know anything about and, as soon as we could, replace this box.

Both of them, actually.

Devique acquired a van that Turk told me was dark red, and we all piled in the back as he drove toward the harbor.

"I held onto Dev and this box the whole time after you guys disappeared. He figured you'd find the ring in your pocket."

I nodded. "That was good. Very good. I mean, we're poor, but..."

Dev looked back. "Maybe not..."

Noemie pulled a golf ball sized rock out of her pocket and handed it to me. "You call it the same way."

Turk looked at her. "Is that what I think it is?"

Noemie nodded.

I handed the rock and the ring to Turk. "Hold on tight to these, okay?"

She nodded and tucked them away. No one could ever figure out where Turk hid things. But she never lost them.

Noemie looked down. "I tried to..." she started crying again.

I wrapped my arm around her. "I know. I know, baby." I still needed time to process all of this, but right now it was my job to say the things that Milan would be saying. This is how to honor my dad. "You did so good."

I kissed her on the head.

Dev called back, "ten minutes. Then we get on that boat and get to Yeronisos. We lie low for a while."

"We live on a rock." Turk tried to perk me up. The truth is that I could live on a rock with these people. I didn't care.

The sun was nearly down by the time we got to the boat. Nobody was around. The harbor itself was nearly empty. It took me a second to remember that this was why we chose this day.

Everyone was somewhere else.

It felt like a million years since we'd been on the boat. Shark met us at the door. Part of me felt like she was looking for Milan and I started to break down.

Dev took over.

We pulled up anchor and made sure we had everything in the right place. I had made sure to place the two boxes in the van in such a way that we could remember easily which was which. I brought them both up to the flybridge along with a marker. On the first one, filled with fruits and honey, I drew a large "B". On the other one, filled with a nearly infinite and eternal evil vampire-like child, I drew the number "2".

Turk came over as I explained. "Well. This would keep me guessing for a few weeks, so, good work.

Noemie shook her head. "I don't even understand how your brain works."

"But we know which is which, right?"

Everyone nodded as we slid both boxes onto the skiff. They would be the first things we moved onto Yeronisos.

I changed and was soon back onthe flybridge, open bottle of wine in hand. We'd be on the island in a few hours. Honestly, though, I don't think I really breathed out until we had cleared Israel and could no longer see land.

We sat quietly on the flybridge as Dev steered. Turk sat on the floor in front of me and I pulled her closely, locking her in with my legs. She ran her hands over my feet.

Noemie still looked sick. I wanted to talk to her and make sure she was ok, but it felt like a million miles to that side of the boat. Besides, moving meant that I would disrupt Turk and the cat on her head.

I started. "Dev, you never talked to us about your dad and Milan and my mom?"

He took a breath. And then another. "I was young, too. Not much older than you. I remember things, though. They were good together. I remember staying over in the guest room like I used to while the three of them laughed in the living room conversation pit. And got drunk. Ha. Do you remember any of that?"

"Maybe. Maybe I do. I remember people being happy. I remember always hearing laughing from the other room. I remember dinners with your dad and my mom and you and how much fun..."

I took a drink.

"I guess I remember."

Dev turned to me and put the boat on auto. He stepped over and kneeled down putting his head the same level as mine. He ran his hand through my hair like dad did and whispered.

"Did it hurt? When Agnes died? I know it doesn't matter..."

I held his face in my hands and the night was suddenly filtered through my own tears, every tiny ray of light bouncing off the tears, colliding, amplifying, exploding.

I nodded. I felt like a monster hoping, but my wishes made it real. I tried to remember Agnes's face as the life drained away.

"It did."

15. The Child is Me

L'oiseau c'est toi
L'enfant c'est moi

The bird is you
The child is me

None of us felt like going to our beds. We slept on the flybridge, looking out over the water. I clung to Turk all night, trying to avoid the hallucinations. I thought I saw colors in the middle of the night, but it was just my brain tricking me, needling me, laughing at me. Everything sounded far away until I focused and even then it felt like I had a blanket over my head.

The sun had been up for a while when Turk and I went below deck to shower. We had all slept pretty late into the day. She kept the lights off and slid into the tiny fiberglass shower with me, dancing slowly against me. In this light, she couldn't see any better than I could. I let my hands rest on her lower back and she put hers on mine, letting the water fall all over us until it ran cold.

Sometimes I would try to use her back to talk like she used mine. It always ended with us laughing, falling over, feeling alive. Today was a little different. Nothing I could say would erase the last day, make it go back to the way it was. Today we tried to not communicate. We tried to just be.

We each put on a pair of shorts and a t-shirt. Turk went directly up to the flybridge and I stepped onto the side deck to see if I could see anything with the sun rising.

That's when I heard it.

The voice.

I felt for the drawer built into the wall and grabbed the two flare guns inside. Under that drawer and aftward about a half meter was the retractable power cord. I wrapped it around one of the guns and tossed it overboard, letting the flare gun sink, still connected to the cord.

I listened as I made my way up the steps. There was no way to sneak up on him. Nikola was sitting, back to the front of the boat, holding his gun up at Devique and Turk.

I didn't see Noemie. But the rain had begun falling, making tiny impressions on the tarp over the command wheel as well as the one over the skiff. It was warm.

"René, why don't you come up and join the party." He didn't look much better than last time we'd seen him. He was sweaty and dirty. He still looked sick.

He was desperate.

"On your way to Cyprus. I thought I'd stop in. You killed the vampire, though, so congratulations." He made the motion to applaud with one hand, still holding the gun. "Yaaaah. Excellent. I'm so fucking proud of you."

I stepped up and let him see the flare gun in my hand.

"Yeah." He looked up at the rain. He knew that flareguns were waterproof. "Why don't you shoot that right at the engine block. Right there. Blow the whole fucking boat up. Or you could put it down. Put it down. He raised the gun at me. I peered in his direction. It was like looking through a long tube. The sun had risen through the light rain but I only had the most minimal of senses. His voice was boxy, empty. I put the flare gun on the floor.

He stood up and kicked it into the water, more violently than he needed to. That seemed to calm him. He sat back down, smiling.

"Come sit down with us. All of you. Once we get to Cyprus, we'll figure all this out with my dad. He'll meet us there. And what the fuck kind of name is XMAS for a boat?" He waved the gun at Dev.

Devique took a breath. "It used to be called the B2N. I didn't know what that meant."

I tried not to look over at the skiff hanging from the starboard side of the boat. Dev was trying to tell me and Turk that Noemie was hiding there, with the boxes, under the tarp. She was the "N"

Nikola seemed to be enjoying his sense of power. "Well, XMAS is a shit name, too."

I looked over at Turk. It was hard to see her face at all, much less read it.

I was alone. Except I really wasn't.

I looked down and breathed in. "What happens when we tell your dad that you're the one who tipped off Ruach?"

Nikola snapped back, "fuck you talking about?"

I continued. "Playing both sides. No matter who got the box, you'd have an in with the big bad guy, right?"

Turk broke in. "It's a good plan."

Nikola laughed. "My dad knows better."

Devique kept quiet. That felt smart. I was reasonably sure he would pause before shooting me or Turk. He would shoot Devique in a heartbeat.

I kept going. "What, that you wouldn't fuck him? Like you've fucked over Ray? Like you fucked over everybody you ever worked with?"

I hit something. His father liked Rialtos. Quite a lot. This was a real threat, too. What if Anton knew that Nikola had been the one to kill him?

"Ray was unexpected. Who knew, right?"

Turk offered up, "the vampire knew. You told him about the job. He knew a lot."

He paused, trying to figure out the angles. What did we know? "Bullshit."

I nodded and sat back. "We'll see who your dad believes." This may have been one step too far.

His voice smiled. He remembered who was in charge. "You want a bullet right now, don't you?" A bolt of lightning struck in the distance as if to accent his words.

Turk tried to be conversational. "Hey, I don't know why we can't all just rationally sit down and talk about it. I mean, we were so freaked out about Ruach. We thought he was so scary. He was just a fucking vampire. Three little bullets was all it took." She made a gun with her hands. "Pow. pow. Pow."

Nikola sounded scornful. Did he believe it? "To kill Ruach? Three bullets?"

"He was half in the Maqor." I explained.

He paused. He hadn't considered that we'd been listening to him. He laughed. "What do you know?"

Turk tried to act flippant. "So now, it's up to your dad. Anton becomes the big bad guy. And he'll take care of you, right?"

"He will"

I added, "unless he suspects you tried to fuck him."

"He trusts me."

Turk made a noise. "Wellllllll. Now, maybe. You might have to kill us all before he gets here. Bam. Bam. It's a bloodbath. Messy."

I shot back, facetiously, "But won't that look suspicious?"

Turk followed up, "damn. I think it will."

Nikola stood up and looked around. "Where's the other one? Where's the witch?"

Turk pulled out some nail polish and started to do her toenails. "We had to drop her off. She said you were tracking her."

I saw him look over at Dev. Devique nodded quietly."

Nik looked confused. "How would she know that?"

Turk pointed the brush at him and looked at me. "That sounded like an admission."

I closed my eyes and put my head back. "It did, a little."

Turk kept working on her nails. "How did you get here so fast, anyway, Champ?"

"What did you call me?" He stepped over to her. Dev looked at me as he reached under the control panel.

I called out. "She just wants to know how you got to us so fast. I mean, you had to dig out of the Tel, make it back up, get to a boat, outrace us."

"It seems like a big deal." Turk contorted herself to blow on her toenails. That move always confuses men.

"I took a private flight to Cyprus and a ten-footer back to intercept you."

I nodded. "That was well done." Suddenly the power died.

He looked at Dev. "What the fuck?"

My brother made a cursory scan of the instruments and looked frustrated. "Fuck. There is a power lead over. I can pull it up and wait a minute. It'll be fine."

Nikola waved the gun. "Well, find it."

Dev did a quick search on both sides. He motioned to Nik, calling him over to port. "See that?" it was the cord I had thrown overboard.

"So you get that out of the water and it'll be ok?"

"Yeah, there is an auto retract. Let me get it.

"I'm right here. I'm watching you."

"I got it. I'll get it." Devique started down the stairs as Nikola watched closely.

Turk called out, "so your dad knows you found us?"

He split his attention, glancing back at her. "Yes, he's meeting us in Cyprus."

I moved over to the starboard side to help her with her nails. "He doesn't think you messed this all up, does he?"

"He thinks I'm the one getting him the box. And I am."

Turk looked up at me as if she was thinking out loud. "Waitaminute. Anton doesn't know about Ruach. So he won't know how Aggie died, either?"

"Right. In fact, we better all get our stories lined up. She always hated me. Maybe I killed her."

"I mean, Anton's not a suspicious guy, so I'm sure it's fine."

"Got it." Nikola looked down to see the cord back in place. Devique stepped back up onto the skybridge. "Now, just give it a second."

Devique pointed to the console and Nikola walked toward it, looking down. The engine started up again and the boat lurched forward. When Nikola looked up again, Devique was holding the flare gun, pointing it at him.

Nikola raised his gun. "Put it down. That's a fucking flare gun. You don't think I can shoot you before you get a shot off?"

"I'm sure you can. But you're standing in front of the engine block. And I'm not going to shoot you."

Nikola's face opened up into a wide, creepy smile. "You're too much of a fucking coward."

Devique looked sad for a minute. He called out. "It was really starting to get fun, wasn't it?"

He looked over at the skiff. I heard Noemie call out as Turk pulled me into the smaller boat and yanked the deployment cord. She wrapped herself around me and Noemie while the explosions slammed into the side of the smaller boat, pushing us away even as we dropped to the water.

Noemie cried out and clawed at the tarp while pieces of the boat came raining down on us. Turk flattened herself over us, but I pulled away, inhaling a mouthful of water. I poked my head out to see a massive ball of white as a dark hole opened in the center of it, getting bigger until it was the size of a softball, slamming into the center of my head.

My eyes closed on their own.

***

I remember coloring with my brother when I was five years old. I didn't realize he was my brother yet. He must have been eight or nine. Still, he was twice my height. I hated the wrappers on the crayons. Without the wrapper, you could draw big, wide areas using the side of the crayon, unrestricted. You could use it in so many ways.

Devique knew I hated the wrappers. When we had new crayons, I would hand him one and he would stop his own drawing and gently take it. He would bark like a dog and make a big deal out of chewing the wrapper of the crayon off like it was a bone. Then, as normal as you could be, he'd hand it back to me gently, while I laughed so hard. He would go back to drawing normally.

Until I passed him another pristine, wrapped crayon.

And when he read to me, he did all the voices. All of them. Like in Le Petit Prince.

"Good morning," said the fox. (The fox's voice was gravely but not too heavy. Never scary.)

"Good morning," the little prince responded politely, although when he turned around he saw nothing. (The prince himself was a clear and pretty voice. Like you might expect from a little prince. The Narrator was as low as Devique could go. So low I felt the vibrations when he did it.)

"I am right here," the voice said, "under the apple tree." (He moved back and forth between the voices seamlessly. Like an expert.)

"Who are you?" asked the little prince, and added, "you are very pretty to look at." (He would look at me when he said that, every time. As if I was pretty to look at.)

"I am a fox," said the fox. (In the most matter-of-fact voice.)

"Come and play with me," proposed the little prince. "I am so unhappy." (And he would sound unhappy. But never for more than a line or two.)

"I cannot play with you," the fox said. "I am not tamed." (And that was wild Devique. When my brother made me laugh by pretending to be a wild animal. But nothing in the world felt tamer than him.)

And he was right. I do remember the laughing from the other room. I just thought it was normal.

So normal.

Why did I think I didn't remember?

I knew those sounds. I know them now.

It's how Turk and I laugh when we draw pictures on each other and make up dates we'll never go on. It's how Devique and Noemie laughed while he tried to rub her feet hard enough to make a difference while she prodded him on.

Harder. Harder.

It was like my mom, my dad, and Christo. How they would sit in the living room, drinking wine and pretending to be planning some big job as they threw grapes at each other and made up code names for their big adventures together.

And for each other.

It was the same.

It was the sound in the air that I grew up with, the sound that fed me and made me grow up, the sound that built me.

And so much of it was gone now.

***

Turk said she couldn't see the burning boat behind us as we pulled the skiff into the rocks around Yeronisos but I don't know if I believed her. She took the helm while Noemie and I sat in the back. I didn't want to ask how long I'd been unconscious. I'd been hit in the head altogether too many times over the last couple of days. If I didn't already have a degenerative neurological disorder, I'd be concerned.

I held on to Noemie's hand. She was shaking. I focused all my remaining vision on her face. Her nose was bleeding and she was rocking back and forth. We needed to get her onto the island as fast as we could.

"What's going on? You're definitely sick."

She nodded.

"What is it? What can we do?"

"Nothing. I thought... I thought it would help. Nothing helps."

"Let us help you."

The waves were hitting hard. I tried to hang on to her. The rain was coming down harder, too, I could hear thunder in the distance.

"You can't. You forget..."

"What?" I pulled her hair out of her eyes. "What do I forget?"

"I don't step off this boat. Remember?"

"This is the boat? In your vision?"

"This is the night. I don't walk off this boat. I don't make it."

I looked up at Turk. "We have to be able to do something."

"And you have to get away from me."

I held her tightly. "Noemie. Why do we need to get away from you?"

"I was right. He's still tracking me," she whispered.

"How. How can he track you?"

She broke down in tears. "I don't know..." I held her as she wailed like an animal.

I heard Turk's voice, as if far away. "René. We have a problem."

She cut the onboard lights and kneeled down next to me.

"There is a small boat incoming on our starboard side. It's moving quickly."

"Nikola?"

"I wouldn't think so. It's coming from the opposite direction. It's not slowing down."

"How long?"

I held Noemie's hand and leaned into Turk. "We have about a minute and a half if it comes up beside us. Less if it rams us."

"Understood."

"I'm going to cut the engine and go totally dark."

Suddenly, the vibrations died. We could hear the lap of the water on the side of the skiff. And now I could hear the oncoming boat. With my hearing as it was now there was no way for me to tell how far away it was.

I felt Noemie and Turk's breathing. We slowly slid the tarp back over us and waited. It was dark enough now that a speedboat that didn't have our exact coordinate might zoom right by us. It was possible they would never see us, never know.

I pressed my legs against the starboard side of the skiff to brace myself. If the boat rammed us, it would hurt, but our heads would be protected. I had no real idea what to do.

We had no plans anymore.

None of our preparation mattered.

I ran through the job in my head over and over, trying to figure out who could be in the boat.

Turk reached into my hand. She signed that the boat was slowly circling us.

They knew we were here.

A spotlight flashed on us from inside the other boat, holding steady as the boat circled us. Over a megaphone, I heard Anton Karras's voice.

"I want to tell you that our deal is still in place. That I will still pay you if you give me the box. But you killed my son. So fuck you. Now you give me the box and you will die faster."

Turk held my hand and signed. "These deals are getting worse and worse."

I laughed despite myself. Noemie was clenching her eyes. She was positive that this was where she died.

I was hoping she was wrong. For all of us.

Turk cleared her throat. The gunshot wound in her arm had opened back up and I could feel her blood as I held onto her.

She rose up a little and called out, loudly. "The box was on the boat, so whoops."

I don't know if I was laughing or crying. I whispered, "I don't think he's going to buy that."

Turk held my head and kissed me. "I'm all out of believable shit, ladies." She put her arm around Noemie.

I reached into the skiff and looked for something to throw. I grabbed onto an ancient jar of honey and tossed it at him.

I whispered to Turk. "Did I kill him?"

Noemie laughed. She breathed in and smiled at me while Turk looked up.

"I think you did, babe."

"Good."

Karras's voice rang out again. "You have a minute. I don't know if you realize how many ugly things can happen to you after that."

Turk whispered, "I don't know. I've got a pretty good imagination."

Noemie spit up a little. "Stop... I don't want to laugh. I want my bear back."

I leaned into her and held her. I think a part of us had been prepared our whole lives for a day when everything might go to shit. But not her. That's not who she was. She didn't deserve this. All of a sudden, all my anger came to the surface in a dense red wave.

I yelled out, "Go fuck yourself. Seriously. Curl up your dick and shove it up your ass. Fuck yourself. Fuck Fuck Fuck."

Turk yelled out, "yeah, like a pig dick."

Noemie screamed, "or a duck. A duck dick."

I whispered to her. "That was good. I forgot how fucked up a duck's dick is."

Turk leaned into me. "I liked how you just ended that sentence and realized it needed more 'fucks'"

"You know I love you."

"It's pretty much the only thing I know. I'm not smart."

Karras turned the engine on and began to circle us again. The sound got closer and closer. I felt the fiberglass of the skiff vibrate as Turk turned on the engine and pushed the little boat toward the rocks on the shore as fast as possible. Karras' boat was getting louder and louder until I felt an impact from the starboard side.

My legs, pushed up against the hull, snapped nearly backwards as my knees popped out. Karras's engine ripped the side of the skiff open and his speedboat rode over the top, digging into my skin with the tips of his rotary blades. I screamed and felt my legs twist around, pulling me almost off the skiff. The smell of blood and charred flesh filled the air while we continued forward, Karras's boat riding on top of ours with its lights blaring and machinery spinning.

I tried to pull back, away from the spinning blades, but they sliced into my right arm, just below the elbow. I felt Noemie pull me backwards, away from the mechanics as they suddenly jammed and shut down. The rain seemed to come down harder.

The only engine sound now was ours. Turk was covered in blood too, as she slammed the engine into reverse, braking us and sending the larger boat over the front into the rocks.

My eyes were filled with blood, viscous and black with my colorless vision, even under the still-bright spotlight thrown by Karras's boat, now facing us, sitting on the rocks. He crawled over the front of his mangled ship, climbing toward Turk. She reached into the front deck cabinet of the skiff.

He was close enough to shoot.

The fiberglass had condensed and folded shut the cabinet. My legs were numb while I crawled over to cover Noemie. Turk slammed her hand into the side of the door to open it. I tried not to look down at my lower half as I felt around for more weapons.

"You fucking pigs. You could have come with me. You could be powerful, rich. But you fucked all that up now." Karras crawled slowly into the skiff, grabbing at Turk.

She finally dug her nails into the cabinet and ripped it open, pulling out a gun. The cabinet was drenched.

And so was the gun.

She flipped it over and crawled onto him, hitting him on the head with the butt of the gun over and over. He reached up and punched her in the face, knocking her into the water.

"No!" I yelled out, barely able to see where she had gone. I pulled myself over to the port side of the boat and reached my hand over it, digging into the water as hard as I could. I needed her to be able to see it, to feel it. There wasn't anything else I could do, I pulled myself up on the hull and tried to drop my hand down lower, until I felt something.

Turk's fingers in mine.

She reached up, grabbing my hand tightly. I pushed against the hull for leverage and pulled her up. She climbed over the hull back into the boat. I turned to see Karras behind me. He had acquired the gun and he hit me with it in the side of the head. Turk pulled herself over me to reach him. She grabbed his legs.

The skiff had started to take on water. The sides were falling over, fiberglass buckling from the impact. Red dots filled my head while I tried to listen for Karras and where he might be. He was crawling toward Noemie right over me.

But I couldn't feel half my body.

He reached his hand around Noemie's neck and started to squeeze. "Stop it. Stop it now. Or I kill her.

Turk and I were breathing heavily. I looked down at the boxes, closed, wrapped in cords. I reached for the one marked "2."

Karras grabbed it out of my hands and tossed it in the water with one hand, keeping the other on Noemie's neck. He returned his hand and she panicked.

"Don't fuck with me. I can feel the power in there. Can't you? What the fuck is wrong with you? I can feel it from a mile away."

I tried to keep him talking. "You didn't track Noemie."

He laughed. I didn't need to. I could feel this. I knew right where you were."

A wave slammed into us, pushing us against the rocks. Turk put her hand on my back.

"The box is breaking..."

"Why didn't you come into the Tel? You could have had the power right away?"

"Why didn't I risk my own life when you people were for sale? You tell me?"

Turk called out, "were you afraid of the vampire?"

He looked confused. "What vampire? What are you talking about?"

I closed my eyes and tried to listen. Everything was drifting away. I felt myself going into shock. "Ruach. The one your son made a deal with?"

Turk broke in, "yeah, that vampire."

"That's bullshit."

I could hear in his voice he knew who Ruach was. But he couldn't conceive of the idea that Nikola might have made a deal with him.

Turk finished, "yeah. He did. And he killed Ray and Aggie because they found out."

I pressed my head against the floor of the skiff. Everything was pain.

Karras's voice rose up as he stood, holding Noemie in front of him by her neck.

I called out. "Stop it. Please. Don't hurt her."

He spit on me. "Worry about yourself, bitch. You look like you have about five minutes left."

He wasn't wrong.

Noemie reached up to his hands, enfolded around her neck.

"Stupid little witch. Do you think I would have hired you if I couldn't see through your little glamors? I know what spells you're carrying. I listen. I learn. You don't have anything that can hurt me. "

That's when I realized what the headaches were, the bad temper, the nose bleeds. You see, magic is all about rules. And the rules have to be followed. If they aren't, something horrible can happen. I saw what toll it took on her to break the rules. I could see it all. The sickness, the loss of balance, the long stretches of sleep. All of it. I saw it when she put her hand over the one he was using to choke her and turned to look in his eyes.

She whispered. "Burn."

Karras head exploded into flame, his hair melting across his face. His jaw slid open and he howled in pain. His hand opened instinctively as he dropped to his knees, clawing at his face, trying to put out the magical fire that would burn until it received direction to stop.

And she fell.

Six.

She had managed to keep six spells. But the cost was horrific. Even as Turk grabbed her and laid her head on the deck of the skiff, her eyes seemed empty. This was a rule you shouldn't break. Turk held her face and tried to revive her.

Breaking rules has consequences.

A wave hit and Karras slid into the water, his head still aflame. The small light on the side of the skiff slid off as well. I crawled closer, feeling for the box, teetering after them. The top of it was cracked, sliding toward the edge of the boat. The skiff tipped. Turk looked at me. For a moment it looked like she had gained her footing, I crawled closer. At the last moment, she lost it.

She fell after Karras, the dark waves pulling her under. I screamed, reaching out, dragging my bloody legs across the wood floor of the skiff. The screech came out of every part of my body and it filled the space all around me. It seemed to fill the world. Suddenly, the air all across that world inverted. My ears shut tightly. I couldn't hear anything.

My hearing was gone, but I continued to scream. The voicebox was grinding into nothing in my throat. Blood filled my mouth. I couldn't tell what my screams sounded like anymore.

Lightning hit, illuminating the hole in my vision. The oily black and white coil that I could see through, the one becoming smaller and narrower by the day. I advanced toward where Turk had fallen and it shut to a pinprick.

I was deaf and sightless. I couldn't feel anything below my waist anymore. My legs were crushed. I couldn't sense up or down. My fingers searched in front of me for the cracked top of the box. It was so thin, so fragile. It was breaking - pulling apart. The rain came down harder.

The enchantments and carvings had been broken through and it was just simple hardened wood, falling apart. My arms felt the vibrations in the chassis of the skiff dissolving with every crushing hit on the rocks. I reached in and wrapped my hands around the body. The child.

Her skin was pulsating, electric. The shaking threatened to rip my hands from my arms as I pulled the tiny body into me and held tightly. I clamped onto it with every ounce of strength I still had. She tried to fly, to move, to explode into motion.

She was alive.

I pulled her head to my neck and felt the fangs like a metallic machine-like row around her open jaw sink into me. I pulled her closer. I locked her in my embrace, digging my fingernails into the doughy flesh of her back like an icepick into a glacier. I was a hook in her that wouldn't let go.

I had one box left to keep this thing in, One place to store it where it couldn't hurt anyone. One place hidden from light and sound, where she would be trapped forever.

Me.

I let the last of my senses go as the Bi'uwsh Olam flowed into me. It was like a liquid flame, burning my skin from the inside while my tears dissolved in the Mediterranean, briny water filling my lungs, burning them in their own way.

There was no up or down anymore, no one to tell me if I was descending, sinking, to lay on the slick weedy seabed or if my body was rising into torpid, insensate need, hobbled and made into something harmless, the endless evil trapped inside something it could never use.

I let it all take me. Not a host.

A prison.

16. Passing in the Distance

Comme un enfant aux yeux de lumière
Qui voit passer au loin les oiseaux

Just like a child with eyes full of light
That sees the birds passing in the distance

I don't know if it will make sense to say that I died, but in every real way I did.

I clung to the bottom of the seabed while life moved and shifted above me. The dark and light shifted back and forth, fighting for supremacy over the water's top. And finally, it wasn't my eyes that opened up.

It was all of me.

I opened up.

The 9,000 men, women, and children necessary to create the flowering box were nothing. That number was nothing. Nothing compared to what it took to create this. I saw the fields in my head -- the killing fields. The blood field. Before recorded time, it was entire branches of humanity that had to die, in order for the Bi'uwsh Olam to live.

I watched the human priests, the champions of Homo sapiens sapiens, as they herded the other offshoots of mankind into wide open clay pens and massive topless grooves torn into the earth like scars, so long they could be seen from space. I saw them hack away at them, burn them, crack them in half, kick and push them back into pits so that they would be clawed to death by their own families, desperate to escape.

I saw the potentialities of 10 different races, destroyed, wiped out, in a holocaust so expansive and abject that the evil of it had no place to go but to cling to itself, to huddle, to coalesce into a single being, inhabiting a single body, the last child laying half-dead in the abattoir of slick blood-coated bodies and mud creating a near-infinite chasm across the earth, home now to only one living thing. Daivana's only true child.

The Bi'uwsh Olam.

I saw those same priests lift the child and place her in protective boxes, freezing time forever for her, hiding away their shame, forging a pact that would keep these boxes intact for over 14,000 years, lying dormant, timeless, asleep.

On that day, humanity rose up the hero, the owners of the earth. They had won the right to progress, to the bounty of the planet. They had won their primacy. And every other race of man had lost everything. And the old gods retired to Haqal Dema. To live on as massive things to be conjured in stories.

In a blink I saw the centuries in between. The milliseconds where the box was opened. As a threat, as a taunt, as a possibility. When the child had been moved to a new resting place, a more powerful home.

Quickly. To show for only a second.

As leverage. As part of a story to keep some group of monsters in line.

To keep some group cowed.

For the monsters that lived in those portals beneath the earth, the Bi'uwsh Olam was the only threat. It was an explosive device built into a library wall, threatening to destroy an Archbishop. It was a cache of weapons, a horde of illicit Nazi gold, it was a secret, an atomic bomb that no one expected you to detonate. One that kept the rabble in line. For the monsters in the world around us, the vampires, the things that hunted humans, their fear of the Bi'uwsh Olam kept them quiet, hunting only at night, skittering off to graveyards and decaying mansions in between.

Amongst the demons in unmade places, the Bi'uwsh Olam had become the dark power that kept them from taking over.

It was never meant to be used. Until Anton Karras believed he could take it in, thinking he could control it and live forever.

It ate at me now and I could feel the part of my body fighting back. I could feel the part of me that was my mother, consuming it, dragging it back into degeneracy, to irrelevancy. The part of my mother who had walked into the sea, unseeing, blithe to the brush of the waves' sound, was marching it just as surely to the edge of my own perceptions, marginalizing it, belittling the infinite evil until it sat small in a corner of my brain.

And I was alive.

I don't know how long it was until I pulled myself up from the water and put my feet on the limestone embankment of the island. Each step hovered just centimeters above the thick white sand as I pressed forward.

I wandered around the island at night. I tried to hide. I tried to make sense of my new senses and say goodbye to what I had lost. None of it made any sense.

One day I did my circuit of the island. In the dark, I circled it like some strange wild animal. And that day, as the sun came up, I saw it.

A red box, open, sitting on a stone. I stared at it, letting my mind wander.

And I forgot to hide.

"Pretty great, huh? The ultimate cat carrier, really." Turk stood there holding Shark, petting her playfully. "Noemie put her in the box. I still have some of the fruit. You tossed the honey away, though..."

I nodded. "I remember."

"I watched you some nights, too. You're hard to follow."

I closed my eyes. But the way my body worked, that didn't stop me from sensing her there anymore. In fact, it let me focus. I felt her. "I know. I'm sorry..."

Turk broke in. "I'm going to find her. Before I go. I was waiting for you. And to bring her home. Her parents won't care. But I do. She pulled out the ring.

"Something is interfering with the tether. I think something is wrong with her."

"I'm sorry."

"I know she's alive. Because this works." She pulled out the little stone Noemie had given her and mouthed "here." A pile of gold bars appeared at her feet. "It's a good trick. Almost an infinite amount of gold." She kissed the stone. "It's good work."

"It really is."

"I'd throw it in the sea if you walked over here."

I felt the tears collect in my eyes. Bloody, boiling, inhuman. I looked down and wiped them off.

"I know you can't come closer. I know you're changed. But maybe soon?" She made Requin wave at me.

"Maybe." I lied. I turned to walk away. My feet felt mired in molasses.

"Confessions."

I stopped. It felt like it took me a million years to turn around. But she knew I would.

"I don't think... it's a bad..."

Turk took a step toward me. "Hey, I'll go first. Right?"

"Turk, I..."

"I wish we never took this job. I wish we never went to London. I'd be curled up in the dark with you, back home. Just... home."

She was about 10 meters away. The way my senses worked, I could have counted that in millimeters if I wanted to. I could tell you that she was 1.5 degrees centigrade warmer than usual. She was leaning on a .23 degree angle favoring her left leg. Information flowed in to me from everywhere.

None of it helped.

But I also knew I could be across that distance with one jump. In a fraction of a second I could be sucking the life from her, reducing her to a husk, bones blanching on the rock below us. Suddenly, that image was in front of me. I forced it away.

"I do like cats. I would have… I wanted a cat. I never realized."

She leaned toward me. She made a half conscious movement with her left foot to move toward me. I took a breath and let myself disappear.

I had something left to do.

***

I grew up thinking that we were the people everyone needed to watch out for. We were the ones lifting wallets, robbing markets, pinching cars. We lived in a world where things were temporary. Where IDs were used once and guns maybe never.

But it was still nice to have one.

If you were a good person, maybe you didn't have much to worry about. The key is that when you take someone down, a mark, a shop, a boss, you usually do it by piggybacking on that thing they carry with them everywhere.

Their greed.

In a way, we fed on greed. And if you were food, we'd find you. We'd use your greed, your fear, the things you hated about yourself. Well, to rob you.

I never imagined a boogeyman or a monster under the bed. These were inventions of grifters, I thought, to clear another franc, to earn another dollar.

But there are real monsters out there. And I'm learning all about them. There is a line in the universe, one I was never privy to, between things that are made, that exist and are real, and things that are unmade. Unmade things skulk off into the imagination, growling, frightening children.

Unmade spaces are filled with monstrous areas growing, expanding, predicated on belief, on what people are willing to tolerate as they sweep their brains for the detritus of monsters and ghouls as kids.

The things that we still believe in.

That line is permeable. As Noemie tried to explain to us, belief has power, not just the power to illuminate celebrities and rockstars, presidents and heads of state. Power to shift creatures of the imagination into real things using belief as a sort of molten clay, a kind of magma, hot with the wonder of children and the credible.

In my new form, my body breaking down and rebuilding every day through the Demasar, I could control the Maqor, the ink that paints the world, the passage between the made and unmade worlds. I could visit the liminal spaces and, more importantly, I could leave again afterward.

On earth here, there is a space where thousands of vampire families vie for dominance over the others, each looking for even ground so they could make their play without intervention from the older gods and demons that made them. They each see themselves as heroes, the ones who will create the perfect reckoning for human beings, who will poignantly offer themselves up as food out of respect for the power of that family or this one.

Or that one.

As this belief grew, creatures like Ruach rose up, so certain that any atrocity was worthwhile in pursuit of that, that any amount of murder could be accommodated in a world where they ended up on top.

I visited them all. Or nearly all, one after another, speaking to the matriarchs and patriarchs of the degenerate creatures that fed on human beings. And I conjured up the spirit of the Bi'uwsh Olam to draw a line in the sand for them.

A line that protected what had to be protected. A line that included my family.

I visited the Zar Qurbana. Family after family. I visited the Rasha, families of changeling beasts who took human form to sow despair and feed on joy.

I made sure they understood how humanity would remain off limits to their manipulations.

And I drew a line.

I slipped into the unmade spaces and visited the Ka Alukah, the faceless ones, who stole ideas from people when they slept, leaving them in the dreams of their petitioners. I appeared to the A-rhm Dei, who made men and women fall in love with them, siphoning away their will to live in the real world as their bodies wasted away. I moved deeply into the unmade spaces, the cities that never saw a living person before, to see the Rephaim, creatures who could use fear as a living weapon, building armor and swords from it that would send someone into respiratory shock at the very sight of them.

And to all of them, I made sure they knew that the Bi'uwsh Olam was real. That it was inside me. That it would continue to keep the status quo among all the families.

I thought about Salvatore Riina and what it took for him to unite the families. Instead, I made sure to keep them apart, separate, afraid, so that no one group would get confident. Rather than build some kind of treaty, I sowed an agenda of disunion, one that would prevent any of them from rising up too high.

I became the monster that monsters talk about in hushed tones.

I was like a newly forged thing that needed to cool. I was molten glass on the outside, hot, destructive. For a while, there was nothing I felt like I could even touch.

So I traveled. I did the things that people do to remind ourselves that we are real. I stood on the boardwalk of the Parc Borély and felt the phantom imagery of my father meeting my mother for the first time. I could see where he had left out details, the mime he hid behind to observe her, the moment of eye contact before the officer arrived that demonstrated she knew he was there, that some small part of her degenerate dance of thievery was for his benefit.

I swam in the water off the Corniche and watched the afterimages of my mother, Suvi Laine, paddling out toward the far islands, unseeing, deaf, looking to let go and I watched the waves take her.

I saw her struggle at the last moment and realized that she didn't want to go. That she didn't want to leave this world behind any more than I did. I watched her balance fail her as she slid beneath the archetypal blue of the bay and become the water, too.

And I learned about her.

I used my new senses to observe the ghosted residue of everyone I loved, as far back as their personal timelines went. I saw Turk's parents, confused, tired, poor, letting her go, wanting a better life for her. I saw the spirit image of her biological father holding a paper, stolen from some dead rack on an unaware newsmonger shop, watching her laugh at a cafe with me when she was 20, wondering if he should make contact, then finally deciding to let her go for good, to let her be the wind, in a way, while he stayed, nailed to the ground.

I saw afterimages in the air like hallucinations, liquid, smoky, of my father dancing with Selene the way you do when you know there is no urgency or need to restart the song, no requirement to place your foot anywhere or to copy some classic move. And she became real to me.

I watched the flickering past images of Christo, on vacation with my mom and dad, all three sinking into the familiarity of it all as they swam together in Nice, unable to recognize that anyone else existed.

Over and over, I used what I had been given to see people. I used these new senses to remind myself that these people – not just my family, the people I loved, but all the rest -- were real.

I fed the Bi'uwsh Olam with life instead of death.

I trained it, taught it, mentored the thing inside me so that it could live in the world, as a part of the world, just how I'd been taught to want to remain part of the world. I toured the world the way Milan had toured the mountainside toward Cassis in the little blue roadster, and for the same reason.

To make sure what was inside me stayed connected.

And after a while, I could sit still. I could tame the immense energies in me and begin to control them.

***

And this is where we came in.

It's midnight so I'm here, leaning against the black wooden door, knowing that she's there. My disease keeps the Demasar at bay, preventing the bloodchild – the flower – from warping me, killing the things in me that are really me. But it's a battle. On good days it's a ballet, a careful choreography that pits me against a rocky, uneven stage, dipping in the wrong places, threatening to break open. On bad days it's a war between who I was and who it wants me to be.

And I choose the thing in between.

I'm strong. My legs work. My mind is sharp. And the things I can do would amaze you.

If I told you.

I've let go of vision. I've let go of hearing, even as I remind myself not to appoint ownership. There is no "my vision" or "my hearing." There is only the world filtered through me, through the new ways I have of perceiving it. I contain the Bi'uwsh Olam and I am dangerous. But my genetics eats at it, sanding down the sharp edges of it. It's no longer fully Bi'uwsh, as I am just me, neither evil nor perfect.

And who knows how "Olam" it will prove to be. Am I eternal?

I don't know.

I can feel the shapes on my back, sense their ridges. There is body memory of her fingers tracing words across my tattoo with her fingers, her tongue, leaning back in bed and tapping out improper propositions across the arch of it with her toes, each one slipping over the raised scars of meaning I dug into myself just so I could keep learning her, just so that I wouldn't miss one beautiful word from the one voice in the world I can't bear to not hear anymore. The one voice whose absence tears at my eardrums.

And I know she's there. With a little black runt cat rubbing her fur against the umber skin of her legs. The one who rode out the worst of all of it in a millenia-old box that stopped time, along with a pomegranate and some dates. One who was now magically connected to her so neither one would ever be lost.

Like I wish I were.

I miss my green eyes. I could tell you what color they are now, but that wouldn't make any sense to you. Color, to me, is a paragraph, not a word. Sounds are a book, not just a sentence long description. I don't rely on things like that any more. I don't reclaim.

I reinvent.

Be clear about it. I loved my life.

But we endure as different people now. And I've come to fall in love with every door in France, every closed-off doorway, every window, every thin stretch of wall that she could be plausibly curled up on the other side of, protected from the monsters that are real, living in the world, safe from me, barely at the edge of my 20-plus senses that scream, every one of them, when she moves through the world like a fish in water.

The police still follow her, legalities notwithstanding, but they reach like children, stubby hands too late to catch intrepid toys that fall off tables and slip easily out of sight under bureaus and dressers when they want, hiding in darkness that can't, ever, diminish their bright colors.

Every other bad thing in the world knows better. I've made sure.

It's Noemie who looks up so often, right when my face is directed downwards, taking in my city in ways I couldn't before.

She knows things.

And while Noemie was right that she never stepped off that boat herself, that doesn't mean she wasn't carried by something, lifted up and away by a thing that may never grow up, may never get old, may never die – something that saw a friend in her. Saved by something that saw a fellow artist recreating herself from the ground up out of the sloppy material we are all born as.

A little ancient girl that kept a tiny part of the massive energies that laid inside her, retaining some after passing them on. Not a lot. Just enough. Enough to see that fellowship, to see a protector. In Noemie.

To see a mother.

And I'm grateful for that, even at a distance. That Turk has family. That she has people who will laugh as she plays faux assassin, bragging about murdering celebrities that most need killing today, running her tongue over their deaths like you might over a freshly brushed set of teeth that feel, suddenly, right in your mouth after a few days of inattention.

Grateful that she has that tiny stone, one that lets her call upon a massive wealth of gold, enough so that she'll never have to break another law. Unless she really wants to.

And one day, maybe, I'll be able to control it – to control myself enough to stand next to her, to feel her touch me again. Maybe. Until then, I'll be the ghost of every doorway in Marseille – every ingress, every portal that she might, logically, be on the other side of.

That will be me.

I'll be grateful that Noemie helps keep Milan's memory. Not just the lessons, but the love. That she lived, for at least a bit, under the arm of a man who adored being my father so much that he became a father to every lost person he met. Every young man trapped in the wheel well of a plane, frozen in his zeal to be somewhere. Every young girl left behind to plunder strange hotel rooms. Every boy left homeless by despairing parents.

I'll be thankful for that. Grateful that the world is still full of people I love.

That it all goes on.

And that when they pulled my brother off that board, out of that water, his body ripped open and with barely an inch of skin not torn by the electric kiss of the explosion or the tortured currents of the Mediterranean, there wasn't anything wrong with it, not one thing, that Noemie couldn't eventually fix.

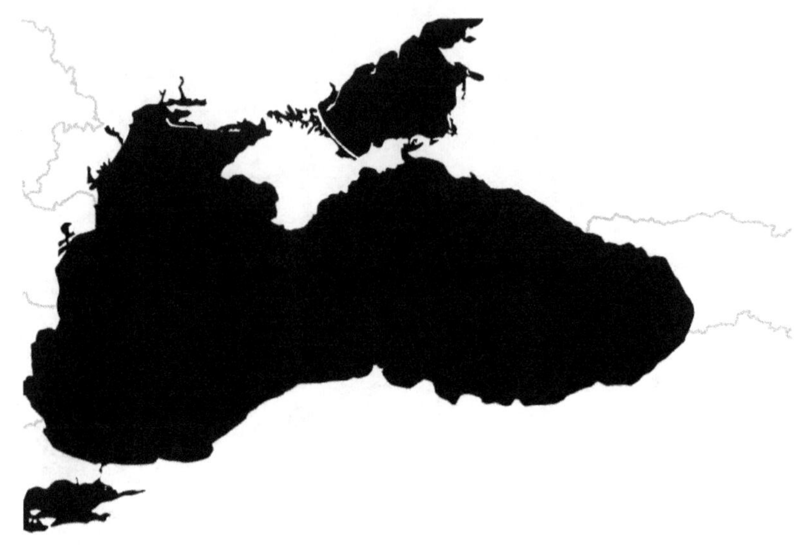

Turkey

Syria

Yeronisos

Cyprus

Iraq

Israel

Jericho

Tell es Sultan

Jordan

Saudi Arabia

Egypt

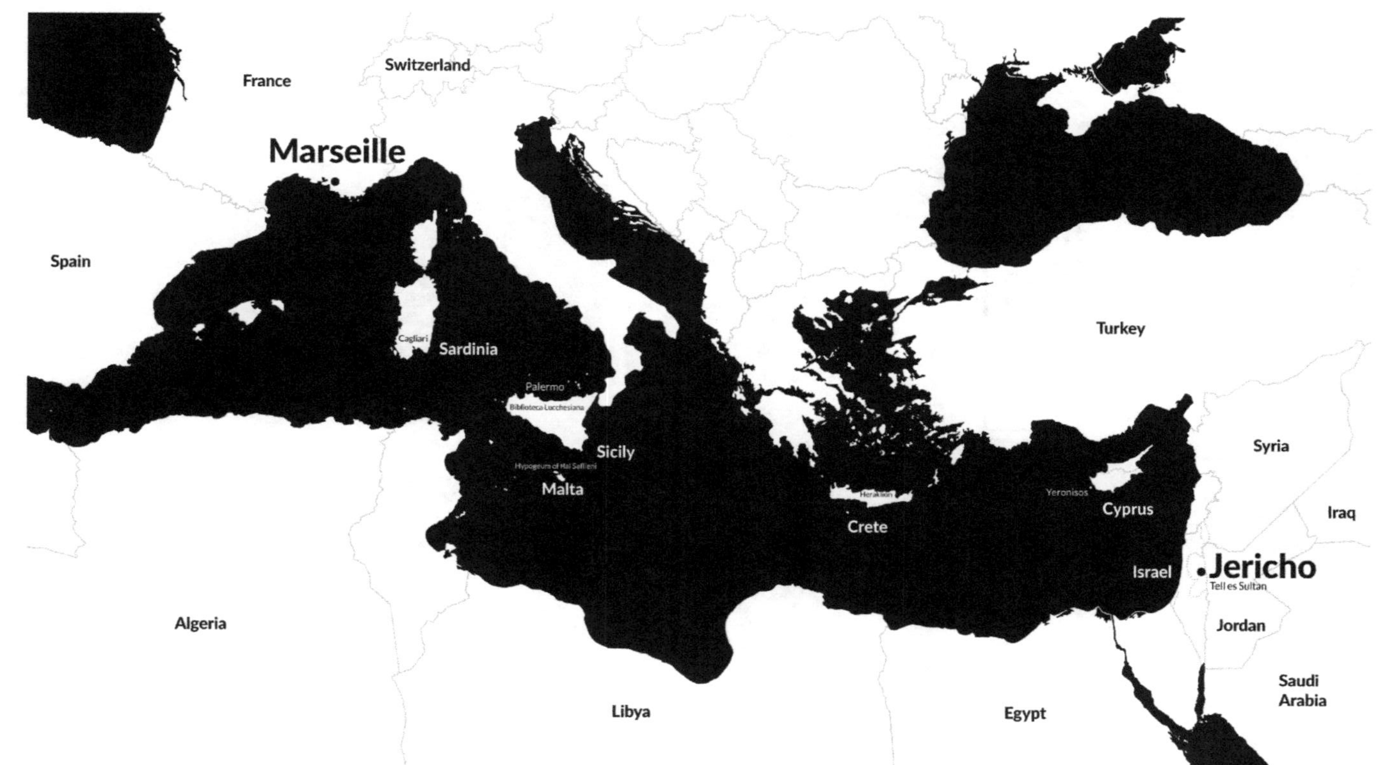

France
Switzerland
Marseille
Spain
Cagliari
Sardinia
Palermo
Biblioteca Lucchesiana
Sicily
Hypogeum of Hal Saflieni
Malta
Turkey
Syria
Yeronisos
Cyprus
Iraq
Crete
Israel
Jericho
Tell es Sultan
Jordan
Algeria
Libya
Egypt
Saudi Arabia

PULSEBLACK

www.ingramcontent.com/pod-product-compliance
Lightning Source LLC
LaVergne TN
LVHW010641110826
845149LV00014B/2917